Mike Faricy

Bite Me

Published by Mike Faricy 2012
Copyright Mike Faricy 2012

Bite Me
ISBN-13: 978-1477588772
10: 1477588779

Mike Faricy

Bite Me

Published by Mike Faricy 2012
Copyright Mike Faricy 2012

Bite Me
ISBN-13: 978-1477588772
10: 1477588779

Acknowledgments

I would like to thank the following people for their help and support:

Special thanks to Kitty, Donna and Rhonda for their hard work, cheerful patience and positive feedback.

I would like to thank Dan, Julie & Roy for their creative talent and not slitting their wrists or jumping off the high bridge when dealing with my Neanderthal computer capabilities.

Last, I would like to thank family and friends for their encouragement and unqualified support. Special thanks to Maggie, Jed, Schatz, Pat, Emily, Pat and Av for not rolling their eyes, at least when I was there, and most of all, to my wife Teresa whose belief, support and inspiration has from day one never waned.

To Teresa

"He was mad until she entered the room and her beauty evaporated his anger."

Bite Me

Chapter One

It was bigger than a steak knife, not quite a
carving blade, but still capable of doing some very
serious damage. The knife came with a bright red
handle, the kind sculpted to fit your fingers and hold a
blade that gleamed viciously. I dodged the swipes again
and pleaded.

"Put the knife down. Just put the knife down,
please." I tried to sound calm.

Another wild swipe, this one slashing very close to
the tip of my nose.

"Look, can we talk about this? Take it easy." I was
aware panic had caused my voice to raise about two
more notches. I was hoping I didn't have to throw a
punch.

"Get out. Just get out. I want you out of here now,
do you hear me? Now! Get out," she screamed.

"Okay, okay, Christ just let me get dressed and…"

"Get out now or I swear I'll cut you up into the
tiniest little pieces. I will, you creep. I swear I will."

"Hey, Kiki, I believe you, okay? Just let me get my
jeans on. If you could just hand them to me and…"

"Get out of my bedroom," she screamed, then
slashed wildly again through the air.

"Just give me my jeans. I promise I'll leave, but I
have to have some clothes. Look, you can keep the
shirt. I never liked that one anyway and…"

"Get out, get out, get out," she screamed, slashing back and forth with every shriek.

Talk about a date going down the drain. Everything was fine until the shots of tequila, mores the pity. Still, I thought there might be an outside chance she was just playing hard to get.

"Look, maybe if we just got back into bed ..."

She lunged at me, tripped over my jeans on the floor and fell. She curled up in a fetal position, naked on her bedroom carpet and began to sob. Even when she was trying to kill me she looked incredibly hot. I couldn't stop staring at her thick brunette hair, creamy white skin, fantastic hips and those cute little feet.

"Sorry, sorry, I'm just such a bitch, well sometimes," she sobbed.

No argument there, but the only person I was feeling sorry for right now was me. I picked up the knife, quickly pulled on my jeans, then slipped on my shoes.

"Keep the boxers and socks, Kiki. It's been a unique experience. I've never spent the night with a woman who kept a knife under her pillow."

I pulled the shirt over my head then buckled my belt as I made for the bedroom door.

"Phone me tomorrow, Dev, promise?" she called, sitting up and wiping the tears from her eyes. Her smeared mascara looked like hastily applied war paint.

"Yeah, sure," I lied hoping she would just stay put so I could make it to the front door.

"I'll lock up behind you," she called, then staggered to her feet and hurried to catch up, sniffling as she came. She stopped at the dining room table, poured herself a quick shot and tossed it back. "Ahhh." She grabbed an apple from a dish in the center of the dinning room table and continued toward the front door.

I realized I was still carrying the knife and increased my pace without actually running. I made it to the door and opened it just as she hurried across the living room.

"Do you have to go? You'll call?" she asked, standing naked in the doorway. She calmly took a bite out of the apple and waited for my reply.

The only call I was going to make was to 911, but then, why bother? One look at Kiki, gorgeous, naked, asking me to stay and the cops would haul me away.

"Hey, I've got an early meeting. Catch you later." I said and then pulled the door closed behind me. She snapped the lock on the other side. I paused, left the knife on the porch and wondered what time it was. The sun was up, birds were chirping. My watch was still inside, probably somewhere in Kiki's bedroom. Screw it. I could always get another watch.

"Bastard!" I heard her scream inside the house. Then, the unmistakable sound of something shattering as the shot glass sailed through a pane in the side window.

That was my traveling music. I climbed behind the wheel of my DeVille and raced off. The clock on my dash read three-twenty-seven, but it had been like that for the better part of the year. I started pushing radio buttons to see if someone might mention the time. They didn't.

Once home I pushed a chair in front of the door just in case Kiki showed up to make good on her promise to kill me. I napped fitfully on the couch until I finally gave up and drifted over to my office. Not that I had anything to do here, except look out the window at

The Spot bar across the street. It was too late to join the lunchtime crowd and too early to stop in for a nightcap.

I got six months office rent free in lieu of payment on a case I'd worked last New Years. A guy I knew bought a bar, hired a number of employees based on breast size, then wondered why he was losing money. Three nights of me posing as a new hire got the answers to most of his questions. If he ran the building where my office was anything like his bar, he wasn't going to stay in business very long.

I'd been staring out my second story office window for fifteen or twenty minutes, leering at female passersby when the phone rang.

"Haskell Investigations."

"Mr. Haskell, please," a male voice said, then coughed.

"You got him."

"Oh, well, this is Farrell J. Earley. I got your name from my sister, Kiki."

"Kiki?"

"Yes, I spoke with her about an hour ago."

"Yeah, well, look, I can explain. See your sister…"

"Relax, I know, she can kinda go over the edge every now and again."

"That's an understatement. It would have been nice to know that before she had a knife in her hand. She threatened to cut me up into tiny pieces."

"That's my Kiki."

"Well, look, I don't know what she told you, but I can assure you that I behaved like a perfect gentleman."

"Yeah, sure you did. That's her hot button, gentlemen. To tell you the truth, Mr. Haskell, I don't really care. Thing is, while Kiki was ranting and screaming she mentioned that you were a private investigator. I'd like to hire you."

"Call me Dev," I said.

"Okay, Dev. I'd like to contract your services. That is, if you're available."

About the only thing I had going on was Jameson night at The Spot on Thursday.

"Well, why don't we meet, discuss your needs and then if you're still interested I'll see if I can adjust my schedule."

"Can you make it today?"

"I can. Where would you like to meet?"

"I'm over here at Craze, K-R-A-Z," he pronounced each letter like it would mean something to me, it didn't. I hadn't the foggiest idea what in the hell he was talking about.

"That still in the same place?" I asked, hoping for a clue.

"Yep."

"I'm in a meeting until about four, rush hour and all. What would be the quickest way over there from downtown?"

"You know with the construction and all, take I-94, get off at Snelling."

"That's what I figured. Pretty sure I know the building, but give me the address anyway," I said, thinking come on, man.

"Fifteen thirty-seven, we're up on the sixth floor."

It was like pulling teeth to find out where in the hell he was.

"Mr. Earley, give me your phone number there in case I'm running late I don't anticipate any problems, but better safe than sorry."

He gave me his number. I hung up, then dialed the number, figuring the receptionist would tell me the street.

Someone answered with a cough, Farrell again, apparently his cell phone.

"Hello?"

"Mr. Earley? Dev Haskell again. I must have misdialed, in the process of adjusting my schedule. Sorry to bother you."

"Not a bother. Still see you at four?"

"Four it is."

Chapter Two

It turned out KRAZ was a radio station. Who knew? Probably not too many people based on the tiny office and even smaller broadcast booth. The first three floors in the grimy building served as a warehouse for the Abbott Paint Company. The halls were a version of government grey, the stairs worn, poured concrete. What sounded like a printing press was clunking away up on the sixth floor and far down the hall. Most of the small office suites appeared to be vacant.

A walnut stained door led into the corner suite. There was a handwritten sign in black marker crookedly taped above the mail slot, 'KRAZ National Headquarters'. I opened the door and walked in, or at least I tried. About three quarters into opening the door, it struck the edge of a desk forcing me to make a quick side step.

"Hello," I called still holding the door open.

The desk, a mid 60's surplus model, was covered with stacks of files. Random scrawled notes were taped to the wall behind the desk. Aging newspapers and advertising circulars littered the stacks of files and spilled onto the floor.

"Hello, anyone home?" I called again.

I heard a raspy cough followed by the appearance of a guy in the doorway off to the right. He wore large, dark framed glasses, wrinkled, cream-colored cotton slacks and a grey t-shirt that read "KRAZ, America's Right!" in bright red letters. He held a cigarette with a two-inch ash in his right hand.

"Hi, I'm looking for Farrell Earley," I said.

He took a drag, thought about that for a moment, then asked, "Do you have an appointment?"

"Yeah, Devlin Haskell. He's expecting me." I would have handed the guy my card, but I'd run out a few weeks back.

He exhaled a blue cloud then gave a slight cough.

"Oh yeah. Haskell nice to meet you. Farrell J. Earley. Any problem finding the place?" he asked, extending his hand. He looked nothing like his gorgeous, knife wielding crazy sister.

"No, no problem, exactly where I thought you were," I lied.

"Come on back to the office I want you to meet Tommy. Give you an idea of what we're dealing with, see what you think." He was saying this as we walked through what must have been an office at one time. The room was crammed with stacks of blue and red plastic crates filled with cords, key boards, three or four antique computer monitors. The things probably leaked radiation and looked as old as me.

"Pardon the mess, we're in the process of updating," he said making for a door on the far wall.

Through the door we entered a dusty office with walls painted a baby-shit brown color. A red-faced guy with a crew cut sat behind the desk, typing on an electric typewriter.

"With you in a moment," he said, not looking up, fingers dancing across the typewriter keys. With every key stroke a ball about the size of a golf ball struck the paper.

Farrell motioned me toward a dusty, black leather couch. We sat there and waited in a blue cloud of his cigarette smoke. Eventually the typing was complete and the guy pulled the sheet from the typewriter, then placed it face down on a stack of paper, turned in his chair and looked from me to Farrell, then back to me.

"Sorry about that, can never be too careful. Tomorrow's broadcast, do that on the computer and there's no telling who'll get hold of it and use it for their own degenerate purposes. All right then, who do we have here?"

"This is the fella I was telling you about. The private investigator, Dennis Haskell."

"Devlin, Devlin Haskell," I corrected.

"Thompson Barkwell," he said, holding out his hand.

I had to get up off the couch and take two steps to grab it. He gave me a limp shake for the effort.

"Nice to meet you, Mr. Barkwell."

"Please, call me Thompson. We get to know one another better and you can call me Tommy. But, let's keep it at Thompson for right now, shall we?"

'Fine with me, jerk.' I thought, smiled and nodded. "Yes sir, I look forward to getting to know you much better."

"Farrell bring you up to speed with our situation?"

"Not really. What seems to be the problem?"

They looked back and forth for a long moment. Eventually Thompson took a deep breath, leaned back in his chair and said, "Here at K-R-A-Z we like to think of ourselves as the voice of the American future. A right thinking America. We…"

The future of America is the electric typewriter? I was wondering why I should even be surprised. After all, they got my name from that knife-wielding lunatic, Kiki. I wondered if she'd calmed down yet. Then I remembered her breasts bouncing up and down while she swung the knife at me. Wondered if maybe it had just been a one time sort of melt down and maybe we could …

"… view us as a threat to their socialistic ways, and therefore intend to deal with us accordingly."

They sat and looked at me, waiting for a reaction. I tried to erase Kiki from my mind.

"So what do you think?" Thompson finally said.

"Give me that last part again."

"Not much to it. The note said that we were a threat to their socialistic ways and therefore they intended to deal with us accordingly."

"So many questions," I said, stalling for time.

"Would you care to share them?" Thompson asked.

"Well, first off, tell me about the note. How did it come to you? Where is it now? Did you inform the police?"

"Like I said, it was shoved under the door when we arrived yesterday. Yes, we did call the police," Thompson said.

"They've got the note now," Farrell added.

"I see, I see," I said, hoping to sound like I did.

"Of course, they're probably worried about equal rights and the other nonsense that's become the left's mantra. While patriots like us just soldier on, moving forward, constantly under fire," Thompson said.

"So you consider this a legitimate threat, the note? You don't think someone might just be pulling your leg?"

"Pulling our leg? You've got to be kidding. No, we've struck a nerve, probably more than one. No doubt you've listened to our broadcasts. You know how they are."

"To tell you the truth I don't listen as often as I'd like to."

"Which was your favorite?" Thompson asked.

Farrell exhaled another blue cloud and leaned forward on the couch.

"Oh, it would be tough to pick just one." I dodged.

"But, you must have a favorite."

"I really like them all. No, no, too tough to narrow it down to just one. Honest."

"I know what you mean," Thompson said, looking thoughtful.

Farrell nodded and fired up another cigarette using the butt of his last one.

"Okay, so we're working with what? A death threat?" I asked.

"Exactly," replied Thompson.

"Yeah, death threat, definitely a death threat," Farrell chimed in.

"And what exactly would you like me to do?"

"Well, first and foremost, protection, that's paramount. Something happens to either one of us and the movement dies, right here, right now." Thompson struck the desk top four times with his index finger in perfect time to *'right here, right now'*.

"Then, when you're not protecting, we'd like you to get to the bottom of this. Find out what sort of pinko, commy group of misfits uses murder and intimidation as a logical consequence of open dialogue."

"What about the police?" I asked.

"Can't be trusted," Farrell said.

Thompson nodded his head in agreement.

"What sort of protection do you want?" I asked.

"You carry a gun, don't you?"

"Yeah, I'm licensed."

"For the love of… hell, we're all licensed, if that's what you want to call it. Part of our second amendment

15

rights. But we need some extra firepower. These folks will stop at nothing."

"Look, no offense, but so far all you've got is a note slipped under the door. You've given that to the police. They'll check it out for you. From what you tell me it sounds like it could be as simple as a college prank."

"A college prank? You can't honestly believe that threat represents a college prank. Although, given the state of what passes for education now-a-days..." Thompson seemed to drift off somewhere distant then slapped the top of his desk. "No, I'm afraid we don't have the luxury of living in such a cavalier fashion, Mr. Haskin."

"Haskell, Devlin Haskell," I reminded, smiling.

"We're the last line of defense before the damn train goes off the rails."

"Meaning?" I was beginning to think Thompson was a legend in his own mind.

"Meaning we've hit a nerve, sir. They know we speak the truth and they can't stand that - the truth."

'In for a penny, in for a pound' I thought.

"So you'd like protection, here, at your office?"

"Our station, and yes, here, while we broadcast," Thompson said.

"It's when we're the most vulnerable, when we're on the air." Farrell added.

"Like I said before, I haven't been able to listen as often as I would like, remind me what your hours are," I said.

"We're on from ten to ten-fifteen in the morning, noon to twelve-fifteen, three to three-fifteen and then the drive home hour, five-thirty to five-forty-five." Thompson squeaked back in his office chair and looked like he just won the lottery.

"We tape our message the day before, then play it four times the following day," Farrell said as he exhaled another long blue cloud.

"It's a well-known fact people have to hear something four times within twenty-four hours before they begin to pick it up," Thompson expounded.

"You guys have any sponsors?" I asked.

They looked back and forth from one another again. Eventually Thompson said, "I really don't feel comfortable divulging that information at this time. Suffice to say we do have sponsors and are enlisting more everyday."

'I'll take that as a no,' I thought.

"When would you like me to start?"

"The sooner, the better," Thompson said and looked at his watch.

"It's time I got into the sound booth," Farrell said, gave a raspy cough and then followed it with a long drag on his cigarette burning it down to his nicotine-stained fingers.

"Does a nine forty-five start suit you?" Thompson asked.

"I can do that. I'd better get going, I've got some schedules to shuffle around. I'll see the two of you here, tomorrow, nine forty-five."

"You're just what we need." Thompson smiled, and held out his hand for another limp, dead-fish shake.

As I followed Farrell out I heard the electric typewriter start up again. We walked past the plastic crates of obsolete equipment. Out in the front office or whatever they called it, Farrell said, 'Appreciate you taking our case on, Mr. Haskin. We'll all sleep a little better tonight knowing you're on the job."

"Haskell, H-a-s-k-e-l-l," I spelled it for him.

"Right." He half chuckled.

"I'll be here at nine forty-five tomorrow. Just keep a close eye out on your way home tonight and back in tomorrow. Let's have you guys keep a low profile until we get things sorted out, okay?"

"That won't be a problem."

"See you tomorrow," I said and left.

Chapter Three

I was buying another round at The Spot. I'd been buying all night. I was beyond the point of caring and was holding court on a bar stool dangerously close to two drunks throwing darts.

"One of your deadbeat clients finally pay up?" Jimmy asked as he filled the glasses with the next round.

"Even better, I got a job where I don't have to work." I laughed.

"So what's new 'bout that."

"No, I mean, I just have to sit around. Someone pulled a joke on these clowns and they bought it. Hired me for protection," I said, then washed that down with a healthy couple of swallows.

"You for protection, that is a joke." Jimmy laughed.

"Yeah? Well, you ever hear of a radio station called craze?"

"Craze… you mean like nuts? What is that some weird punk rock, kid thing?"

"No, K-R-A-Z, supposed to be something right with America deal or, I don't know. I'll take another, Jimmy," I said and drained my glass.

"You driving?"

"Yeah, but not all that far, so relax "

Over the course of the evening I asked around. No one in the bar had ever heard of KRAZ. The next thing I knew it was closing time, Jimmy locked the door, let me finish my beer, but wouldn't give me another. I apparently made it home all right because I woke up on my couch at about six-thirty the following morning. I stumbled to the kitchen, put some coffee on and curled back up on the couch. When I next looked at the clock on my microwave it was nine twenty.

I threw a semi-clean shirt on, gobbled some mints, raced out the door and over to KRAZ.

Farrell was sucking the last inch of life from his current cigarette when I bounced the office door off the front desk. I was still a little breathless and red in the face from rushing to make it modestly late.

"You guys ought to move that thing," I said, nodding at the front desk.

He exhaled, sipped from his coffee mug and smiled, but didn't say anything.

I saw Thompson through the doorway. He was standing next to the stacks of red and blue crates. It was the first time I'd seen him standing. At least I thought he was standing. I put him at about five foot three, on a good day.

He glanced at his watch, raised an eyebrow then shook his head.

"I believe our agreement was nine-forty-five," he called.

"It was. I got here early, strolled around the building and the parking lots checking some things, making myself familiar with the area. Nice to know what I'm dealing with. First line of defense is out there, not in here." I had to admit that sounded so good, even I half believed it.

Farrell looked surprised. Thompson looked like he wasn't sure. I seized the opportunity.

"Anything seem out of the ordinary? Another note, a phone call, someone following either of you, noise out in the hallway?"

They both shook their heads.

"Okay, you're on the air shortly?"

"Twelve minutes," Farrell said and lit up another cigarette.

"Mind if I watch?"

"Be my guest." He exhaled.

By this time Thompson had returned to his lair.

Eleven minutes later I was standing behind Farrell in a converted closet. We had to hunch over because of the shelf that ran across the top. There was a bare light bulb in the ceiling with a string attached to turn it off and on. Fortunately, someone had the foresight to remove the pole and clothes hangers.

Farrell wore a set of headphones. He was seated at a tiny desk at one end of the closet with a laptop in front of him. The dusty screen on the laptop displayed a digital readout ticking down the minutes before broadcast and then the last sixty seconds. The final ten seconds clicked past furiously in increments of a tenth of a second. With three seconds left, Farrell slowly, deliberately raised his index finger and pushed the enter key on the laptop. Then he leaned back and listened for a moment before he removed his headphones.

"There you go, we're on the air," he said and pushed back his chair.

Still hunched over I had to back up to exit the closet. Farrell took a final drag, then fired up a fresh cancer stick and backed out.

"We record the *word*, as we like to call it, the night before. Then upload it and we're set to go. We could set the download for any time, but I like to do the manual play. Gets me into the groove if you know what I mean."

Actually I didn't. Somehow Farrell 'in the groove' didn't seem to compute.

"So that's it until noon?"

"Well, we stand by, answer the phones, sign up volunteers, get people organized... that sort of thing."

"Oh, so listeners call?"

"Well, they could. I mean that's what we're hoping will happen, sometime, anyway."

It didn't happen.

The routine was the same at noon, three and five-thirty, only even more boring. I walked around the building and the parking lot a few times just to stay awake. At six I drifted into Thompson's office. He was pounding away on the future of America, his electric typewriter.

"You feel comfortable with me leaving for the day?"

He stopped hammering the typewriter keys, squeaked his chair around and nodded with a determined look across his face.

"I'd say we sent out a pretty strong message today."

"Your broadcast?"

"Broadcast? No, you, our protection. We won't be silenced. Matter of fact it's provided me inspiration, freedom of speech," he said and patted the one-inch stack of paper on the desk. Just like yesterday it was face down.

"Tomorrow's broadcast?" I asked.

"Exactly."

"Farrell reads that for fifteen minutes and then you play it four times a day?"

"We do."

"Ever think of maybe shortening it? I don't know, cutting it down to maybe fifteen or twenty seconds? Maybe play some music or something?"

"We've done that from time to time, or a version. We've had 'America The Beautiful' as a background accompaniment once in a while, some Sousa marches."

"Yeah, I was thinking more like just music, maybe something popular, current, get your audience interested and…"

"Some drug culture thing? That it? You've been in the gutter too long, Haskell. We're not trying to be popular, if that's what your angle is. We're here to tell the truth, something that often times is unpopular." He placed some added emphasis to the *un* in unpopular.

"Well, I kind of like the gutter, to tell you the truth. But, I was thinking fifteen minutes is an awfully long time to listen to someone going on and on."

"On and on, that's what you think we do?"

"You know what I mean. I just wonder if you aren't missing your mark a bit by trying to tell them too many things. You know the KISS acronym, Keep It Simple Stupid."

"No, I guess I missed that one," he said and squeaked around to face his typewriter, signaling the end of our conversation.

"Well, I don't want to piss you off, but whatever you ran as your message didn't seem to cut it. You played the thing four separate times. Fifteen minutes a crack, that's an hour and unless you got a call center tucked away somewhere, I never heard a phone ring all day long, ever. Not trying to tell you how to run your business, Thompson, that's just my opinion."

"That's part of what's gone wrong with this great nation. Everything comes down to the ten-second sound bite. Is that what freedom means to you, ten seconds?"

23

I waited for a moment, a long moment, maybe ten seconds worth.

"Nine forty-five tomorrow, right?"

Chapter Four

It was more of the same the next day. The term boring wouldn't begin to do it justice. Add to that the hot, humid weather and a nap had become one of my top priorities.

Immediately after the dreadful afternoon broadcast Thompson and Farrell had me follow them out of the office to the stairway. As we trudged down the six flights of stairs they filled me in on their latest brain fart. Then Thompson said, "So we up and decided, let's just advance in another direction."

"Do you think this is a good idea? I mean, wasn't the plan that you were going to keep a low profile?" I asked.

"Within reason, but one can never be timid when freedom is involved," Thompson replied. He sounded breathless and he still had another flight to waddle down.

"But a press conference in front of the building?" I said, "I don't know, it…"

"That's right, you don't know. We'll be just in time to hit the Six O'clock news. Look, Haskin, I'll handle the PR, you just handle protection," Thompson wheezed, then pushed the door open and we stepped outside.

There were two cameramen and two people I guessed to be reporters standing there. They were chatting, waiting and looking very bored. One guy flicked a cigarette off to the side as the door closed behind us. I had news for them. It was about to get a lot worse. A woman I sort of recognized in a blonde way was on her cell phone with her back to us.

"Ladies and gentlemen, thank you for coming. I'm Thompson Barkwell, CEO of K-R-A-Z, craze radio, seven-forty on your dial. I'm sure you're all familiar with our on air personality, Farrell J. Earley."

Farrell nodded, pushed his glasses back up on his nose and exhaled a blue cloud of smoke. Thompson continued, "We're here today to discuss an extremely serious situation. Over the course of the past seventy-two hours we…"

"Excuse me, please. Please, excuse me, sir, Mr. Barky, is it?" asked the blonde on the cell phone.

"Barkwell, Thompson Barkwell."

"Sure, Tiffany Kinny, from *The Source*. Would you mind starting over? Sorry. I was on the phone to one of my kids and by the way, do you have a hand out?"

"A hand out, no. I do not have a hand out. Maybe you could listen. I have some prepared remarks, and then I'll take your questions." Thompson suddenly produced a sheaf of papers that looked like a small phone book. He cleared his throat and began reading.

"It is time that the concept of Freedom of Speech in this great nation is taken back by the people. The very patriots who, in 1776, refused to stand idly by while…"

One of the camera men lowered his camera, shrugged and looked very bored. I'd have said Tiffany what's-her-face stopped writing, but then I was pretty sure she had never started. Thompson droned on, and on. Farrell had assumed a sort of military parade rest position and stared straight ahead wearing a more dazed look than usual. I tuned the whole thing out and watched a bus fifty yards away at the corner.

By now Thompson was working his way through the Gettysburg address.

"… it is for us the living rather, to be dedicated here to the unfinished work…"

He lunged, or did he fall? I didn't know. I was just coming back to reality when I heard the shot, and then another. I saw the car race down the street. Farrell was over Thompson, shielding him. I glanced down the street, but couldn't read the license plate. Hell, I couldn't even tell if the plate was from Minnesota. A nondescript grey or silver something, but I couldn't catch the make of the car.

One thing for sure, the cameras were suddenly rolling, focused on Thompson and Farrell. Thompson mumbled something to Farrell, they got up together, and dusted themselves off.

"Is everyone all right? Anyone hurt?"

"Jesus Christ, did you get that shit?" Tiffany Kinny asked a cameraman from where she was crouched behind a trash can.

"Anything Haskell?" Farrell asked.

I shook my head, still staring down the street. The car was long gone.

"Nothing, not a thing."

"Folks, who knew? They think they can silence the craze, K-R-A-Z, seven-forty on your dial. Seven-forty, get it? Seven four, like July fourth. Seventh month, fourth day. Freedom, Freedom, we will not be silenced. We've hit a nerve, people. We're speaking the truth and the lefties don't like it. No, sir, we will not be silenced."

27

The cameras continued to roll as Thompson spoke. Tiffany shook her hair left and right, then lunged into camera range moving closer to Thompson.

"Who is this gentleman?" she asked Thompson, indicating me with a movement of her head.

"Security. It's the sad state of affairs in our great nation that we have to hire protection in order to speak the truth. The silent majority can not continue to sit idly by while…"

I was wondering where the rounds hit. They should have hit the building, or the steps or someone. Nothing. I heard a distant siren that seemed to be getting closer.

Chapter Five

We were back up on the sixth floor in KRAZ
National Headquarters. We had gathered in
Thompson's dingy little office. Thompson, Farrell, me,
two patrol officers and Detective Norris Manning, from
Homicide.

"Well, I would hope certain people will take that
death threat from the other day a little more seriously
now," Thompson said, enthroned behind his electric
typewriter, looking from me to Manning and then back
to me.

Manning's blue eyes looked exceptionally bright.
He nodded his pink, bald head, attacked his chewing
gum with his front teeth and didn't say anything.

Thompson kept his attention on me.

"I thought we hired you for protection. That
certainly doesn't seem to be happening, does it? Do you
have anything to say in your defense?"

"In my defense? Look, with all due respect, you
told me about your news conference literally fifteen
seconds before you stepped out the door and in front of
the cameras. I barely had time to tell you it was a stupid
idea. I believe you told me at some point you were
going to handle the PR. Isn't that right?"

Thompson sighed and then attempted to level a
withering gaze at Manning, I don't think it worked.

"And do you have any leads? Any idea what
organization is trying to stifle the truth? Who's trying

to eliminate our right to freedom of expression? It seems to me, one of the things you should be doing is to…"

"One of the things I should be doing is getting a list from you of exactly who knew about your news conference, for starters," Manning interrupted.

"I think we can safely assume it wasn't one of our contacts in the media," Thompson said.

"Really, who else knew about the press conference? Unless maybe someone just driving past suddenly developed the urge to take a shot at you?"

Thompson went beet red. I didn't think Manning's question seemed so far-fetched.

"Allow me to be blunt, Detective. I find nothing funny about this vicious attempt on our lives," Thompson replied.

"Nor do I," Manning glared.

"Tommy, it's almost five-thirty. Give me a hand getting the broadcast uploaded. Is that all right, Detective? Shouldn't take us more than five minutes. Give us all a moment to collect our thoughts," Farrell said rising to his feet, stretching, and waiting for Manning's answer.

"Yeah sure, we've got someone at the door. You're not leaving the office, are you?"

"No, sir, just our broadcast booth down the hall."

'That closet,' I thought.

"Please be my guest, gentlemen," Manning said, then turned his gaze toward me.

Farrell wandered out. Thompson waddled after him, still flushed in the face.

"Little twerp," Manning said, shaking his head.

"What do you think?" I asked.

"I think you're doing a particularly lousy job on protection detail. How did you find these characters anyway? Don't tell me you're a fan?"

"No, nothing like that. Actually they contacted me. Someone gave them a referral and they called."

"Someone gave a referral on you? Jesus, they must have been nuts."

I couldn't see anything that would be gained by answering.

"What's with this joint?" Manning asked. He was examining a number of dust balls from the back of the couch with his fingertips.

"It's a conservative radio show or station, I guess. They broadcast a fifteen minute radio message, four times a day."

"That's it?"

I nodded. "I think the rule of thumb is you have to hear something four times in a twenty-four hour period to make it stick."

Manning stared at me, wide eyed. "Something's God damned goofy around here. And they got you through a referral? This ain't your usual cheating spouse with the babysitter routine. What the hell do you do here, anyway?"

Well, to tell you the truth not very much…"

"There's a surprise," Manning scoffed.

"I check out the building and parking lot a few times. Sit around up here. They usually never leave. Well, except for today, but I wasn't kidding. I didn't find out about that press conference thing until just before we stepped outside and in front of the cameras."

Manning nodded, but didn't say anything.

"Be interesting to see if your people find the slugs."

"Why do you say that?"

31

"I don't know, it'll just be interesting," I said.

"You place the 911 call?"

I shook my head.

"Who then?"

"Tell you the truth, I was watching the shooter's car disappear down the street and heard the siren in the distance. Pretty exceptional response."

"Yeah, well, we're known for doing exceptional things," Manning said and then looked up as Farrell and Thompson returned.

"The truth shall not be silenced," Thompson said, settling back in behind his desk.

"You were going to give me a list of everyone you contacted regarding your press conference," Manning said and then set about attacking his piece of gum.

Chapter Six

Manning kept me cooling my heels at KRAZ for at least another hour. I had to pinch myself to stay awake. The only thing of any interest was a large fly circling around the ceiling light in the front office. The thing looked about as desperate as me to find a way out. By the time I was given the okay to flee it was close to 8:00. I had just pulled up in front of my house when my cell rang. I attempted to read the caller id, but couldn't.

"Haskell Investigations."

"Oh, stop it. Quit pretending to sound busy."

"Hey, Heidi, what's happening?"

My friend, sometimes lover for a night, and occasional bail provider, Heidi Bauer. I was guessing she was on the rebound from another failed relationship.

"Believe me if there was anything going on in my life I wouldn't be calling you. You eat dinner yet?"

"I'm just on my way home, working late." I glanced at my watch. I pulled back onto the street and headed for Solo Vino, the wine store just a block away. It would take close to two bottles to get Heidi either in the mood or to the point she didn't care if it was me in her bed. I had about four minutes before they closed.

"Look, I'm just doing some leftovers, you interested?"

She must have already completed her standard week of swearing off all men forever and was thinking she could use and abuse the likes of me, which was just fine with me.

"I'm on my way," I replied and hung up just as I pulled in front of the wine store. I waved wildly at my pal Chuck as he prepared to lock the door.

"Cutting it close," he said, holding the door for me.

"Emergency rations needed."

"In other words you're going to try and get some poor woman intoxicated to the point where she'll forget how revolting you are."

"You know me, just drunk enough so they can't testify."

"I shouldn't even let you in. I should just lock the door, go home and rest with an easy conscience."

"Since when has that ever been fun? Here, I'll take these two. No better make it three."

Heidi doesn't cook, she never has. So the excellent meal she was taking out of the oven shortly after I arrived came from somewhere. We were at her kitchen counter sipping and midway through the second bottle of wine.

"You still seeing what's his name?"

"Don't ever mention that creeps' name in my presence."

"Jerold?"

"What did I just tell you?" She drained her glass.

"Sorry, want to tell me about it?" I asked, refilling her glass.

"No. Except, where do I find this constant parade of creeps?"

"Last time we talked you said he was everything you ever wanted and more."

"Oh, he was. Unfortunately the *more* part turned out to mean married."

"Oh, that."

She took another healthy sip.

"Yeah, that."

"Speaking of married, did I mention I was involved in a drive by shooting today? Actually, that's what I was coming from when you phoned. I thought it was a bogus protection gig and then…"

"Plus, his wife was pregnant, with two kids." Another healthy sip.

"She was expecting twins?"

"No, they already have two kids. This was number three on the way. I'm just lucky he didn't knock me up." She drained her glass and then slid it across the counter in my direction.

"There you go, that good old positive attitude," I said, pouring a refill.

"It's just a joke to guys, isn't it?" she said, then downed half the glass I'd just poured.

"So anyway, we're all at this outdoor press conference and someone drives by and fires two rounds at us. My clients received a threatening note two days be…"

"He tried to tell me it was his sister," she said and took another large swallow. "I ran into the happy family at the Mall of America. Stupid me, I'm coming out of Victoria's Secret with a couple of sets of date underwear and guess who I run into? The happy family… kids, mom ten plus months along and Jerold the jerk."

"So, did you return the underwear?"

"Shut up. You ready for dinner?"

"Yeah, what did you make?"

"Whatever my friend Carol was going to serve us for dinner that night. Jerold and I were supposed to go over there, but under the circumstances… you know, him, me, pregnant wifey and the two kids. I thought it might be a little much so I canceled. Carol sent dinner over so I took it out of the fridge this morning. I've been eating chocolates, donuts and ice cream for a week and decided I better get back to eating healthy."

"Well, it smells good, and you look great. His loss." I raised my wine glass to her.

"My glass is empty," she said and held it out for a refill just to prove her point.

Over dinner I heard, in no uncertain terms, what an absolute rat Jerold turned out to be. She was still in the process of composing the multi-page email she planned to send. In it, she called Jerold every name in the book and reserved a special place in hell just for him. He could just languish in eternal flames chained next to Cambodia's Pol Pot and whoever invented pledge week for public radio.

I found the remote and turned on her flat screen just as the news led with "Shots fired at a St. Paul press conference."

"Oh, God, I can't take another minute. I'm going to bed. You coming?" she asked, more like a command, as she walked out of the kitchen with a determined look on her face.

I figured I could catch the news later.

Chapter Seven

I had a vague recollection of Heidi kissing me goodbye when she left for work. I pulled a perfumed pillow over my head, drifted back to sleep, then woke to my cell phone ringing. I cleared my throat a few times before I answered.

"Haskell Investigations."

"Where are you? We don't have any idea what we're facing here." It was Thompson Barkwell.

"Thompson, sorry, meant to call… just leaving the police station. I've been meeting with a number of people, including their psychologist, trying to work up a profile," I said as I frantically looked for my boxer shorts.

"Oh, really, what did they say?"

"Bit too sketchy right now. They're going to reexamine that note, see if they can pick up anything from the handwriting."

"Handwriting? The damn thing was typed."

Shit.

"Yeah, but the words used, the language… you know the thrust of the thing. It seemed to suggest an educated individual, perhaps someone familiar with philosophy, political theory, that sort of thing. Most likely well read."

"Yes, yes, I suppose that makes sense."

"Anyway, secure facility, as you can imagine, so I couldn't phone. I'm on my way over now. I should be there shortly."

"We'll be waiting," he said and hung up.

I supposed it would be too much to ask that Heidi would leave me some coffee after availing herself of my services last night. It was. I'd have to stop for coffee on the way.

I pulled into the warehouse parking lot at KRAZ. Crime scene tape was still wrapped around the area where the press conference had been held, but the only person there was a kid ducking under the tape and going in the door. I parked next to what looked like an unmarked police vehicle. I had a bad feeling and left my cup of coffee in the car.

"Well, Devlin Haskell, sleuth extraordinaire. Sorry I missed you this morning down at the station."

Detective Manning seemed far too cheery standing in the front office of KRAZ sipping coffee. At six foot two he dwarfed Thompson standing next to him, who looked like a stuffed animal you'd win at the fair.

"I was explaining to Detective Manning about the profile the police psychologist put together. Educated, grounded in philosophy and political theory, well read. What else did you say?" Thompson asked.

"Yes, yes, tell me what did you and the psychologist come up with?" Manning's blue eyes focused in on me like lasers.

"Well, it's a bit complex. I mean you know yourself, Detective. Any profile is a work in progress. Any news on a weapon or rounds fired?"

"No. Funny thing, nothing found, not even a point of impact. We've been over the front of the building with a fine tooth comb more times than I care to recall, and nothing."

"Did you see the news last night? We were on all the stations. Great publicity," Thompson said and then dashed off to answer of all things, a ringing phone.

"Psychologist?" Manning asked.

"Yeah, I know. Look, I had to come up with something. I was working another case."

"Really? She has very nice perfume." Manning sniffed.

"And you guys haven't found anything?"

"Not so much as a scuff mark on the sidewalk."

"Could it have been blanks?"

"Why do you ask?"

"Why? 'Cause you said you didn't find anything."

"You heard the shots. What's your take?" He set his empty Starbucks cup on a stack of files, then opened a piece of gum, tossed it into his mouth and began to attack.

"Well, yeah I heard them, but I wasn't really paying attention. I was thinking of something else. Actually I was looking at a bus, and..."

"A bus?" Manning half shouted.

"Hey, have you heard these guys ramble on and on? You have to tune it out or you'd go nuts. Actually, what caught my attention was Thompson going down. Then, Farrell jumps on top of him, protecting him. I guess. Somewhere in there I thought I heard a couple of shots."

"You saying they were down before the shots were fired?"

"No, I'm saying I was looking at a bus, it gets crazy for two or three seconds and I can't be sure of the sequence. Hell, I can sort of see the car speeding off, but I can't tell you what kind of vehicle. Maybe grey, silver, light blue, I can't be sure. I can't even tell you if it had Minnesota plates."

"And you're providing protection? Good luck."

Chapter Eight

If the day didn't go downhill from there it certainly didn't improve. Time seemed to stand still. The phone at KRAZ national headquarters was ringing off the hook and interrupting any attempts at a nap. I had stationed myself on a wooden chair behind Detective Manning's empty Starbuck's cup and the stacks of files. I was reading a newspaper from about six weeks earlier, occasionally nodding off, when the door opened. A familiar figure with gleaming brunette hair and eating an apple strutted in.

"Devlin Haskell?"

It was Farrell's lunatic sister Kiki, only now she had clothes on and I didn't see a knife. I still thought it might be a good idea if I kept the desk between us.

"Kiki?"

"Hi, I hear there was a lot of excitement yesterday." She smiled, wrinkled her nose and shrugged like a sexy teenager.

"Yeah, the good news is no one was hurt."

"They catch the guy yet?" She took two steps around the side of the desk.

I folded my newspaper and then casually rolled it up just in case I had to swat her away.

"No, I don't think they have any suspects, yet."

"But they're working on that profile, right? Farrell said you were involved in that this morning." She took a step closer to me.

"Yeah, yeah, we're working on that and a number of other things." I attempted to back up, but bumped against the chair.

She suddenly squeezed my arm, leaned in close and whispered, her breath tickling my ear.

"That was so hot the other day. God, I lost count. You, well, let's just say you made me crazy." She smiled, bit her bottom lip and thrust her cleavage against my arm.

She was absolutely beautiful and certifiably nuts.

"I don't think I can wait very long before we do that again. What do you say?"

I could hear her panting. As she let go, she ran her nails along my arm, then squeezed my hand, gorgeous brown eyes suddenly going wide. I felt like I had a gun to my head, or in Kiki's case, a knife to my throat.

"Yeah, it was really unique."

"Later. Tiger. You may have just created a monster," she growled softly, licked her upper lip, then turned and walked back to Thompson's office taking a big bite out of her apple.

I was sweating and thought it might be a good time to go check out the rest of the building. I wandered aimlessly through the top three floors of the building before I drifted out to the tree line at the back of the parking lot just to see if someone might be out there with a rocket propelled grenade.

No such luck, but I did see Kiki exit the building, bounce down the steps and walk over to the silver Audi parked next to my DeVille. She took her sweet time getting in, fumbling with her keys or something before she eventually got behind the wheel and pulled away. I went back up to KRAZ national headquarters where I twiddled my thumbs for the better part of the next three hours. The ringing phones prevented me from catching any serious shut eye. About five-thirty Thompson drifted out of his lair and stood in the doorway. Farrell hovered behind him in the shadows.

"Say, looks like the threat has subsided. I don't think we'll need your services tomorrow, or the day after for that matter."

"What?"

"I feel rather certain the danger's past."

"The danger's past? That's interesting. When do you think you'll need me then?"

"Either you're trying to be funny, and you're not. Or, I don't think you're following what I'm telling you."

"Which is?"

"Which is, do not come in tomorrow, or the next day or ever again for that matter. I think we have things well in hand here now. You can just leave and send us your invoice. We'll run it past the board."

"Board?"

"Review board… before we sign off on any invoice over twenty-five dollars, our review board has to approve it. I'm guessing your invoice will be more than twenty-five dollars, won't it? Look, don't worry, the board meets every six weeks," he added cheerfully.

"So, when did they last meet?"

"Oh about a week ago. On the twelfth, I believe."

"So I'm not going to get paid for another five weeks?"

"I don't know that I'd look at it exactly like that." Thompson shook his head as he spoke. He placed his hands on his wide hips, apparently daring me to challenge the idea of waiting five weeks to have my invoice reviewed.

"My terms are payment due when the invoice is presented."

"I understand, and we'll certainly review that at the board meeting. Of course, we'll have to be in receipt of your invoice before we can review it. For approval, that is."

"Yeah, well tell you what, why don't I drop it off sometime tomorrow?" I suggested.

"Oh, that won't be necessary. Don't go to any additional trouble. You can just put it in the mail and we'll…"

"What, and trust the government? I don't think so. Besides, they could just as easily be monitoring all mail arriving at this address."

"Do you think so?" Thompson asked.

I couldn't tell if he was serious or not. I was afraid he was, very serious.

"I'll drop it off tomorrow," I said, standing and stretching.

"Well, suit yourself. Of course, you could always donate your time. Our listeners would tend to look favorably on a gesture like that."

Yeah, *'both of your listeners,'* I thought. "I'll consider that. See you tomorrow," I said and walked out the door of the asylum.

When I got to my car, someone had scratched a large "Fuck You" onto the driver's door, probably with a key. Kiki?

Chapter Nine

My cell ringing the following morning woke me up. By the time I found it resting in a shoe under my bed, the call had dumped into my message center.

"Yes, Mr. Haskell, Detective Norris Manning. It's eleven-forty-five, please give me a call at your earliest convenience. Today."

I put some coffee on, showered, shaved, brought in yesterday's mail, ate a couple of slices of cold pizza for breakfast, plucked some nose hair, then called Manning and left a message.

"Devlin Haskell, returning your call. I'm in meetings most of the day, but please call back. Hopefully we can connect."

I filled a travel mug with coffee, then drifted out the door in the direction of my car. I poked my head in The Spot, just to check for messages and then crossed the street to my office. I had just put my feet up on the desk when my cell phone rang.

"Haskell Investigations."

"Did I catch you between meetings?"

"Detective Manning, you did as a matter of fact. How can I help you?"

"Sorry if my initial call got you out of bed." He didn't seem to be kidding.

"Like I said, I've been in meetings all day."

"Sure you have. Listen, I wonder if you wouldn't mind stopping by. We've got a couple of questions for you, possibly some new ground we might like to cover."

"Oh?" I sat up interested.

"Just routine."

"Name a time," I said, leering out the window at a nice looking mommy in tight little yellow shorts, pushing a stroller across the street.

"I thought you had meetings?" he said.

"Things are moving along a lot faster than I thought. I could actually wind this up in… oh, I don't know, maybe the next thirty or forty-five minutes."

"Sure you can, that's great," he said, sounding like he didn't mean a word of it.

"See you in an hour?" I asked.

"You know where we are?" he said.

"Yeah, been there once or twice before. See you in an hour."

I strolled over to The Spot, figured a quick beer couldn't hurt, stayed for two, and then I drove down to Manning's office at police headquarters. I cooled my heels in the lobby until someone came down to get me.

Wayneta Van Haug, pronounced Juanita, was decidedly overweight, always crabby and unfortunately named. She was a uniformed officer, and one immediately wondered where you purchased uniforms that large. She had not a drop of Hispanic heritage. She did however have four older brothers, Wayne, du Wayne, de Wayne, da Wayne. Her ill-advised parents attempted to maintain the family tradition when their darling daughter was born, and so named her Wayneta. We all make mistakes.

"I know you from some where's," she said, once we were in the elevator.

We were ascending six floors. The elevator creaked and shuddered and I was genuinely concerned I might not make it with Wayneta on board. I clung tightly to the hand rail on the back wall and focused on the digital floor readout as we groaned our way up to six.

"Where'd we meet? You been hauled in here before?" she asked, and leaned intimidatingly closer.

I continued to focus on the digital readout over the door. Third floor seemed to be taking its own sweet time.

"I've been in a few times. I'm a private investigator. I've worked with Detective Manning before. Worked with Lieutenant Aaron LaZelle, over in vice, a few times. Maybe you know him. We probably met that way, or maybe you just saw me or heard about me from those guys. Nice to see you again," I said, thinking I couldn't possibly forget ever meeting her.

She half scoffed under her breath.

"He told me just to bring you up here. Don't know why he didn't want to put you in an interrogation room," she said, staring at me.

We were coming up on five, not fast enough for my taste.

"Just some general background information. I witnessed something the other day, and thought I might be able to help Manning with his ongoing investigation."

That got me another scoff. Mercifully six finally blinked on. We seemed to just hold there for an ungodly length of time. I was sure the computer was busy calculating how many seconds remained before the elevator cable snapped and we dropped to the basement. Eventually the doors groaned open.

"Six," Wayneta said and stepped off into the hallway. The elevator rose an inch or two and I quickly jumped off behind her.

"He's in there," she said, pointing to a door labeled Homicide. Then turned and waddled toward where the donuts were kept.

I quickly headed for the safety of Homicide, knocked and stepped into a small lobby with a receptionist's window. A guy in shirt sleeves was walking past the window and glanced out at me.

"Can I help you?"

"Yeah, Devlin Haskell, to see Detective Manning."

"He expecting you?"

"He is."

"Hey Man Eater, some guy named Haskell to see you." He called, then walked away.

Chapter Ten

Manning suddenly appeared at the window.

"Haskell, thanks for coming down. Come on in," he said, then buzzed something that opened the security door next to the receptionist window and I walked in.

Manning's battleship-grey cubicle was devoid of any personality, not so much as the photograph of a dog. It did look neat, orderly and gave the sense of a highly efficient individual in residence.

"Grab that chair there, will you?" He indicated a chrome and grey fabric chair next to a black, two-drawer file cabinet.

I sat and looked around quickly, not that there was anything to see.

"You want some coffee?" he asked, blue eyes fixed on me. He raised a paper coffee cup from a vending machine to his lips, slurped, grimaced, then waited.

"No thanks, I've had stuff from your machine before."

"Can't say that I blame you," he said then slurped again.

I hadn't done anything wrong, at least in regard to the KRAZ shooting, but I was still on guard.

Manning set his coffee cup on the desk area behind him, picked up a thin file, flicked through a couple of pages, then read for what seemed a long moment before he looked up. While he read I examined the top of his bald head. It was decidedly pink, as if it had been somehow contaminated by his fringe of red hair. I figured him for one of those redheads who never tanned, but just burned to varying degrees.

"Look, let me level with you… the K-R-A-Z deal, it isn't adding up."

"Not adding up?" I wasn't following.

"Here's the deal. You were there. You seem to have some limited experience, so that's why I wanted to chat."

I nodded.

"It's a drive by, theoretically. No one's hit, that's good. No impact site located from the shots that were supposedly fired, that's not so good. Depending on which statement we're dealing with, some say two, others say three shots fired. You say two, along with a couple of others. I've got a couple of the news guys who swear three shots. Not unusual. Really doesn't matter and no way we can seem to confirm or deny, at least at this point." He picked up his coffee and slurped some more, then sat back waiting for my reply.

"If it's a drive by, I mean this wasn't gang bangers sticking a MAC 10 out the window and spraying someone's front porch. This was two, I think, two definite shots fired, no more than a second apart, from a moving vehicle. It seems logical the shooter might have missed," I said.

Manning nodded in agreement.

"What do the cameras have? There were news crews there. They must have filmed the thing. They got it all on film right? Audio?"

"Wrong. Two cameras, plus a recorder from the reporter woman…"

"Tiffany what's her name."

"Kinny. Tiffany Kinny, Channel Nine. They were all turned off. Somewhere between rambling from the Bill of Rights, through the Declaration of Independence to Lincoln's Gettysburg Address they turned off the cameras. Your girlfriend Tiffany switched off her recorder. Save on batteries, I guess. Anyway, all we've got is that pudgy little guy…"

"Thompson Barkwell."

"That's him, got him going on and on."

"Tell me about it," I groaned.

"The next thing we see is your pal Farrell huddled on the ground on top of Barkwell."

"Yeah, you know in defense of him, Barkwell might have been huddling, but Farrell covered the guy. I mean, regardless of what you're suggesting, all he knew is someone was shooting and he protected Barkwell. That takes some brass ones."

"So you say."

"Ever been shot at, Detective?"

Manning nodded, then went in a different direction.

"How long have you been working for K-R-A-Z, craze?"

"Actually, just a few days. They let me go yesterday as a matter of fact."

"Let you go?"

"Yeah, said they had things in hand, send them an invoice, that sort of deal. I was gonna drop it off, the invoice, after this. Got it out in my car if you want to see it?"

"Can you just email me a copy?"

"Yeah, I think so," I said, figuring I could get Sunnie Einer, my computer gal to show me how.

"Why'd they let you go? You'd figure after someone took a couple of shots at them they'd want protection, such as it is." He looked me up and down. "You have an argument or anything?"

"Argument? Why would you think that?" I asked, regretting the question before it had left my lips.

"Nothing really… just seemed you got a bit, oh, I don't know, exercised maybe. When we were all up in the office the other afternoon and Barkwell asked you about security, remember?"

"Well, I think I said something like I knew about the press conference fifteen seconds before it happened. That's a literal time frame by the way, not just some figure of speech. We're walking down the damn staircase on the way to the thing, he tells me about it just before we walked through the door, and suddenly we're standing in front of reporters and cameras."

"Would you have done anything differently?"

"Probably not. I mean, if you had to hold the damn thing outside, to be honest that was as good a place as any. Would have been better in an enclosed area, but I get it. It's just that the whole thing was a surprise. They had to know it was going to happen an hour, two hours, maybe the day before. Never bothered to tell me and then it's my fault? Christ, kiss my butt."

"No, thanks." Manning might have actually smiled.

"Like I said, other than getting paid, I'm out of it." Manning nodded.

"Any women work there?"

"Women?"

"Yeah, you know, nice looking, perfume, don't want to associate with guys like you. Any women work there?"

I let his comment go.

"No, at least as far as I know. Obviously, I haven't been around there all that much. You were up there. The office is small to begin with, national headquarters or not. They've got junk piled everywhere. I've only seen the two of them there, Thompson Barkwell and Farrell J. Earley. No other employees, male or female as far as I know. Tell you the truth I think they're running on a shoestring. My impression is they don't have the funds to pay anyone, at least not much."

"You worried about getting paid?" He was flipping through a couple of pages from the file on his lap, pretending to read. I was sure he was listening for any telltale sign.

"Yeah, somewhat. Barkwell told me they have to run my invoice past some committee or board or some damn thing, get the thing approved before they can pay it."

"And that worries you?"

"Not as far as actually getting paid. It's just that he said the committee meets in almost five weeks. Do the math, five weeks before they meet. Then get the run around for another week before the check's cut, another week before it's in the mail. It's two damn months before I'm paid."

"We talking a lot?"

"Not really, it's just the principle of the thing."

"That's what springs to mind when I think of you, Haskell, principle."

I ignored his comment.

"They're just jacking me around, and any other guy stupid enough to deal with them. Comes with the territory, I guess."

"You remember who made the 911 call?"

"No. Tell you the truth, I was watching the car drive off, not that it did any good."

"It was a woman's voice." Manning was back to flipping pages, looking disinterested.

"Well, to be honest, there wasn't much of a crowd. Hell, there wasn't even a crowd. I mean, Barkwell, Farrell J., that Tiffany chick, some other guy, two cameramen. That was it. Well and me, six, seven total. There wasn't a crowd. Hell, the whole thing was staged for the news cameras."

Manning nodded.

"Tiffany was on a phone apparently with a kid when we first came out of the building. In fact, she asked Barkwell to repeat himself because she sort of missed whatever he said initially. She the one who called 911?"

"Nope." Manning shook his head. "Fact is, the call came about two blocks away. We triangulated the towers. Call came from a disposable phone, false records plus thirty five dollars cash and you're good to go. It's a dead end."

"That's strange."

"You think? The whole deal is strange. Look, thanks for your time," Manning said getting to his feet, then held out his hand. It was like shaking a brick, no give when I squeezed.

"Can you find your way out? If not, I could always get officer Van Haug to escort you back down."

"That won't be necessary," I said and made my way to the door.

"Mr. Haskell, good luck with your invoice. You'll email a copy, right?"

"Thanks, I will," I said and left.

Chapter Eleven

I pulled into the parking lot at the international headquarters of KRAZ. I dodged a couple of the potholes and parked. Some newspaper and a BBQ potato chip bag scuttled past me as I walked into the building. I took the back steps up to the sixth floor, by the time I made it to the top I had to pause a moment to catch my breath, then walked down the hallway to the office.

I remembered not to swing the door widely when I went in. Instead, I sort of stepped sideways to enter the office.

"Halt, identify yourself."

"What?"

"Identify yourself," a short, fat guy groaned as he came out of a chair in the process of blinking himself awake. He was dressed in camouflaged combat fatigues that looked brand new. They were a woodland pattern, not the digitized stuff like we had in Iraq. He had gold Sergeant Major stripes sewn on both sleeves. He wore spit-polished combat boots with his trousers bloused into the top of the boots. An olive drab web belt was cinched snugly around his forty-six inch waist. He fumbled with the top of a black leather holster at his side. I assumed he was attempting to pull a pistol out.

I spun him around, pushed him up against the wall, pinned his arm behind his back then pulled a forty-five caliber pistol out of his holster.

"Ouch, ouch, get off, get off, damn it, you're killing me," he groaned.

"You idiot, this damn thing is loaded," I said, feeling the weight of the weapon. I yanked his arm up a little higher behind his back.

"Aw, God, uncle, okay, okay, I give up, let me go, I'll talk, I'll talk."

I released my grip and took a step back, extracted the clip from the pistol, then pulled the slide back and ejected a round that bounced across the floor.

"What the hell is this? You're lucky you haven't killed someone or shot yourself, you boob. Who the hell are you?"

He wore a pained look on his face, his jowls and chins were suddenly flushed. He stood there looking hurt and rubbing his elbow. The web belt around his waist was cinched tightly around his massive midsection, a large roll of fat ballooned above and below the belt.

"Who the hell are you?" I asked again.

"Hogue, Matthias, C. Command Sergeant Major. Four-five-five, three-five…"

"Shut up, you fuckwit. Don't give me that name, rank and serial number bullshit or I'll…"

"Sergeant Major, is everything…oh, you." Thompson Barkwell stood in the doorway leading back to his office. He sounded disappointed.

"He doesn't have the password, sir?" The camouflaged toad said, then sniffled and continued to rub his elbow.

I glared at him.

He took a step back and stared at the floor.

"At ease, Sergeant Major." Thompson Barkwell looked me over. "I thought we dismissed you yesterday. What do you want, Hastings?" he said.

"Haskell. Just dropping off my invoice, Tommy. I didn't think I was going to be breeching your security. Password? Are you guys nuts? A fucking password isn't going to help. I'm already in here."

I made my thumb and forefinger into a gun, pointed it at Sergeant Major Tubby and dropped my thumb. "Bang! Your fat ass is dead."

I pointed at Thompson, dropped my thumb, twice for good measure. "Bang, bang, you're really dead, Tommy."

"That sort of behavior is neither necessary nor helpful," Thompson said.

I just shook my head.

"Look, if you guys are really under threat, you'd better start taking things a little more seriously and knock off the toy soldier bullshit. That sure as hell ain't cuttin' it."

"Was there some purpose to your unauthorized visit this afternoon?" Thompson asked.

I took a deep breath, attempted to relax.

"Yeah, here's my invoice. Payment upon receipt," I said, handing him the envelope with the invoice enclosed.

He looked at the envelope in my hand, but made no effort to take it.

"And as I explained to you, yesterday. Your invoice will be reviewed at our next board meeting."

"You did explain that. And, as I told you, I would be dropping this invoice off, today, and my terms are payment upon receipt."

"Do you have a signed contract, Mr. Haskell?"

"You know I don't. But I think under the circumstances you might just want me paid and out of your hair."

"What circumstances would those be?"

"Well, for starters, I just came from the police station. They called me down for a chat. They seemed to be a little curious about the attempt on your life. You know, the press conference, the shooting, the…"

"Our right to free speech shall not be silenced. We…"

"The phone call to 911, made from a couple of blocks away. You know, you should have thought things through a little better, before you had her call," I bluffed.

It was Thompson Barkwell's turn to go red faced.

"I'll take that. Wait here while I cut you a check," he said, then snatched the envelope out of my hand and stomped back toward his office.

"Could I, could I have my gun back?" the Sergeant Major whined.

"Are you kidding me?"

"It's, it's not mine. It belongs to one of the other guys on the team."

"Team?"

"Seal Team Six, there's six of us. We've sworn an oath…"

"Stop, before I really hurt you. Seal Team Six… this isn't some fucking toy, numb nuts. This thing is loaded. In fact, you know what? Spoils of war, I'm keeping it. You better find a new line of work because this sure as hell doesn't seem to fit you."

"But I promised I'd take care…"

"Mr. Haskell, here, your deed is done, now get out," Thompson called from behind me, then thrust a check in my direction.

I glanced at the amount, about a hundred and twenty-five bucks short.

"That's not the right amount."

"I took a twenty percent discount, based on early payment."

"Twenty percent, that's not my policy."

"No, but it's mine. Good day, Mr. Haskell."

"You're stiffing me for a hundred and twenty-five bucks?"

"No, I'm paying you more than you're worth as it is. Now get out before I call the police."

"This isn't the last you've heard from me."

"Good day, Mr. Haskell."

Chapter Twelve

There wasn't much I could do. I thought about throwing Thompson out the window, but with the way my luck was running he would simply land on his thick skull and remain unfazed. Instead, I drove over to his bank, cashed his check before he had a chance to reconsider and stop payment. Then I drove to my office, rifled off a nasty letter and attached an invoice for the balance owed. I slapped a stamp on the envelope and mailed the thing before I had a chance to reconsider.

Amazingly, the mail box was right across the street from The Spot. I decided a beer couldn't hurt. I was successfully pursuing that activity some hours later when my phone rang.

"Haskell," I answered, forgetting the 'investigations' part.

"Oh, wow, Dev, how exciting. You sound positively uncivil. I heard you had a run in with that tubby little wart Tommy Barkwell, earlier."

"Who's this?" I was having trouble hearing over Lonesome George Thorogood cranking on the jukebox and I staggered outside into the heat.

"It's me, Kiki. Where in God's name are you?"

"The Spot. What do you want?" I mumbled, attempting to clear multiple beers from my head as I leaned against the outside of the building.

"Oh, I don't know, just a girl looking for some fun."

"Well, like I said, I'm at The Spot."

I didn't remember much beyond that. I knew Kiki must have shown up at some point because I woke up in her bed the next morning. Mercifully, there were no knives. In fact there wasn't any drama. Well, except for the spray painted "KRAZ SUCKS" in large red letters, about four feet high, across a bedroom wall.

"Holy shit," I groaned, stuffing my head back under her pillow.

"Here, take a couple of these," Kiki said, holding out what I guessed were four aspirin and what looked like a glass of orange juice.

I tossed all four aspirin into my mouth, then washed them down with the orange juice, sugary, sweet and the first non-alcoholic thing in my system in the past eighteen hours.

"Actually, two of those were for me," she said.

"Oh, sorry 'bout that God, that stuff was sweet, man." I smacked my lips and then ran my tongue over my fuzzy teeth.

"Yeah, I added sugar, lots of it. It's what the system craves just now. The sweet carbs will go a long way in fighting your hangover. I'm guessing you've got one… a hangover."

"The king of all hangovers. What the hell is this?" I asked as I turned my head back and forth to crack my neck and felt something tighten.

"Whoops, your collar and leash." Kiki laughed.

"My what?" I asked, sitting up, then glanced at the black leather leash along my side, reached up and felt where it clipped onto a dog collar around my neck.

"You were in need of some, um, training last night. Don't you remember, bad puppy?" she said, then gave the leash a tug.

"What?"

"Oh, you were a bad boy, a very bad boy." She giggled.

I noticed the grass stains on my knees.

"Need to be taken outside again?"

"No, no, ahhh look, I probably should get going, I've got a meeting. What time is it, do you know?"

"Just a little after two."

"In the afternoon?"

"Yes, in the afternoon. Do you think the sun would be out if it was two in the morning, silly?"

"Yeah, good point, I guess."

I swung my feet onto the floor, sat on the edge of her bed and took a couple of deep breaths, then looked around the bedroom for my jeans.

"You sure you haven't already missed your meeting?"

"I only wish. No, it's at three-thirty or four, I can't remember which," I lied.

"What are you doing?"

"Actually, to tell you the truth, I'm looking around for my jeans."

"Oh, I think you left them in your car."

"My car?"

"Yeah that big red clunky thing you drive… it's out in back."

"Oh, yeah, now I remember."

I thought I spied my T-shirt on the floor, began to pull it on, but it got caught up on the leash.

"Hey, could you maybe help get this thing off me. The leash?" My arms were up in the air with the T-shirt over my head.

"Yeah, I guess. By the way, that's my top you're putting on, unless you have one with spaghetti straps."

"Oh sorry." I peeked out at her as she climbed off the bed and unclipped the leash.

"Here, give me this. Now turn round," she said directing me with her hands.

"I think puppy needs a lot more training. What do you think?' She giggled and rubbed against my back.

"I think I need my jeans."

"I'll go get them," she said, pulling on a thong and exiting the bedroom.

"What if someone sees you?" I called.

"What if they do?" she said, already in the kitchen. I heard the back door open a moment later. After a couple of minutes she strolled back in, carrying my jeans, T-shirt and boxers.

"No worries, they were all in your car," she said like it was an everyday occurrence.

"Thanks for getting them," I said, then glanced at the spray painting on the bedroom wall as I pulled my boxers on.

"Enlighten me," I said, nodding at the wall.

"Oh, you did that right before I took you outside."

I looked at the graffiti I'd apparently sprayed on her bedroom wall. I must have been flying, I never wrote with capitol letters, but then again, I never wrote with spray paint either. It seemed particularly harsh against the beige walls and glossy white woodwork.

"You were pretty screwed up," she said.

"Yeah, I would say so. Look, sorry about that. I know a guy who can fix that. Paint it, I mean. Let me get him over here, take care of that right away."

"I don't know, I kind of like it."

"You do?"

"No, just yanking your chain. I mean, your leash," she said and held up the leash, giggled, then tossed it onto the bed with a suggestive look on her face.

"Look, I better run. Sorry to dash out like this," I said, slipping on my shoes.

"Sure?" she said, raising her eyebrows and running her tongue back and forth over her lips.

"I'll call my pal. I'm sure he can get over here in a day or two and get that taken care of."

"No rush," she said, following me out the bedroom door and into her kitchen.

We stopped, kissed and groped for a few minutes at her kitchen door.

"I gotta get going," I said," felt for my keys in the pocket of my jeans, kissed her a final time and stepped out the backdoor. She grabbed an apple off the counter, took a bite then stood there chewing, watching me as I walked out to my car in the alley.

"Hey, Dev, oouuuuuu!" she howled, just as I opened the gate.

I smiled, shook my head, then quickly closed the gate behind me, jumped into my car and locked all the doors.

Chapter Thirteen

I didn't drive home. Instead, I stopped by The Spot, just to see if I could piece things together from the night before. It sounded like Dear Martin on the juke box. I wasn't sure, but it was too early for whoever it was. I nodded at the three guys drinking.

"Hi, Dev," Linda called as I walked in the side door.

"Linda, how's it going?"

"Beer?" she asked.

"No, not right now. Just checking in. Any messages?"

She pulled a handful of pink "While you were Out" notes from behind the cash register, flipped through maybe a half dozen, shaking her head.

"No, no, don't look like there's anything here for you."

"Kinda working at putting last night together. Anything you're aware of?"

"No, I haven't heard much. Usual insanity, but you didn't shoot up the place or hide in the ladies room or anything, if that's what you mean. Least as far as I know."

"Okay, thanks."

I walked across the street and up the stairs to my second floor office. The office door was closed, but unlocked. I stepped inside and glanced around. Everything seemed to be in order. My laptop was open, but the screensaver was on, fireworks bouncing around. As soon as I touched the mouse the screen returned to a word document, a one page letter to Thompson Barkwell at KRAZ. The letter began with the greeting: Asshole. Not even so much as a 'Dear' in front of it. Then went down hill from there, demanding payment in full of the hundred and twenty-five dollars still owing. Two paragraphs calling Barkwell just about every name in the book followed by a third paragraph using rather colorful, often misspelled language describing exactly what I would do to him if he refused to comply with my payment request.

I always printed two copies of letters, one for a hard file, and the other to actually mail. There was one copy of the nice letter I'd sent before I went into The Spot. There was also one copy of the insane rant I'd just read. The book of stamps on my desk was empty and I knew there had been two or three stamps in there yesterday after sending the first letter. I must have stupidly mailed this second awful thing when I was drunk.

I went out to the mailbox on the corner. Pick up in about an hour at four-thirty. I wandered into The Spot and waited.

I didn't know her name, but I recognized her from across the street when she pulled up in the mail truck fifteen minutes early. Who ever expected the government to be early?

"Excuse me, ma'am," I called from the front door of The Spot, then half stumbled down the three steps in my hurry to get to her.

66

She was busy shoveling envelopes into a white plastic box stenciled with black letters. "Property US Postal Service."

"Excuse me, ma'am, I'd like to get a letter back. I think I tossed it in there last night," I called, half running across the street.

"Sorry, no can do, it's in the system now," she said as she shoveled the last two or three envelopes into the box and then looked up at me, dead pan.

"Yeah, I get that, but see, I sent the letter in the first place and I forgot to enclose something. Actually the check for payment. I don't want to waste the stamp, if I could just get it back. I'll put the check in, toss it back in the mail box, and you can pick it up tomorrow." I thought my little white lie sounded pretty convincing.

She smiled, nodded, seemed to consider my logic, and then said, "Nope. Sorry, against Federal regulations."

"But I wrote the letter, see, and forgot to put the check in, so if I could just get my letter back from you…"

"Yeah, I know, happens more than you think. Well, or so folks tell us. Anyway, I'm sorry, but once it's in the system, we can't. You could go down to the main Post Office, fill out… I don't know, maybe PS form 8076. Oh wait, that holds mail, you don't want that. They'd know the form number. This going out of town?"

"No, it stays right here, in St Paul."

"Oh, well then there's really nothing we can do It'll be sorted and delivered by tomorrow. Did you use zip plus four?"

"What?"

"Doesn't really matter, in town. it'll be in their hands tomorrow. Why not just put the check in another envelope? Mail it and maybe call them, explain what happened just to be sure."

"Why not just give me my letter back?"

"Wish I could, but it would be against government regulations. No can do."

"Come on, damn it, I mailed the damn thing to begin with. Besides, I don't have another stamp."

"So for the sake of forty-eight cents you want me to commit a Federal offense, that it? Sorry, not happening," she said and took two steps to her truck, tossed the box onto the floor and began to climb in.

"Aw, come on, you gotta be kidding. I think I saw my envelope on top of that pile of letters."

"Look, buddy, I said no. Now, if you'll excuse me."

I grabbed her ankle, then attempted to get past her to snatch my envelope back.

"Federal employee, Mr. and that's assault." I heard the hiss for a nanosecond just before the pepper spray hit my eyes.

"God, what the… Arghhh, Jesus Christ!" I screamed, and then collapsed down onto my knees.

"This is driver eleven twenty. Repeat, One, one, two, zero, assault on a federal employee, in progress. Subject has been neutralized. Please dispatch, repeat please dispatch. Corner Randolph and Victoria, repeat corner Randolph and Victoria."

Chapter Fourteen

I think I was in the back of the squad car. I wasn't sure because the paramedics told me to keep my eyes closed and my head tilted back. I was following their advice, doing just that. My eyes were on fire, my nose was running and my face felt raw. I could hear the paramedics laughing with the police officers a few feet away.

"Stuff's lethal, man. We had to put a German Shepherd down once. Some mail carrier sprayed the thing. It was a blessing to shoot the poor dog."

"This is so great. I can't wait to tell my wife. She'll go nuts that Dev was pepper sprayed by some Post Office gal. She hates him."

Isn't that just cheery? Laughs all around after being assaulted by some reactionary wench who literally went Postal on me. Luckily for me I knew my arresting officer, Timmy Callahan. We'd played hockey on the same pee wee team. His wife Shelia had never quite fallen for my charm ever since I threw up on her prom dress junior year. It had been a particular off white color. Unfortunately I'd had a number of bottles of Red Ripple. I vaguely remembered leaning over to stare down her low cut top when things began to…

"Mr. Haskell, I want you to keep your eyes closed and your head tilted back. I'm going to help you out of the car and we're going to flush those eyes again."

"Am I going to be all right? Will I be able to see? This shit still really stings."

More snickers.

"Yeah, I think so. You might want to get checked out, but usually twenty-four to forty-eight hours does the trick. Okay, there you go. That's right, just step out nice and easy. Keep the eyes closed, head back. Good, real good." He was saying all the right things, but I could tell he found my predicament hilarious.

"Shit's still burning, man." My eyes were killing me, my face felt like someone took a belt sander to it and my nose was still running.

"Yeah, she nailed you pretty good. I'd guess once you were down she gave you a couple more squirts just to keep you there."

"Did Timmy arrest the bitch?"

"No, Dev, I just took her name. We'll put her in for a Citizen of the Month award. You know, keeping the streets safe, dealing with local riff raff. That sort of shit." This came from off to my right somewhere. Even with my eyes closed, I recognized Timmy's voice.

"Thanks a lot. That bitch is a menace to society."

"Okay, head back, this is going to feel nice and cool. It's just water. A good long shower when you get home should go a long way in getting you back to normal. You're going to have some swelling for a day or two, a little redness. Might be a good idea to have a doc check it out. Just to be on the safe side."

The water was refreshingly cool washing over my face and I moved my head slightly left to right as he slowly poured the water onto my face. The burning in my eyes was substantially reduced.

"How we doing? Feeling better?"

"Much better, much better."

"Keep those eyes closed. Yeah, that's right. Now, the stinging is going to return a little, so when you get home hop in the shower. I wouldn't make any plans for tonight. And you sure as heck can't drive. Officer Callahan offered to give you a ride."

"So, I'm not going to jail?" I asked.

"Well, I guess that's up to your arresting officer," he said, suddenly sounding deadly serious.

Chapter Fifteen

"You fucking idiot. What the hell were you thinking? Attacking some postal chick picking up the mail… you must have lost what little brains you've left."

I was riding in the back of Timmy's squad car, eyes closed, head back, just as the paramedic had instructed. I had the sense we were really moving fast. My head was bouncing off the back seat, none too gently.

"Hey, I told the bitch I just wanted a letter back. I forgot to put the check in. What? All of a sudden it's some sort of federal crime to pay your bills on time?"

"Bullshit. She said you stumbled out of the bar, smelled like beer, tried to grab the mail out of her truck, pushed her aside, then you grabbed her. Sounds like assault to me, dumb ass."

"That's all bullshit."

"Oh really? Were you in The Spot?"

"That's got nothing to do…"

"Answer the question, asshole. Were you in The Spot?"

"Yeah, I might have popped in for a moment."

"Big surprise."

"Had you been drinking?"

"Come on, Timmy, suddenly it's against the law to have a beer?"

"I'll put that down as a yes."

"Did you attempt to grab the mail out of her truck?"

"It was my God damned letter. I wrote the thing, I put the stamp on the damned envelope. I was just…"

"Jesus, you dumb ass. To tell you the truth, Dev, you got off easy. She didn't press charges. What the Post Office does is going to be another matter."

"Post Office?"

"Hey, jackass, her superiors are going to look at this thing. I mean, we had to get involved, and the paramedics, too. You'll be looking at a bill from the city for the paramedic run, by the way. I think it comes in right around eight-seventy-five."

"I gotta pay almost ten bucks to the city after I was assaulted?"

"No, idiot, eight hundred and seventy-five bucks."

"For what?"

"For being an absolute jerk and wasting the city's time and money. The term budget cuts mean anything to you? Christ, we're broke just like every other city in the country and you want the tax payers to pick up the cost so you can run around town playing grab ass with women picking up the mail. I don't think you're going to find a lot of folks arguing your side of the case in this deal."

Timmy flicked on the siren.

"What the hell is that for? You chasing some guy?" My eyes remained closed, my head continued to bounce.

"No, just alerting your neighbors that you're in the area and about to arrive home, compliments of the city.

Hey, by the way, you'll be getting a bill for the ride. Not much I can do about it. Sorry, sort of."

My eyes were still closed, but I could hear he was enjoying every minute of my misfortune.

We slowed to a stop, then sat there a good few seconds with the siren blaring.

"You about done?" I asked.

"Almost, let me help you out."

I heard him get out of the squad car and a moment later he opened my door.

"Watch your head, Dev. I'll help you inside. Maybe keep your eyes closed in this sunlight."

"Can you at least take these damn handcuffs off? Not like I'm a criminal or something."

"Tell that to the Post Office." He laughed.

"Come on, Timmy."

"Na, Shelia will enjoy this part. Plus, let's go, it's time for your perp walk." Then he led me by the elbow across my boulevard and up the front steps.

"Grass could do with a cutting." He snickered.

"Shut up."

"Mommy, what's wrong with that man?" It was a little kid's voice, from somewhere behind us.

"He was bad, honey. He's always bad," a woman said in a slightly louder tone. We went up the three steps to my porch and walked across to the front door.

"Here, give me my cuffs back," Timmy said, taking my wrists.

"You're sure? I'm dangerous you know."

"I can leave 'em on, Dev. I got a couple of spare sets in the trunk."

"Get 'em off."

"There we go. Hey thanks, it's been a pleasure. Oh, listen buddy, sorry 'bout this, but I had to cite you. I didn't mention the assault, but you got a disorderly, here," he said and slipped a citation into my hands.

"Disorderly? You mean you're citing me for disorderly conduct?"

"Yeah, that's right. I've been dicking around with you for the past forty-five minutes. You had a team of paramedics attending to you. My sergeant swung by to check up. We had a back up squad initially. All that shit, at city expense, and what? I'm supposed to pat you on the back and tell you to have a nice day? I don't think so. You're lucky you're not being booked right now."

"Shit," I shouted.

"Mommy, he said a bad word," the brat from the sidewalk called out.

"Dev, don't you go postal, I've got spray, too." Timmy laughed.

Chapter Sixteen

In between spells stretched out on the couch, I stood in the shower with my face about four inches from the shower head. It pretty much did the trick. The next morning I actually used soap in the shower, although not on my face just to stay on the safe side.

I found a skin cream some long forgotten date must have left behind and smeared that on my face. It stung a little but seemed to help. My skin was still red and puffy around the eyes, but the swelling on my cheeks had gone down, more or less.

I got dressed and decided I could be bored at the office just as well as at home. My car wasn't in the driveway. It dawned on me that St. Paul's finest had given me a ride home. Instead, a silver Audi was parked on the street in front of my house. Kiki leaned against the car door, smiling, looking gorgeous and sipping from a Starbucks cup.

"Jesus, what the hell happened to you?"

"Hi, Kiki. Here to comfort the afflicted?"

"Huh? What happened to your face? You look all blotchy and well, shitty."

"Long story."

"Tell me. Here, I brought you a coffee. I wasn't sure how you like it, so I added cream and sugar."

"I usually take it black."

"Then you can go inside and make some, I guess."

"Cream and sugar will be fine."

"I brought you some croissants, too. So tell me what happened."

I gave her a sanitized version. I didn't mention the stupid letter to her brother and that fat ass Thompson Barkwell. I stuck to the white lie about forgetting to enclose my check in a bill payment. I skipped over the part about drinking a couple of beers beforehand in The Spot. I sort of neglected to mention the potential assault on a Federal employee charge or Timmy's disorderly conduct citation. Then closed with, "So, one of my pals at the police department warned me that I was likely to see a bill from the city because the paramedics had to be called. I mean, can you believe it?"

"Wow, that seems so unfair." She sounded genuine.

"Yeah, you're telling me. I mean, it's like suddenly I'm the criminal here."

Kiki sipped her coffee. After a long moment I said, "Hey, could I hit you up for a lift down to my office. One of the cops was nice enough to give me a lift home yesterday, said it was the least he could do, you know, under the circumstances."

"Yeah, sure, another croissant? Or anything else you want?"

I didn't touch that last line. "No thanks, but I've got some meetings and I like to be prepared. Really appreciate the coffee and the ride."

"You and your meetings, we'll have to cure you of that. Come on, hop in."

I gave her directions to my office. Mercifully, she didn't mention a thing about KRAZ until we had pulled up in front of the pet shop on the first floor of my building.

"Hey, about that KRAZ," she said.

"Not to worry, Barkwell gave me a check, said he'd get the rest to me in a couple of days, after the board meeting or something."

"Yeah, whatever. No, I meant, you know, the KRAZ you sort of left on my bedroom wall. Remember, the red spray paint?"

"Oh, yeah, that."

"You had some guy or something. No rush, but, you know, I'd like to get it taken care of. It doesn't really go with the rest of the décor in there."

"Yeah, I've got a call into him. I'll check as soon as I'm in the office, see if he got back to me."

"Do that, thanks. You'll let me know?"

"I will."

She drove off before I had a chance to swallow my mouthful of croissant and thank her.

I thought about painting the wall myself. How hard could it be? Then remembered the difficulties I'd encountered at an ex-girlfriend's, splattering paint on some heirloom antique I'd never liked in the first place. I knew the guy to call.

Gary Hobson was one of those guys who never held a job and knew how to do everything. There was a lot of family money from somewhere, though I'd never learned where. He could fix the brakes on your car, put a new roof on your garage, wire a light, paint a room, do a thousand different things. I don't think I'd seen him for the better part of six months. I looked up his number in my rolodex and called.

"The number you have reached, six one two, blah, blah, blah, has been temporarily disconnected at the customers request. Calls are being taking by, blah, blah, blah."

I phoned the new number.

"Serenity Center."

"Sorry, I think I misdialed."

"Are you calling for one of our residents?"

"No, trying to reach a pal, Gary Hobson. I think…"

"Please hold, I'll have Mr. Hobson in a moment."

After about three minutes and a number of clicks on the phone a tentative voice came on.

"This is Gary."

"Gary? Dev, Dev Haskell. How are you, man?"

"Just fine, Dev. Gee been a couple of years, hasn't it? I'm in an after treatment facility. Sort of fell off the wagon, again, you know I just…"

Actually I never knew Gary had been on the wagon. He could hit it pretty hard.

"… eight months and now I'm here."

"Can you get out?" I asked.

"What for?" He sounded cautious.

"Just a minor painting job, probably take longer to tell you about it than to do the damn thing. One wall in a bedroom, a little touch up of some minor blemishes," I said, visualizing the four-foot red letters I'd spray painted across Kiki's wall, 'KRAZ SUCKS'.

"Yeah I could do that. You'd have to sign a pass for me. They're pretty tight on times and stuff. You know, don't want us wandering into the wrong place or ending up back with the wrong crowd."

"I can do that. What are we looking at time wise?" I asked.

"Whenever you want."

"Tomorrow too soon?"

"No, that'll work fine, not like I'm busy. Just sit around and go to meetings all day, listen to how we all screwed up. Tomorrow works for me."

"Nine o'clock?"

"Yeah, just bring a picture I.D. You know, they'll run a quick check on you. They need to have a pretty tight return time, but it only takes a couple of minutes to sign out."

"See you tomorrow at nine."

"I'll look for you, Dev, and thanks, going kinda stir crazy here," he whispered then he gave me the address and hung up.

Chapter Seventeen

Serenity Center looked pleasant enough. A converted three story Victorian sort of place, neatly clipped lawn, trimmed hedge, a flower garden, birds chirping, lots of white wicker furniture on the front porch. I guessed it was running Gary's trust fund five to eight grand a month to straighten him out here. The brass plaque next to the doorbell informed you it was a secure facility and instructed to please ring the bell for service. I did.

A white-uniformed guy answered the door and then showed me into a reception area. The place was like a surgery unit, you could have eaten off the floor it was so clean. The large vase of lilies on a side table almost, but not quite, covered the scent of disinfectant. Everything was white and gleaming.

I filled out a short form, actually a five by seven card, signed and dated the thing, then handed it to the receptionist. She was a black woman wearing a nurse's uniform.

"Mr. Haskell is it?" she asked. I could sense her staring at my still slightly red and puffy face, compliments of the federal government and my tax dollars.

"Yes, Ma'am."

"May I see some I.D., please, a driver's license or something?"

I handed her my license.

"Thank you," she said, and then jotted down my license number on a form just below the bold line labeled 'Serenity Center'. She wrote her initials next to that and handed back my license, then said, "Here you are, sir. I'll have Mr. Hobson brought down in just a moment. If you'd care to take a seat." She indicated a series of white chairs against the far wall.

"Thanks." I smiled.

There were four or five different Serenity Center brochures to read, but not so much as a dog-eared copy of People magazine. I took a pass, then counted different white wallpaper patterns on the opposite wall and waited. Gary Hobson arrived through a secure door about five minutes later. He looked better than I'd seen him in years - fit, clear eyed, shaved, clean and steady.

"Gary, man you look fantastic. You really do."

He beamed a smile.

"Thanks, Dev, good to see you. Just getting things back together, finally. You know, one day at a time."

"Man, I should check into this joint," I joked.

"Yeah, you probably should, Dev." Gary looked serene, but serious.

"Let's go," I said and we walked out the door.

As I drove, we caught up on "whatever happened to" sorts of things. It really was over two years since I'd seen him last. He kept looking left and right as we drove over to Kiki's.

"God, great to be out, Dev. I've been under wraps, sort of, for almost a year." He turned round completely in his seat to stare at two young women walking down the sidewalk.

"Forget that stuff, it'll only get you in trouble," I joked.

"Yeah, trouble," Gary said wistfully and nodded.

"So look, here's the deal. You just cover up this shit on Kiki's bedroom wall. Shouldn't take but a minute, then maybe we'll go grab something to eat. Sound okay?"

"Tell me what's with the wall. I feel like I'm not getting the full story here."

"Oh, I don't know…"

"Don't bullshit me, Dev. We've known each other too long. You screw something up? What, kick a hole in the wall? 'Cause that'll take some sheet rock and taping compound, gonna be more than just a few minutes, stuff has to dry overnight, then…."

"No, nothing like that. Just, well… there might be a little spray paint."

"Yeah, I knew it was something. You?"

"Me?"

"Yeah, I think you just answered my question. You did it, right?"

"Yeah, I guess."

"Should be honest with yourself, Dev. You did it, not, you guess."

I glanced over at him.

"There… see, it's over. Was it so hard? No, of course not. Simple, if only you follow the rules and are honest with yourself."

"You know me, Gary, I've never followed the rules." I laughed.

Gary sat straight faced and looked at me.

"Yeah, well. Okay, here's what I'll have to do. If it's just one wall I have to paint it corner to corner, otherwise you get some tonal difference and it will look like shit. What's the girl's name? Kathy?"

"Kiki."

"She got the paint?"

"Told me she has everything... paint, tray, roller, the works." I didn't mention the dog leash.

"Okay, shouldn't take that long. We'll see, but I'm guessing two coats. I can do them both today but it's gonna take at least an hour between coats to sort of dry. Hope it's latex. Is it?"

"Latex?"

"The paint... oh Christ, it doesn't matter. Just good to be out. God I haven't really been out in the world for the better part of a year. Jesus, the women," he said, turning around in the seat again, staring at a teenager riding past on a bike. "God, you see that? Man, I've been living like a damn monk for forever."

I pulled into the alley and parked behind Kiki's house. We entered through the back gate, then climbed up onto her back porch and rang the doorbell.

"Nice shack," Gary said, looking around.

"Hi, guys," Kiki answered the kitchen door. Thankfully, she was dressed.

"Kiki, Gary. Gary, Kiki. Gary is one hell of a painter extraordinaire. He'll get that bedroom taken care of. That the paint there?" I pointed my chin at three different gallon cans sitting on the edge of the kitchen counter.

"Yeah, do you think it's enough to do the job?" she asked.

Gary looked at the cans.

"These are all different colors?"

"Yeah, I couldn't remember which one we used in the bedroom. They're all similar, but I was hoping maybe you could decide." She sort of shrugged, then bounced her breasts as an added incentive.

"I'm sure we can figure it out. Why don't you show me the wall?" Gary said.

"Sure, come on. You stay here, Dev. I don't want you to see my bedroom." She giggled.

I shook my head, but remained in the kitchen. Gary followed Kiki like a little child. I hoped he knew what he was in for. I could hear the tone of their conversation coming from her bedroom, but I couldn't make out what exactly was being said. Eventually, they returned to the kitchen.

"So I got a drop cloth, tray, roller, roller covers, rag to wipe up drips, masking tape, brush, your choice of paint. You're good to go. You want a drink or anything?"

"A drink?" Gary asked.

"Yeah, I got a couple different beers in the fridge, a white wine, red wine over in the cabinet there. A full bar in the dining room, if you're into the hard stuff, you know."

"No, probably shouldn't," Gary said.

"Suit yourself, I'd be drinking all the time if I had to hang around with this character," she said, pointing at me.

"I know what you mean," Gary said.

"Look, Gary, I'm going to talk Dev into going with me to the store so I can get a few things. You got everything you need?" she asked.

"Yeah, you kids get the hell out of here." Gary shooed us out the back door with his hands.

"Why do I have to take you to the store?"

"Because." She smiled.

Chapter Eighteen

We went to the hardware store, and the dry cleaners, the grocery store, picked up some sort of make up cream at the hairdressers, got some fish oil tablets at a health food store. With all the driving around I had to refill my gas tank. We'd been gone the better part of three hours when I pulled into the alley behind Kiki's house. I noticed a broken gin bottle in the alley, but didn't pay much attention to it.

"I hope Gary was all right. I didn't think we'd be gone this long," she said.

I gathered up a handful of shopping bags from my back seat, and grabbed the twelve pack of diet Coke she couldn't live without. Kiki held a cardboard flat filled with little pink flowers in plastic trays.

"He'll be fine. With any luck, he's finished. I have to check him back in early this afternoon."

"Check him back in?" she asked, as we were climbing the steps to her kitchen door. She'd just set the cardboard flat on the bottom step.

"Oh, he's in some post treatment joint. They just keep close tabs on the guy is all, don't want him out drinking, running with the wrong crowd, you know."

"You knew this and you left him alone in my house? Jesus, Dev, I offered him a drink, told him where the beer and wine and all my liquor was." She was hurrying now, quickly pushing into the kitchen. I dropped all the shopping bags next to the kitchen counter.

"Gary, Gary, we're back. Gary?" she called, walking quickly down the hall.

"Will you relax? He's fine, Jesus. How much trouble…"

I heard her scream from the bedroom and ran down the hall. She stood in the doorway with a hand to her mouth, a shocked look on her face. I stared over her shoulder. It looked like Gary had taken one of the gallon cans of paint and just flung the contents. The paint was splashed across wall, over the woodwork, and puddled onto the carpet. Long drip marks ran down the wall.

"Christ, it's not even the right color," I said.

"Oh my God, what in the hell? Jesus, my clothes," she screamed.

Bras and thongs were scattered across the floor on the far side of her bed.

"You didn't leave them there?"

"Me? No, you idiot, of course I didn't leave them there. Oh my God, he's ruined my bedroom. He's ruined it. Your pervert friend has ruined my bedroom, Dev."

"Look, Kiki, I don't know what to say, I didn't think…"

"Stop right there. Oh my God, you complete and utter idiot," she screamed and picked up an empty bottle of lubricant off the floor next to her scattered thongs.

"Maybe now's not the best time for that," I said, then ducked as she threw the bottle at me.

"Get out of my house," she screamed.

"Look, maybe I could help clean..."

"Get out of my god damned house, you asshole. Get out, get out, get out!"

I decided not to wait until the knife came out. I dashed through the kitchen and out the back door.

"Call you later," I yelled as I jumped off the porch, ran to my car and drove off.

I had no idea where to start looking for Gary, so I went to The Spot. I stuck my head in the door. Jimmy was tending bar.

"Hey, has Gary Hobson been in here today?"

"He quit drinking, Dev. Went to some high price treatment facility."

"Call me if you see him, okay?"

"Yeah, but he won't be in here. Like I said, he quit."

I crossed the street to my office, phoned a couple of hospitals, the Detox unit, the police. Nothing. About forty-five minutes later I began getting phone calls from Serenity Center. The calls continued every fifteen minutes. I really didn't want to talk with them so I let the calls drop into my message center.

Chapter Nineteen

Kiki phoned sometime later that night. I was in the process of stuffing the last of a BBQ cheeseburger from McDonald's into my mouth and washing it down with a Summit beer. I really didn't want to talk to her, but I answered anyway.

"Kiki?"

"He's here," she whispered.

"Who? Gary, he came back?"

"Apparently he never left. I was doing all my laundry, again." She paused for emphasis. "I found him passed out in the guest bedroom down in the basement. You better get over here, right away, before he wakes up or I'm calling the cops."

I didn't have to be told twice.

Gary was on the floor and out cold. He must have rolled off the bed. He lay wedged between the bed and the basement wall. His face looked like it had gone about three rounds with the concrete floor when he fell. He had dried blood below his nose, a split bottom lip and a gash on his cheekbone.

"Did you do that to him?" I asked Kiki.

"If I'd done it he'd look a lot worse, believe me." She sneered.

I believed her.

"Gary, hey Gary." I was shaking his foot, attempting to wake him up.

"Just get him the hell out of my house, now," she demanded.

"Look. I'm trying to, but he's out cold."

"I want him out of here before he throws up all over the place. God, you and your friends," she said, like this was an everyday occurrence instead of just the fourth time I'd ever been in her house.

"Can you help me carry him?"

"Me?"

"If you can just help me get him up the basement steps, then I can drag him out the door," I explained.

"I just don't want him to throw up." She shuddered.

"He won't. Look, he's dead to the world," I shook Gary's foot again and got no reaction.

"Oh, that's great," she said, then crossed her arms, cocked a hip and thrust her bottom lip out.

"Just grab his feet, okay?"

"Ugh," she groaned, but she did it.

I held Gary beneath his arms and wrestled him up Kiki's ancient basement stairs. Talk about dead weight, but eventually we got him up into the kitchen.

"Can you get the back door for me?"

She let go of his ankles and they dropped with a thunk as she hurried to the back door and opened it. I dragged Gary out the door and across the porch.

"You better get your ass back here tomorrow and fix the fucking mess he left here."

"Me?"

"God," she screamed, then slammed the kitchen door and turned off the porch light. I dragged Gary down the steps and out to my car in the dark. I stuffed him in the back seat, checked for a pulse once I got him in, then headed off in the direction of Serenity Center.

Chapter Twenty

I answered my phone on the drive to Serenity.

"Haskell Investigations." I was pretty sure I knew who it would be.

"Mr. Devlin Haskell, please. This is Gordon Sweitzer, provost at the Serenity Center.

"Yes, Mr. Sweitzer, I'm enroute to your facility now. Should be there within the next fifteen minutes." I put a little cheer into my voice and tried to keep things positive.

"You do realize you are in gross violation of your sworn pledge."

"Yeah, well something unexpected came up."

"You may find this amusing, Mr. Haskell, but I can assure you there is nothing funny about this situation. Mr. Hobson is much like a fragile flower, and you're responsible for leaving him out in the sun too long, far too long."

"Believe me he wasn't in the sun."

"Excuse me?"

"No problem. See you shortly," I said and hung up.

I drove on for a few more minutes when I heard Gary cough from the back seat and suddenly he sat up and breathed on me. I put down the window.

"Let's stop for a drink," he said, clearly having difficulty forming the words.

"I'd love to, Gary, but I think we should probably take a pass on that tonight. I've got to drop you off, get home myself. Maybe some other time."

"Then I better just get out here," he said. At the moment we were in the center lane of I-94, doing a little over seventy-five.

"Tell you what... why don't you just lie back down, rest your eyes? I'll tell you when we get there."

"You'll tell me? Promise?" he said lying back down.

"I promise, Gary. Rest your eyes." We were maybe five minutes away.

The remainder of the ride was uneventful. Gary snored in the back seat. I sort of toyed with how I was going to play the Serenity folks, then decided there wasn't much to say other than to hand Gary over and suggest that there might be a flaw or two in their after treatment approach. Then run like hell.

I pulled up in front of the facility. The front porch light was on, the porch uninhabited. The Serenity House looked to be in lock-down mode.

I turned off my car, looked into the back seat where Gary was snoring soundly.

"Rise and shine, sleeping beauty," I called, then shook him when I didn't get a response.

Gary groaned and grunted, but eventually, with some vigorous shaking he sat up and leaned forward on the front seat.

"Are we there?"

"We are," I answered.

Gary looked at me through bleary, bloodshot eyes and then threw up, all over me and the front seat of my car. Projectile vomiting, as they say, he even managed to get the inside of the windshield. I didn't have a chance to recoil. I just sat there for a long moment as a lot of liquor and what looked like beef hash slowly dripped off my dashboard.

"You finished?" I asked.

He threw up again, but this time on the back seat.

I got out of the car, opened the back door, pulled Gary out and half carried, half steered him toward the front porch. I more or less man handled him up the steps, leaned him against the wall, just below the brass plaque. I rang the bell, twice, as a matter of fact.

I was back at my car, standing with the driver's door open, debating about getting back in, when they opened the front door. Gary had slithered off to the side, and was leaning against the door when it opened. He fell backward. I heard the thump from out on the street as his head bounced off the polished wood porch floor. He groaned, rolled sideways, and then threw up again.

I was going to yell something at the attendant, thought better of it, slid behind the wheel of my disgusting car and drove home.

Chapter Twenty-One

I stripped my clothes off out in my backyard in the dark and just tossed everything in the trash. I removed anything worthwhile from my wallet, then discarded that with the clothes. I took a very long shower, drank a very large Jameson and went to bed.

Kiki's seven-thirty call the following morning woke me.

"What time are you planning to come over here and fix this major league fuck up?" she asked before I had a chance to answer hello.

"Who is this?" I groaned.

"How many homes have you ruined this week?"

"Oh, hi, Kiki. Today?"

"Yes today. And just so you know, I have to leave for an investors meeting at K-R-A-Z no later than eleven-thirty."

"Yeah, well… see. I have to get my car cleaned."

"Your car? You mean that wreck you drive around town takes precedence over the disaster you two idiots left in my bedroom?"

"But, I didn't do anything," I pleaded.

"Oh really? Well how in the hell did your friend find his way to my door? That dreadful painter extraordinaire, as you called him. He didn't just wander in and destroy my house on his own. You brought his ass in here, then left him here to ruin my bedroom, drink all my gin, perform sex acts with my leopard skin thong, pass out in my…"

"I get the point, Kiki, okay. We had a bit of an accident on the way home. I have to deal with that."

"An accident? You didn't let him drive, did you?"

"No, he just threw up all over me and the inside of my car, twice."

"Serves you right."

"Thanks."

"So what time do you plan on being here? I've got a meeting that…"

"I know, a meeting that you have to leave for no later than eleven-thirty. I'll be there before then. I'm not sure how long it will take to get my car cleaned out."

"You let it sit, overnight, with, with all that blicky stuff all over?"

"I did."

"Oh, gross."

"Anything else?" I asked.

"Just get over here and get this mess cleaned up." Then she hung up.

I rolled over and attempted to go back to sleep. It didn't work.

I was ringing Kiki's kitchen doorbell at eleven-fifteen.

"Come in. Thank you for coming," she called from the far side of the kitchen counter sounding like she didn't mean one word of it.

"Yeah, sure. Look, which paint is the right one?" I asked. There were two gallon cans on the kitchen floor, next to the door.

"Like I told that Gary person yesterday, I'm not sure. Can't you just put a little dot of it somewhere and see if it matches?" she said.

Actually that sounded like a pretty good idea, but I didn't plan to let her know that.

"I'll figure it out."

"Well, I found some sandpaper in the basement. You'll have to get all the drip marks off the wall before you even begin. Just for the record, I don't want to see that psychotic Gary person over here or anywhere for that matter, ever again."

"This may come as some surprise, but I sort of feel the same way."

"What in the hell were you thinking?"

"Do you think I would have brought him over here, if I knew he was going to do an Amy Winehouse on you?" I said.

"Look, I have to get to this investors meeting, just get the problem taken care of. Can you do that much? Not make things in there any worse?"

I nodded then stared as she walked out the back door, across the yard and into her garage. Even mad at me and certifiable, she was hot.

Chapter Twenty-Two

Fortunately, the paint Gary had tossed on the wall was thick and relatively fresh, it literally peeled off in big sections. I had it all removed within a half hour, including the stuff on Kiki's woodwork and the better part of the carpet. I rolled the wall, then rummaged around in the basement and found a can labeled bedroom trim that looked about right, and tried it. It matched perfectly. By two-thirty the place looked great and you couldn't see Gary's mess or any telltale signs of my spray painting.

I put everything away in the basement, tossed her paint brush in the trash since I hated cleaning the things, and opened a beer from Kiki's refrigerator. I was sitting at her kitchen counter sipping it when she came in.

"You had better be finished in that damn bedroom if you're sitting on your ass out here drinking one of my beers."

"Go see for yourself," I said.

She came back three or four minutes later a different person.

"Dev, thanks, it looks great. I'm sorry I was so bitchy, but you can see how it would make anyone wild. I mean, what were you thinking? That Gary person is crazy, absolutely nuts."

"No argument from me," I said, thinking Gary's not the only one.

"Stay for dinner?"

A little voice inside my head warned me, *'leave, right now for your own safety, just run'*.

"Look, let me finish this beer, then run out and replenish your gin supply, grab a shower. What was it Gary drank up?"

"Bombay Sapphire," she said.

It figured, expensive stuff. I finished my beer, raced home to shower, then returned with a fifth of Bombay Sapphire, a fifth of Jameson and a case of beer.

"Wow, how long you planning to stay?" she joked.

"How long can you stand me?"

"Long enough to teach bad puppies new tricks." She giggled.

Oh, oh, I thought and then tossed my Saints cap on a kitchen stool and poured myself a Jameson.

I would have liked to brag and say we had sex before and after dinner, but we never ate. At least that I can recall. Kiki insisted on being 'hostess with the mostess' as she referred to herself and kept my drink glass full and the sex nonstop.

I groaned awake sometime just before noon the following day. I was tied to her bed, unable to move. She was leaning against the door frame, sipping coffee. Her hair was pulled back tightly. She was wearing a black garter belt and sporting a matching black eye.

"Oh God," I groaned and then blinked a couple of times as I attempted to focus and think.

"How's the head, bad puppy?"

99

"God, its pounding, feels like it's going to explode. What the hell is this?" I asked, pulling against the restraints. They looked like nylons.

"I don't know, when you want to get kinky I guess you go all out. You made me do it."

"Made you?"

She brushed her cheek, tenderly.

"What happened? I, I didn't do that. Did I?"

She nodded, casually sipping more coffee.

"Said it was just the beginning then really worked me over. I've never been treated like that before."

"Look, Kiki, I, I'm not sure what to say, how much did we drink last night?"

"You drank quite a bit, got really rough, you had me frightened. Well and excited."

"That just doesn't sound like me. I don't know what... look, if it's not too much trouble, could you untie me?"

"You're not going to do anything crazy, are you?" she said it dead pan, almost like a memorized joke, but I wasn't laughing. She climbed onto the bed, straddled me for a long moment looking down before she began to untie me. I looked away.

"Oh, so now you've had your fill. I get it."

"Kiki, I hit you? Are you sure? I just have never, ever done anything like that. Are you sure?"

"Oh, yeah, it was really scary," she said as she untied my arm, but she didn't look scared. She didn't even seem concerned. She almost gave the impression of just going through the motions.

She climbed off me, ran her nails down my chest and stomach, raising welts on my skin. Then she groped me for a long moment, before she ran her nails hard, along the length of my thighs.

"Ouch, hey, don't," I cried out.

"Okay, suit yourself, tough guy," she said, then reluctantly rolled off the bed.

I sat up and untied the black hosiery from my ankles.

"God, my head is killing me. It's really pounding."

"Look, bad puppy dog, how about a long shower? I'll get breakfast going for us. Take thirty minutes in the shower, you'll feel a thousand percent better."

"Kiki, I'm so sorry. I don't know what to say. Maybe I should just go and let you get…"

"No, no, don't do that. I want to cook you breakfast, serve you, go on, promise me you'll stay in there for a half hour. You'll feel lots better."

"But, your eye, I mean, God I just can't believe I…"

"Not another word or I'll tie you up again and keep you for the rest of the day. Come on," she said, slapping me across the butt. "Get going, I'm making breakfast." She strutted out into the hall, gave a quick seductive smile over her shoulder then headed for the kitchen.

Chapter Twenty-Three

I'd been in the shower for some time. Not the half hour Kiki suggested, but at least twenty minutes. The air in the room was steamy, moisture running down the mirror. I felt a little better, but still had a long way to go. I was confused, still a little dizzy and mortified about her black eye. I had never done anything like that in my life. It just didn't make sense. But, then, neither did the complete black out or making her tie me up. Something just didn't seem right.

I was trying to remember something, anything from the night before and failing miserably, when there was a knock on the bathroom door. God, the poor thing was probably bringing me coffee.

"Momentito, my precious," I called, trying to be funny.

I turned off the shower, grabbed a towel and wiped my face, then went to open the door, thinking I may have really misjudged her. Amazing how sometimes you can get off on the wrong foot.

"Hey gorgeous, you've got…"

The jolt from the officer's Taser knocked me to the floor. Writhing around on a wet, ceramic tile floor in electronic shock as thousands of volts jolted through my body did nothing to help my hangover.

When I stopped sizzling, three of them were on me. One stomped my right hand and I was pretty sure he broke a couple of fingers, but that was the least of my problems. Someone was sitting on my head, not Kiki, while another pulled both arms up behind my back and pinched on a pair of handcuffs. There was a lot of yelling from the hallway and the bedroom. Somewhere a woman was screaming. I was attempting to breathe after being tasered, hyperventilating.

"Bring that bastard out here," someone yelled.

I was pushed and pulled out the bathroom door. Someone bounced my head off the door frame. A knee narrowly missed its target and slammed into my hip. I found myself handcuffed, standing naked in Kiki's hallway, surrounded by a mob of blue uniforms, all wearing badges.

"You sick son-of-a-bitch."

"What, what the hell?" I stammered.

"Too bad you ran out of time. Not to worry, you're gonna have a good long time to think about it. Read him his rights."

"What the hell is going on here? Where's Kiki? Kiki, are you okay?" I called.

"Don't let that animal near me," a female voice I didn't recognize howled from the bedroom.

Kiki suddenly appeared. At least I thought it was her. She looked completely different. The woman I saw twenty-five minutes before wearing a black garter belt and a hop-on-me smile, now stood wrapped in a terrycloth robe, cowering behind two police officers.

Bright red lipstick was smeared across her lips and chin in a hideous clown-like grin. Tear stained mascara underlined her eyes and ran down her cheeks. Her hair was messed and bedraggled and it looked like the word "slut" was written with some sort of marker across her breasts. And then there was the black eye.

"Don't let him near me, don't let him near me… please, please." She stepped behind a large patrolman.

He looked at me with very cold eyes and moved a hand toward his weapon.

"Read him his rights, get his pants on and get him out of my sight," said a thin bald guy in an ill-fitting brown suit.

"What the hell is going on?"

"You have the right to remain silent…"

"All right, this is a crime scene, people. I want everyone out except the site team. And don't touch anything! Mrs. Barkwell, if you would let us take you to the hospital, Officer Christine Jenkins here will be with you at all times."

Had he just referred to Kiki as Mrs. Barkwell? I didn't have time to ponder that, but was led naked out the back door where my jeans were thrown at me.

"I'm fucking hand cuffed here, how am I supposed to get the things on?"

"Figure it out. You're lucky you're not dead, asshole. Tough guy, beating up a woman, raping her. You're damn lucky there are witnesses around right now."

"Rape?"

Chapter Twenty-Four

"I'm accused of rape? You're telling me that psychotic bitch is accusing me of rape?" I asked.

"I'm afraid that's just the tip of the iceberg," Aaron said, shaking his head.

We were sitting in an interrogation room on the fifth floor of the police station. I knew we were on the fifth floor because I'd been interrogated up here before, although never on a rape charge. Lieutenant Aaron LaZelle headed up the vice unit. He and Detective Norris Manning from homicide were conducting the interrogation. Neither man looked to be enjoying the task at hand.

I sure as hell wasn't.

The room was either dingy white or light grey. I wasn't sure which. The place smelled of sweat mixed in with a healthy dose of fear, or maybe that was just me.

Leaning against one of the cinder block walls was Detective Sergeant Dixon Heller, homicide. I recognized him as the thin, bald guy in the ill-fitting brown polyester suit from Kiki's. I guessed he may have been the officer in charge of the investigation, although he clearly wasn't conducting my interrogation.

"Rape? Honest to God, you guys know me. I didn't rape her. I'm not some damn rapist, for Christ sake."

"Look, Dev, I'm going to ask you again, do you want a lawyer present? This is really serious," Aaron said, looking very uncomfortable.

"Serious? You're telling me. Look, the woman is nuts. She went after me with a knife the other day, threatened to cut me up into little pieces. Then…"

"Do you have a witness that could…"

"Well, no, but she did. Look, guys, she was, no, she *is* crazy."

"So you went back there. After she threatened to cut you up? Is that right?" Manning asked.

"Well, yeah, but not exactly. See, I brought this guy over to paint her wall, Gary Hobson."

"When was this?" Manning asked.

"Couple of days ago."

"To paint her wall?" Aaron asked.

"Yeah, in her bedroom."

"Just a wall or the entire room?" Manning fired back.

"Well, just a wall."

"Just one wall?" Aaron asked.

"Yes."

"What was wrong with it?"

"Some marks or something on it."

"You know she'll tell us if it was more than that," Manning said, writing a note on a sheet of paper from the open file in front of him.

"There might have been a little spray paint on the wall."

"A little spray paint, define little."

"Maybe a few letters." It didn't sound good, even to me.

"Did these letters say anything?" Manning asked, almost sweetly.

"Come on, Dev, what was it?" Aaron said, clearly frustrated.

"It said, KRAZ sucks."

"Did you spray paint that?" Manning asked, looking up from his file.

I nodded.

"I'm sorry, could you speak up?"

"Yes, apparently."

"Apparently?" Manning asked.

"That's what she told me, but I really don't remember doing it. I just woke up and it was there, on the wall."

"Large letters?"

"Sort of."

"Care to define sort of?"

"Okay, okay, yeah, about four feet high, all capitals. So that's why I had Gary Hobson over, to paint the wall and get things perfect for her, you know? Anyway, Gary couldn't do the job so I ended up painting her bedroom wall. She offered to make me dinner and then talked me into staying. The next thing I know, I wake up tied to her bed. Then you guys broke in and tasered me while I was standing in the bathroom."

Manning tapped his pen on the file in front of him. Aaron stared at the grey Formica table top.

"So, what seems to be increasingly difficult for me to figure out is how you woke up tied to the bed?" Manning said.

"Yeah, right, exactly." I nodded in agreement.

"So what happened? She unties you, and you tie her up and then rape her? That it?"

"No, look, I didn't rape her. I've never raped anyone. I've done a lot of things, but never rape."

"But you tied her to the bed?"

"No, I didn't do that."

"I wonder who did? See, when the officers got to Mrs. Barkwell's home they had to break in, break through the door. You were taking a shower. And she, Mrs. Barkwell, is tied to the bed. I'm having trouble here. Do you think she tied herself to the bed?"

"Yes."

"So she tied herself to the bed. That must mean she gave herself that black eye? Beat herself up and raped herself using you as an unwitting accomplice. Right?" Manning asked.

"Yeah, something like that."

"Something like that?" Manning said.

"Look, I think I must have blacked out for the night, okay? I have no memory of anything after my first drink there. All I know is, in the morning everything is fine. She untied me, wanted to make me breakfast and sent me to the shower. She even told me to stay in there for thirty minutes, said it would make me feel better."

"Thirty minutes? She said that?" Aaron asked.

"Yeah."

"And then she ties herself up and calls 911? Gee, all of a sudden it seems so cut and dried," Manning said, then stared at me.

"I think that's what happened," I said.

"You think. Interesting. What about the images we found on your phone. She take those? She looks pretty frightened."

"Images? On my phone?"

"Yeah almost a dozen of them, taken over the course of the night. She's restrained in every one of them. Looks like a long night for her. What? You wanted some souvenirs of what you did to the poor woman?"

"I don't know anything about that. My phone takes pictures?"

"Apparently. It seems obvious to me after she gave herself the black eye and tied herself up, somehow she managed to take pictures of herself being raped over the course of five or six hours."

"Look, I know this looks bad, but I'm telling you, I didn't do anything."

"To tell you the truth, Mr. Haskell, it doesn't look bad, it looks airtight."

Aaron stared down at the table, shaking his head ever so slightly.

Chapter Twenty-Five

I spent the night in jail. Not the worst cell I'd ever been in, but not a luxury hotel suite, either. The pad I was supposed to sleep on was about a half inch thick. Not that it mattered since I couldn't sleep. I stared into the dark for most of the night trying to make sense of everything. I never did accomplish that task.

The next morning I still had a pounding headache, no recollection of anything that happened and a court appointed Yale educated attorney by the name of Daphne Cochrane. She'd been given a file, a fairly thick file, and was reviewing my case with me in another dingy, smelly room. At the moment she was giving me the cheery news, explaining what she saw as my best option.

"Look, Mr. Haskell…"

"Please, under the circumstances, call me Dev."

"Quite honestly, I think under the circumstances, I would prefer to call you Mr. Haskell." She had a way of talking with her teeth clenched, mouth set in sort of a grimace, speaking in an Ivy League accent even though she'd been St. Paul born and raised. She was clearly unhappy to be saddled with my case.

"As I was saying, it would seem the best we can hope for is a plea of insanity due to chemical excess. That might help mitigate the kidnapping charge, since you claim you were invited over, at least initially. Thank God she hadn't had a restraining order served on you, yet."

"Restraining order?"

"Well, I'm sure after the spray paint incident she must have been thinking of it. That's not a concern just now. She never got the chance before you raped her. But, I'd better check, just to be sure," she said, jotting down a note on the margin of a page in the file.

"I didn't rape her."

"Right.

"I did not rape Kiki."

"All right, very well. But, let me be honest, the evidence seems to be more than a bit overwhelming. Don't you agree? There are these photos." She tossed a stack of enlarged color copies across the table to me. They half slid to one side. Each image revealed Kiki tied up and taken from various angles. She looked frightened, vulnerable and with the black eye, beaten up.

"I don't know where those came from. I sure as hell didn't take them," I said, glancing down at the stack. I'd already gone through them and had no recollection of taking any of them.

"Yes, well so you say. But, look at it from the jury's point of view. A prosecutor is going to post each one of these as an exhibit. You'll note in this one, for instance, the victim's, or rather Mrs. Barkwell's hands, are tightly fastened to the bed. The camera, your cell phone by the way, was between her legs. Her expression would suggest, well frankly, she's frightened out of her wits. I believe that's her leopard print thong stuffed into her mouth as a gag."

I couldn't think of anything to say.

"Now, unless we can prove she used her feet to take this photo, or you had an assistant, I'd say this is rather damning evidence. And there's nine, no, ten of these photos, taken over the course of the night. You'll note the digital clock on the bedside table. All taken using your cell phone."

"But, I can't remember."

"We're due to get the toxicology reports sometime later today. They should help with our inebriation claim. If we can get that, you might be looking at twelve years, just eight with time off for good behavior." She seemed to cheer up at the prospect.

"Eight years? But I didn't do anything. I'm fucking innocent," I screamed.

"Please watch the temper, Mr. Haskell. As distasteful as I find this, I'm still here to represent you."

"She must have drugged me."

"Oh, you mean sort of a date rape scenario, only in reverse? That it?"

"Exactly," I said, glad to see Daphne was coming around to my point of view.

"As your attorney I suggest you not go there. You see, the problem with that sort of defense is, well frankly, you weren't raped. May I remind you that Mrs. Barkwell was raped, repeatedly. Unfortunately for you, according to her statement and backed up by the Doctors reports from the Rape Crisis Center this was a six to eight hour ordeal for the poor woman, and now these cell phone photos of yours. Also, unfortunately, other than wounds consistent with those inflicted during her defensive struggle, you seem to be completely unharmed."

"Look, I…"

"Mrs. Barkwell, on the other hand, remains bruised and bitten on her buttocks and breasts. A bit difficult for her to do under the best of circumstances, let alone while tied up, don't you think?" She nodded in the direction of the cell phone photos.

"She exhibits signs of forceful vaginal, anal and oral entry. As I mentioned a good deal of her bruising appears to be defensive in nature. Of course, there's the matter of her black eye. And, they scraped skin samples from under her fingernails that appear to be consistent with the efforts of an individual fighting off an attack, a rapist. Skin samples that at least under preliminary examination match you, Mr. Haskell, match your DNA exactly."

"But I didn't do this."

"Then we need to know who did because otherwise, you're toast."

"Look, she sort of likes it rough and…"

"That's exactly the sort of statement I would strongly advise you stay away from."

"I didn't even know my phone could take pictures, honest."

"And yet, we have these." Daphne nodded disgustedly at the stack of images.

I looked down at the table, shook my head and slumped, defeated.

"Mrs. Barkwell…"

"Yeah, that's another thing. Where did that come from? Mrs. Barkwell? I knew she was the sister of Farrell Early, but I never heard them refer to her as Mrs. Barkwell."

"It seems she and her husband, Thompson Barkwell, are experiencing a bit of a rough patch in their relationship and Mrs. Barkwell needed some time…"

"She was screwing everything that moved."

"Not helpful, Mr. Haskell, not helpful at all. Now, I have my office attempting to locate Thompson Barkwell. We'll need a statement from him."

"A statement?"

"For the record." She sighed, and then looked up at the ceiling as if to ask God to give her strength.

"Look, to tell you the truth, Daphne…"

"Miss Cochrane."

"I'm not so sure you've got the balls for the job, here. You already have me convicted and serving eight years with good behavior for something I didn't even do."

"So you say."

"Don't take it personal, or do for that matter, I don't care. But you're fired."

Again with the sigh and the grimace.

"You do that again, Cochrane, I'm gonna wipe it off your face."

"Thus far, all your attitude has done is convince me I've an uphill fight on my hands not to have the death penalty administered."

"The death penalty? This is Minnesota, even I know we don't have the death penalty."

"There are always exceptions, Mr. Haskell, always exceptions," she said. Then stood the thick file on end, banged it on the table three or four times to straighten the contents and looked me in the eye.

"If you wish me off the case, and another attorney appointed, that is your prerogative, sir. I would caution and advise otherwise, however. You may find my attitude mild in relation to the other attorneys from the public defenders office. I'll await a final decision from you by noon today. Part of the beauty of the legal system in this country is that one is allowed to make as many mistakes as one would wish. Good day." With that she pushed back her orange plastic chair, picked up her file and stomped out of the interview room.

Chapter Twenty-Six

He smelled slightly of the bourbons he'd had for lunch. At two in the afternoon he needed a shave. His grey suit looked like he'd slept in it and as he leered over each provocative photo of Kiki naked, tied to the bed, and lewdly exposed. He raised his eyebrows and gave a quick smirk. My new court appointed attorney, Louis Laufen, Louie the Lout.

"Wow, busy night, man. She's a real looker, I'll give you that much," he said, setting the stack of photos down.

"Yeah, Mr. Laufen, your colleague, Daphne Cochrane, had me convicted based on those," I said.

We were in the same interrogation room where I'd met with my former, death penalty, court appointed public defender yesterday morning. The room was still dingy and still smelled bad.

"Call me Louie. No doubt Daft can have an edge to her. In her defense, she deals with a lot of shit, a lot of jerks, and you can't really blame her for ending up getting a little jaded. She's smart, though."

"Well, the reason you're here is she had me convicted before we even went to trial. I didn't do this shit, any of it."

116

"Yeah, well pretty strong evidence, here. I'm still waiting on the toxicology report, already a day late. Tell me your version, again."

I was already further in the game with Louie on my side after only thirty minutes. He may have smelled like bourbon and looked like shit, but maybe that made us kindred spirits. At least he displayed a passing interest in my explanation. The only problem was I didn't have much of an explanation.

I started in anyway, told him about Kiki and the knife. I told him about getting hired by K-R-A-Z, based on her passing comment to her brother. Then I told him about the press conference shooting. I continued on, including the spray paint and my ill advised hiring of Gary Hobson, how he passed out after drinking a fifth of Kiki's gin. I finished up with me painting the wall and then going back to her house with bottles of Blue Sapphire and Jameson. He nodded, made the occasional note on a legal pad and glanced from time to time at the top photo, Kiki naked, tied, gagged, and sporting that black eye. I finished up my love story with getting tasered, cuffed and arrested by the cops in her bathroom.

"And you don't have any recollection of the night? Nothing?"

"Not a thing, other than Kiki continually keeping my glass full, I think she poured a total of three drinks for me. At least that I remember, Jameson."

"Water?"

"No, just a couple of ice cubes."

"That's how I'd take it," Louie said absently, then pushed the top photo over and stared at the next one.

"Anyway," I continued, "it was going to be a long night. We had sex, skipped dinner, more sex. Next thing I know, I wake up tied to the bed with the mother

117

of all hangovers. I'm still trying to shake the headache."

"Still?"

"Yeah."

"That typical?"

"No, I've had some bad hangovers, but forty-eight hours later and still suffering? No, never."

He made a note, then drummed his pen on the legal pad and seemed to be in deep thought.

"Big black space where the night should be?" he asked.

"Yeah, literally, no recollection."

"Classic symptoms of date rape. Sounds like someone fed you Roofies, or some kind of shit, a pretty healthy serving. You take anything? Ecstasy, whites, CFM's?"

"I hardly even know what the hell you're talking about. I don't do drugs, at all."

"I guess we'll see when that toxicology report gets in. Tell me about this," he said, flicking through the photos and pushing one my way. It was Kiki, wrists tied to the bed and half rolled over on her side, clearly displaying a large reddish-purple bite mark on her ass. Along with her wrists tied, she had the leopard print thong stuffed in her mouth and a frightened wild-eyed look on her face.

"Not much to tell. I don't recall taking the photo or anything. I told that attorney, Daphne, all this yesterday. In fact, I didn't even know my phone took photos. Christ, I just make phone calls on the damn thing. Hey, I'm a guy, I even hate to text, not that I'm any good at it."

"Tell me about it," Louie said absently. "So, you've never taken photos with it before, your phone?"

"Never. I didn't know the thing could do that."

"The bite mark, that a usual or sometimes deal you're into?"

"You mean bite her on the ass?"

"Yeah, her or any other partners for that matter."

"No, not that I recall. I gotta be honest. I'm not into the whole pain thing. I've met some kinky gals in my day but nothing like this. The pain deal never really turned my crank, you know?"

"And you state you didn't know she was married to Thompson Barkwell over at K-R-A-Z the same fellow who hired and then fired you?" he asked, flipping to another sheet of paper.

"Hired, fired and stiffed me on a part of my fee. No, I had no idea. I knew she was Farrell's sister. In fact, she sort of gave them my name. They hired me for a couple of days, then got these idiotic, overweight, right wing nit-wits working for them and let me go."

"So you were screwing the boss's wife, right?"

"I never knew she was married to the guy. In fact, I had been with her before I ever knew her brother or Thompson Barkwell even existed. I saw her in the office once or twice, K-R-A-Z. She never mentioned she was married, never did or said anything that I picked up on. First I heard of it was when one of the cops referred to her as Mrs. Barkwell, then that other attorney, Daphne mentioned it yesterday."

"Yeah, Daft," he said absently and drummed his pen some more on the legal pad.

"So?" I asked.

"So, let me be honest. Right now it looks like you're in pretty deep shit. But, things change. I don't want you talking to anyone, unless I'm at your side. No one in the cell, no one in here, no one anywhere. Got it?"

I nodded.

"Someone asks you how you want your eggs for breakfast you don't answer unless I tell you. Okay?"

I nodded.

"I mean it. The least little thing you say, can and will be used against you. Sound familiar?"

I nodded.

"I'd say you were drugged. It's got all the symptoms. I just don't know why. If it's a set up, why? It's not like you got funds they can blackmail you for, right?"

"Right, I don't have any funds."

"No Swiss bank accounts anything like that?"

"You kidding? I got a bunch of girlfriends who like to be taken out and wined and dined. A car that is in constant need of repair, a house I'm always late with the mortgage payment, and…"

"I get it. A bunch of girlfriends, you're a glutton for punishment."

"Tell me about it."

"Okay, toxicology report is our next step. Oh, I want to get a dental impression from you, too. I'll send someone over later today."

"A dental impression?"

He slid the image over of a bound and gagged Kiki with the bite mark on her ass.

"I got a funny feeling we blow that up, get some forensic geek to look at it and compare it to your dental impression we might just find it ain't you."

"But then who did it?"

"Well, we know she didn't, you don't think you did it. Who? That's kind of the sixty thousand dollar question. That, and why in the hell you're being set up? You involved in any other work? Another client that's snakey or would rub this K-R-A-Z bunch the wrong way?"

"No, no one, and even if I was, I don't know how they would possibly know about it."

"Okay, well, as long as nothing else goes wrong, let's look at this as rock bottom and we'll begin to climb our way out of the hole. Deal?"

"Yeah, Louie, thanks for believing me."

There was a knock on the door, followed immediately by Detective Norris Manning, red faced, tie undone, striding in and looking very business like. My favorite arresting officer, Dixon Heller, the detective sergeant who wore the ill fitting brown suit at Kiki's house, followed behind him. This afternoon he wore an ill fitting light blue suit. My friend, Aaron LaZelle, brought up the rear and looked very tired.

Manning stared at me with ice cold, blue eyes and attacked a piece of gum with his front teeth.

"Devlin Haskell, I'm placing you under arrest for the murder of Mr. Thompson Barkwell. You have the right to remain silent. Anything you say can and will…"

I'd heard it all before, or most of it, the reading me my rights part. But, the Thompson Barkwell murder charge came out of left field.

"Don't say a thing," Louie commanded.

Chapter Twenty-Seven

At least with the murder charge I was guaranteed a cell all to myself. Not that it improved my sleep. The following afternoon we were on the fifth floor, in my favorite interrogation room. Detectives Manning, Heller and LaZelle seated across from me and my estimable attorney, Louie Laufen, dutifully at my side. Louie had to be wondering what in the hell he'd gotten himself into.

We'd been in the interrogation room for quite some time. Long enough for me to determine the city of St. Paul must have cornered the market on grey paint and the lowest bidder had won the contract for the air filtration system. The overhead fluorescent light flickered in perfect time to my throbbing headache.

"And you have no recollection of driving to Mr. Barkwell's home?" Manning asked for the umpteenth time.

I looked at Louie, just like I'd done all morning and most of this afternoon, before I answered.

Louie gave a slight nod.

"Look, I've told you guys a thousand times before. I have no recollection of the night. I sort of remember, maybe, a third drink, then it's pretty blank up until the time your goons tasered me in the bathroom."

"I think my client, Mr. Haskell, has been fairly consistent on this point. He simply does not recall anything from the night in question," Louie added.

"Pretty convenient," Heller quipped. He'd been acting the part of the bad cop for the past few hours.

"Look, if I could remember anything, I'd tell you," I pleaded.

They sat stone faced and stared back at me.

"I've no idea where Barkwell even lives."

"And yet we have a 911 call reporting a red 1995, Cadillac DeVille, weaving across the center lane shortly after three in the morning, not four blocks from Thompson Barkwell's home. Amazingly, you drive a red 1995, Cadillac DeVille, don't you?" Heller asked.

"No."

"No?"

"My car's more of a burgundy."

"Oh."

"Broken left tail light?"

"No, it just shorts out once in a while."

"So it might have at least appeared to be broken, even if it was only a short?" Heller asked.

Louie shook his head.

"Possibly." I felt on pretty solid ground.

"Blue door on the passenger side?"

"Well, yeah, I guess so."

"You guess so. Surprise, surprise, a vehicle very similar to yours is spotted in the vicinity at close to the approximate time of death. And, the following day we find Thompson Barkwell beaten to death in the basement of his home with your invoice stuffed in his mouth," Heller said.

"I don't know anything about that."

123

"You'd expressed to me personally, the day we met in the K-R-A-Z offices that you were expecting some difficulty in getting paid, isn't that correct?" Manning jumped in.

"Oh, I don't know."

"I think you suggested you weren't happy about having some sort of board review your invoice, is that correct?"

"No, well, what I meant was…"

"Don't answer that," Louie said.

"The board was going to review my invoice and I didn't want to wait for a month before the board met, that's all. I wasn't worried about getting approved, just the time frame." I thought my explanation sounded reasonable.

"So you thought you'd go over after a few drinks and get the check, right?"

"No."

"You were pretty upset when Thompson Barkwell gave you the check, weren't you?" Heller again.

"No."

"Did you assault him?" Heller asked.

"No."

"You didn't assault anyone?"

"No."

"Do you know a Matthias C. Hogue?" Manning jumped in.

"No."

"He claims you assaulted him during your meeting when Thompson Barkwell paid your invoice."

"Don't answer that," Louie said.

"Bullshit. I didn't assault… wait, you don't mean that fool in the camouflage? The little fat guy? He had a gun for Christ sake. I just disarmed him is all."

"And threatened Mr. Hogue and Mr. Barkwell?"

"Don't answer that." Louie said.

"No."

"You didn't point your hand like a pistol and shoot Mr. Hogue and Mr. Barkwell? In fact, make to shoot Barkwell twice?"

"Don't answer that." Louie said.

"Yeah, but it wasn't a threat, it was a warning."

"A warning?"

"Yeah," I said.

"Gentlemen, might we take a brief moment, I'd like to confer with my client," Louie said, sounding frustrated.

Heller exhaled loudly, then nodded, got up from the table and walked out. Manning and Aaron followed. Aaron looked at me on the way out and shook his head. As soon as they were out of the room Louie glared at me and said, "What the hell are you doing?"

"I thought…"

"Don't think. I didn't think it was possible, but you've managed to find some even thinner ice and push us out onto it. Jesus Christ will you Shut The. Hell. Up. Dev! You are not helping."

"But I…"

"No, just shut up." He glanced at his watch. "It's almost five. I'm calling it quits for the day. Remember what I told you… someone asks you how you want your eggs done you don't answer unless I tell you what to say, got it?"

I nodded.

"Good, now not another word. It's only the rest of your life we're dealing with here."

Chapter Twenty-Eight

Despite the luxurious private cell and paper-thin pad for a mattress. I didn't sleep worth a damn. We were back at it by ten the following morning, in the same room, with the same flickering light, only I thought the place smelled a little worse.

Louie threatened to strangle me if I said one word without his express approval. I'd been responding to the same questions for the past couple of hours, only this time with one word answers after the okay from Louie. Aaron wasn't with us, but Heller seemed to have more than enough fire in his belly to pick up any slack.

"So, you know, I was thinking last night. How do you guess a great looking woman like Kiki ended up with a fat load like Thompson Barkwell?" Heller sort of glanced around the room. Today we were all just pals talking.

"No wonder she was attracted to you, right?" he said.

I didn't respond.

"So then I got to wondering. When you went over to Barkwell's the other night, it's amazing you didn't get stopped for speeding. I mean, good looking woman

126

like that, tied to the bed just waiting for you. Must have been tough to even leave, right?"

I stared straight faced.

"You drive over there on Snelling or did you take Hamline? You know and avoid the construction?"

"I don't think my client was able to take either route actually, Detective Heller. While I understand you've got some serious problems on your hands, the murder of Thompson Barkwell and the supposed rape of his estranged, widowed wife, I'm sure you received the same report I finally got this morning. Mr. Haskell's toxicology results? You did receive the report, didn't you?" Louie asked, and then pulled a manila folder out of his briefcase.

He lowered his head and made a show of pulling his reading glasses down slightly. Then he peered over the top across the table at Heller and Manning.

Heller nodded, but didn't say anything.

"If I might bring your attention to page three, paragraph two, of the toxicology report, gentlemen. This is the analytical report regarding Mr. Haskell's urinalysis and blood workup."

Heller and Manning suddenly appeared crestfallen. Heller thumbed through his file until he brought out four or five pages stapled together in the upper left corner.

"Good." Louie smiled coldly. "If you'd care to follow from the second sentence as I read." He cleared his throat, then began, "Detection of sufficient quantity of flunitrazepam with the resulting effect of profound intoxication, an inability to remember events, possible amnesia, and excessive sedation. Other adverse effects include gastrointestinal disturbances lasting twelve hours or more. Gentlemen, someone fed my client

127

Ecstasy and Roofies," Louie said and casually tossed his copy of the toxicology report on the table.

"I'm afraid that sounds just a little too convenient," Heller stammered.

"Look, you've pounded on my client for almost three days here. Mr. Haskell can't remember a thing. Your own report indicates he was so severely drugged he was incapable of functioning. Let's face it, he's been set up. If I were you, I'd be out there looking to find out who and why?"

Amazingly, Louie seemed to have taken the wind out of their sails and they never got it back. I was back in my private cell by three that afternoon. About three-thirty, Louie and a sheriff's deputy escorted a young woman to my cell. Although I couldn't see them I could hear their approach based on all the whistles and cat calls.

"Dev, Amanda Nguyen, Amanda, Dev Haskell," Louie introduced her through the window in the steel door. The sheriff's deputy gave a nod back down the corridor to the central area so they would open my cell door. It was all computerized and the door opened electronically.

"Nice to meet you." Amanda smiled, oblivious to her surroundings or the cat calls and whistles that continued. She stepped into my cell as the door opened with an audible click.

She was a gorgeous Asian woman, just a little over five feet. I felt like I'd been locked up for years instead of a couple of days and couldn't help but stare. I hoped I wasn't too obvious as I attempted to suck in all her perfume.

"Doctor Nguyen is going to take that dental impression," Louie said.

I looked around for someone else and she picked up on my stupid look.

"I'm a forensic odontologist," she said, snapping open the briefcase she set on my bed.

"What?" I replied.

"A forensic odontologist, a dentist, in plain English."

"She's going to analyze the bite mark on Mrs. Barkwell," Louie offered.

"We're going to do a couple of things. First," she said, then opened a Tupperware sort of container and pulled out what looked like a mouth guard. "I'm going to take upper and lower impressions. Have a seat." She indicated the bed with a nod of her beautiful head. I caught another hint of perfume. It sure as hell beat the normal smells in my cell.

She took two impressions, and told me more than I wanted to know while she did so.

"I'll use a G-clamp and a semi-adjustable articulator on these casts. I'll be able to articulate the maxillary and mandibular positions, relative to one another. I can adjust the condylar angle, incisal and cuspid guidance and the shape of the glenoid fossae and eminintiae. Normally, I'd have to use a face bow, but I think not for this application."

I just sort of made a noise, pretending I understood as I sat there with five pounds of plaster shoved in my open mouth.

She turned to Louie and said. "I'll run the usual tests on porcine skin, compare it to a life size photo. I've got the thing downloaded and ready to be enhanced." Then she turned toward me and yanked the plaster cast off my upper jaw. It made a loud sucking sound. She slapped the lid on her Tupperware and nodded to the deputy, then turned back to me.

129

"With any luck, we'll at least be able to prove it wasn't you who bit the lady in the ass. It's been real," she said, reached in her briefcase and pulled out a sucker with a soft string handle.

"Its okay, Ramsey County Jail approved." She smiled at the deputy. He shrugged and they exited my cell. The sound of whistles and cat calls echoed down the hall as they departed.

I lingered in the remnants of the good doctor's perfume for as long as it lasted.

Chapter Twenty-Nine

Eleven the following morning I was escorted by a deputy to a wooden chair at the courtroom table where Louie sat reading notes. We were on the third floor of the Ramsey County Courthouse, my bail hearing. The room had some sort of polished, dark wood paneling on all four walls. At the front of the room stood an alter-like affair, heavily carved and rising about fifteen feet into air. I slid into the hard wooden chair next to Louie, but was interrupted before I could really say anything to him.

"All rise," the court officer called and everyone stood. Louie was on my left. We sat at one of two mahogany tables. He wore a pressed, dark blue suit with red silk pocket cloth. He was shaved, scrubbed and reeked of men's cologne. The prosecutors, there were two of them at the other table, both square built butch-looking women, appeared frighteningly business-like in their matching grey suits. They seemed to be reveling in the task. I was sure they possessed a not so secret hate of all men and not so much as a hint of a sense of humor.

For this event I had changed from my county issued orange jump suit to a navy blue suit, starched white shirt, conservative tie and shined shoes. My entire ensemble was set off by a pair of nicely buffed steel handcuffs which the prosecuting attorneys insisted I wore. I didn't know them well enough, but it seemed to suggest they might be kinky.

"Look, relax, it's just a ploy, court room theatrics at your bail hearing. I've been up against these two dykes before," Louie whispered.

"Did you win?"

"Sometimes," he replied, a little too off handedly for my tastes.

The judge entered, and took her seat on the bench. It wasn't my first time in court, but I couldn't recall ever seeing her before. She seemed to sit a lot higher than other judges I recalled.

"Oh, shit," Louie hissed under his breath just as she looked down on us.

I was about to ask him what was wrong when the judge spoke.

"Thank you, I'm Judge Helen Slaughter, filling in for Judge Spofford this morning. It seems his honor had a minor traffic accident on the way in and is unable to sit at this proceeding. Therefore, without further delay, let us begin in the matter of ..." She glanced down at something in front of her.

"Ramsey County, versus one Devlin Haskell, bail hearing. Miss Metry, prosecuting for the city. Nice to see you this morning and are you ready, Miss Metry?"

"We are, your honor."

"And representing Mr. Haskell, Mr. Laufen, wouldn't you know. Are you ready, Sir?"

"We are, your honor," Louie said, standing and then continued. "Your honor, if it would please the court. We would like..."

"It does not please this court, as you undoubtedly know, Mr. Laufen."

"Your honor, I was merely about…"

"That will be enough, Mr. Laufen."

Louie, sat down and fought to appear in control while one of the prosecuting dykes read out the laundry list of charges against me. She stopped a couple of times to glance over at me as if she couldn't believe the crimes I was being charged with.

Kidnapping, false imprisonment, rape, assault, sexual assault, and resisting arrest for warm ups. Then the kicker, she paused a half beat, glanced at me again and read the charge.

"Murder."

She went on to suggest I was a danger to society and a flight risk. Frankly, listening to the charges, even I wouldn't grant me bail.

Louie argued I had a business and a home and constituted no risk what-so-ever.

In just under eight minutes the thing was done, bail set at five hundred thousand dollars, half a million bucks. And, if and when I did get out. I would be wearing an ankle bracelet and required to check in with authorities, daily.

We were in a holding cell, Louie and I. He had replaced the plastic dry cleaning bag over my suit and straightened my coat on the hanger. I was stepping back into my orange jump suit as we talked.

"That seemed to go okay," Louie said, undoing his tie and then unbuttoning the top two buttons on his shirt. The open area of his collar immediately filled with a couple of chins.

"Okay? A half million bucks for bail? I gotta wear an ankle bracelet if and when I even do get out, and that's your idea of okay? No offense, Louie, but could things have gone much worse?"

"You kidding? With this judge, you're lucky you're not in some dark hole doing solitary confinement. She has no problem denying someone bail. I'd say we got lucky with all the news reports of overcrowding and that bullshit due to state budget cuts. Otherwise, well like I said…"

"So how soon can I get out?"

"Just as soon as you can get someone to post for you. Any ideas who might have that kind of dough stuffed in a mattress?"

"No, not really. Ten percent of a half million, five grand, hell," I said.

"Actually, that would be fifty grand, Dev."

"Oh, shit," I said.

"Any ideas?"

"Yeah, well there is one person, Heidi Bauer, a friend. She's posted bail for me before. I just don't know about the number. I mean, fifty grand."

"You better go for the gold here, Dev, otherwise you're gonna just have to get comfortable with your cell."

"I'm not sure she's exactly talking to me, just now."

"Why, what happened?"

"Nothing, don't worry. I didn't assault her or anything. We just sort of agreed to disagree."

"And she can make your bail?"

"Yeah, I think so, but the question is would she?"

"So call her. The worst she can do is say no. You'll be no further behind than you are now."

"You think?" I half hesitated. Heidi was gonna freak with another bail call from me.

"What, you can't seriously enjoy being locked up, can you?"

"No, it's just… if I call her to post bail for me again this might be the safest place for me, locked up with armed guards to keep her away."

"Deal with it. Look, you call her, give me her number, and I'll do a follow up. She the mother of your child or anything like that?"

I shook my head no as I zipped up the orange Ramsey County jump suit and then held out my wrists so the deputy could handcuff me. "No, I don't have any children."

"Like I say, unless you like being locked up, I mean, it's your choice. I'll check in with you at the end of the day. I want to give old Doc Nguyen a call in the meantime."

"Who?"

"Stands about this tall." He held a fat hand about chest high. "Gorgeous, Asian, sexy, gave you the oral treatment yesterday and then something to suck on."

The deputy kept his face expressionless, but his eyes moved from Louie to me, then back to Louie.

"Oh, yeah, Doctor Drop Dead Gorgeous."

"Just checking to see if you were breathing. I'll be in touch, take care," he said.

"Thanks, Louie."

He took a few steps then turned at the doorway.

"And remember, not a word about anything to anyone, got it?"

"Yeah, got it."

Chapter Thirty

Forty-eight hours later I was in the passenger seat of Louie's car, a 2000 Dodge Neon, faded blue where it hadn't already rusted. Our path was marked by a cloud of oily blue exhaust hanging in a toxic vapor behind us. Louie was back to wearing a wrinkled suit and smelling like bourbon. His car smelled like a wet dog. Or was that me?

"I still don't understand how you got her to go for it. I told you when I called she swore at me then hung up."

"Power of persuasion, that's why I make the big bucks," Louie said.

"No doubt," I said, scattering crumpled fast food bags with my foot.

"Couple of ground rules. First, do not under any circumstances, go near or in any way contact Kiki Barkwell. Got it?"

"Yeah."

"I'm not kidding here, Dev. It'll land you back in the slammer faster than a whore's trick when the fleet comes in. And don't try and be smart and phone her, or call and hang up, or get a flat tire in front of her house, or run into her at the grocery store, or follow…"

"Louie, relax, I get it. I mean, I am an investigator for God's sake. I make my living watching people do stupid stuff, you know?"

"That must be why you have that ankle bracelet on." He glanced over at me. "Look, they are not kidding, the cops. You need to phone whenever they buzz you on that thing, got it?"

"Yeah." I nodded, then leered at a blonde as she pushed a baby stroller down the sidewalk, sporting head phones and plenty of bounce. God it was good to be out.

"I'm not kidding, Dev. I've had more than one client end up back in the slammer because whatever they were doing was too important to interrupt. The next thing you know, cops got you locked up and once that happens, you ain't getting back out, period."

"Okay, I get it."

Louie was ruining the moment with his advice.

"Next thing, GPS, it's in that damn ankle bracelet so they can find you and track you. If you go near that chick's house they'll know and you'll be a guest of the county for a lot longer than these past few days."

"God, feels like a year since I've been out," I said checking more of the scenery strutting past on Selby Avenue.

"Just keep in mind what I've said. And by the way, forget about getting that thing off and sneaking around. A lot better idiots than you or me for that matter tried and it never works."

"Look, Louie, I appreciate the concern, but I'm not going anywhere near Kiki. Or her weirdo brother, Farrell. Or that bullshit craze, K-R-A-Z. Okay?"

"See that you don't."

"Believe me."

137

"You might want to call your pal Heidi, just to keep her happy. We don't need any problems on that front."

"You know, I was thinking, it might be nice to thank her in person. Any problem with me going over there to her place?"

"Please tell me you're not really that stupid," Louie said, then shot a glance in my direction.

"You don't think..."

"No. You don't think, or at least, you're not thinking right now. Just call and say thanks, tell her it's a function of being monitored that you can only be on the phone for sixty seconds or something. But call, say thanks, and then get the hell off the line."

"Okay, okay, I get it."

He pulled up in front of my house, put the car in park, and turned toward me, wedging himself between the steering wheel and the back of his seat. His suit seemed to be even more wrinkled than just a few minutes before.

"Look, Dev, we've got half a chance here to beat this thing. What we don't need is you sneaking around supposedly investigating. Let the cops do that. You just keep out of trouble, stay close to home, maybe read a book or something. Okay?"

I nodded, put my hand out to shake.

"Louie, can't thank you enough, honest. I really appreciate all you've done for me. I promise I won't screw up."

"I'm going to hold you to that," he said shaking my hand.

Chapter Thirty-One

It took about thirty minutes before I started losing whatever was left of my mind. At least lying on my couch was a lot more comfortable than that cot in my jail cell. I was really trying to follow Louie's advice, let the cops take care of things. On the other hand, that's exactly how I ended up wearing an ankle bracelet and out on bail to the tune of a half million bucks. I wanted to rush over and strangle Kiki, figuratively of course, sort of.

Instead, I phoned Heidi to thank her.

"Hello."

"Heidi, this is Dev."

A very long dead space followed. Eventually I said, "I wanted to phone and thank you for having faith in me and for posting my bail."

More dead space.

"Look, I'm innocent. I didn't commit any of the crimes I'm charged with."

"You never do, do you? I mean, every time I post bail for you. Guess what? It's never your fault, it's always some other dumb ass."

I suddenly liked the very long silence better.

"Look, I'm sorry you feel that way and it makes me appreciate what you did even more. I'm sorry you're involved, I just didn't know where else to turn. I felt like... hello? Hello?"

She'd hung up.

I showered, shaved, went through my mail, then tossed it all into recycling. I looked out the front window for anything of interest. I drifted back to my kitchen and checked around for something to eat. All I found was half a pepperoni pizza from over a week ago. It seemed to be growing some additional spice so I tossed it into the trash, then drifted back to the front window where I stared out at the passing traffic.

I had just wandered back into the kitchen when the doorbell rang.

I opened the front door and there stood Heidi. Eyes puffy from crying and a grocery bag in either hand.

"Heidi..." I'd never been happier to see someone.

"I don't know if I should hug you or just strangle you. You fucking idiot."

"Would you settle for giving me a spanking and then maybe I could..."

"Shut up and let me in," she said, then pushed me aside and stormed back to the kitchen.

"Honest to God, Dev. You have got to knock this shit off, you..."

I followed her into the kitchen like a little puppy.

"Heidi."

"Just let me finish, you absolute, complete and total idiot."

She placed the bags on my kitchen counter, then began to pull out a number of small, white, takeout containers along with three bottles of white wine.

"Oh, sorry, I'm not allowed to have a drink with this ankle bracelet thingy. I guess they can tell if I consume alcohol, somehow. Anyway, I better not…"

"It's not for you, stupid, it's for me."

"Three bottles?"

"I'd say I've earned it, don't you think? Besides, I'm staying the night."

Next to making bail, that was about the best thing that happened to me in over a week.

We were at my kitchen counter the next morning eating breakfast. It was close to one in the afternoon. I'd walked down the street to Nina's Coffee shop, gotten a newspaper and four caramel rolls. Heidi was wearing one of my T-shirts and cramming a third caramel roll into her mouth.

"What I don't get is why?" she said, a giant wedge of caramel roll shoved into the right side of her mouth.

"Why?"

"Yeah." She licked her fingers, oblivious to how sexy she was just now. Or, maybe she did know.

"I guess to set me up."

"Okay, but why? I mean it seems like a lot of extra work. You know?"

"No, I don't."

"Whoever wanted to kill this Barkley guy, did."

"Barkwell. Thompson Barkwell."

"Whatever. But he's dead, right? So why go to all the trouble of setting you up? See what I mean?"

"No."

"Look, the guy is dead. If I was this Kiki person, her alibi would have been she was with you, all night. Not that you could remember, but that sounds pretty solid."

I nodded, slowly.

"If it was someone else, a burglar or business partner or someone, they got away with it. Why call the cops? Seems to me it would be better if they didn't say a thing. He might not have been missed for a day or two. That makes their chances of pulling the whole thing off even better."

I nodded again, deep in thought.

"You gonna eat the rest of your caramel roll?" she asked.

"What? No, you go ahead." I pushed my plate toward her.

"You should have gotten more of these, I'm really hungry and they're kind of little."

"Well, if I recall, you worked up quite an appetite."

"That a complaint?" she asked then returned to licking her fingers. I was pretty sure this time she knew exactly what she was doing.

"Not a complaint, just an observation."

"Let's go observe some more in the bedroom." She smiled. Then got off her stool and slinked out of the kitchen.

I was staring at the bedroom ceiling forty minutes later, deep in thought.

Heidi was curled up against me, with her head on my chest, sound asleep and snoring.

Her "why call the cops?" question had been bouncing around the interior of my thick skull ever since she rolled over and went to sleep. She was right. It didn't make any sense. Unless, it was all a ploy to get me.

But, if that was the case, why not just kill me after I'd been drugged? Or save the Roofies and kill me before? Nothing seemed to add up.

142

Chapter Thirty-Two

I was standing on my front porch, barefoot and feeling very laid back toward the end of the afternoon. I was giving a friendly good-bye wave to Heidi. There had been a light rain for most of the day. The rain made for the perfect sort of afternoon for an accused murderer like me to just lie around and have sex.

Heidi waved, blew me a kiss and slid into her car, some dark blue foreign thing that cost more than I wanted to know. As she drove away from the curb a sheriff's car pulled into the parking place she'd just left. A uniformed officer climbed out and pulled his hat on as I watched from the porch.

He was dressed in a tan uniform shirt with epaulets, a gold badge on his chest and a beer belly hanging over his belt. He held an envelope in his hand and marched up my front sidewalk with a purpose.

"Mr. Devlin Haskell?" he said, sizing me up.

"Yes."

"This is for you," he said and slapped the envelope into my outstretched hand.

"Gee, thanks."

"You have been served. This is a restraining order, Sir."

143

"Wonderful," I said.

"The pleasure's all mine." He smiled, seemingly sincere in his remark, then turned, marched back to his car and drove off.

My phone rang as I walked in the house.

"Haskell Investigations."

"Please tell me you're home."

"You called me on my home phone and I answered. Where else would I be? Louie?"

"I thought this was your cell phone?"

"Okay it is, but I'm still at home."

"Good boy. Keeping a low profile?"

"Yeah, I've been horizontal most of the day. Just had a visitor."

"Who?"

"Sherriff. Served me a restraining order."

"That Kiki woman?"

"Yeah."

"Don't worry about it. Be a damn good idea to stay away from her anyway. Look, that's just the prosecutor piling it on. We got bigger fish to fry."

"Oh?"

"Yeah, the good doctor Nguyen is going to stop by on her way home, probably the next thirty minutes or so."

"She makes house calls?"

"Not usually. But, she has some good news. She can't get a match based on her analysis of the impressions she took and the photo displaying the bite mark on your pal Kiki's very nice ass."

"Is that her technical description?"

Louie ignored my comment.

"Look, just get all the women out of there, the dirty dishes out of the sink, maybe clean yourself up so you look halfway decent. She wants to get another jaw

144

impression or some damn thing from you. Be a gentleman, we are going to need her testimony."

I loaded the dishwasher, took a four minute shower, vacuumed, stole some flowers from the neighbor's garden and put them on the dining room table. Then I watched out the window.

She parked in front about two and a half hours later. She walked up the sidewalk, carrying a large sort of satchel. I waited until she rang the door bell.

"Oh, Doctor Nguyen."

"Hello, Mr. Haskell, did Louie tell you I was coming?"

"He did, and I cleaned especially for you. Come on in."

"Thanks."

I held the door for her as she stepped inside and caught a hint of that perfume again.

"This should only take a moment."

"Do you need anything? Kitchen, a chair?"

"Actually, kitchen would be fine, you lead the way."

I did, and settled on the far side of the kitchen counter.

"Can I get you anything? Coffee, tea, water?" I would have offered her a glass of wine but sex machine Heidi had consumed every last drop.

"No, thanks."

She set the satchel on the counter, opened it up, took out a plastic packet and peeled back the corner.

"Interesting," I lied, trying to sound interested.

"This is an in-vivo porcine model. I'm going to use it…"

She seemed perfectly proportioned in every way. Elegant nails, gorgeous hair, beautiful face and figure. I should have changed the sheets on my bed, imagining her looking up at me while I...

"... just sign this here, indicating you agree and submitted to this of your own free will," she interrupted my daydream.

"Yes."

"What do you mean yes? Were you paying attention? I need you to sign this, right there." She pointed to a form and the pen she'd slid across the counter to me while my mind was elsewhere.

"Yeah, yeah, I knew that," I said picking up the pen and quickly signing.

"Good, now I need you to bite down on this. Apply some pressure." She held out a sort of spongy little disk and inserted it into my mouth, then looked at her watch apparently counting seconds.

Being a trained investigator I noticed she wasn't wearing a wedding ring.

"Okay, and release," she said, then took the disk and placed it in a small plastic case.

"What is that stuff?" I asked, smacking my lips and picking up a taste not unlike envelope glue.

"Porcine," she said, closing her satchel.

"Porcine?"

"Pig skin. The model we made from your impression doesn't compare with the photographic evidence presented. This is just to confirm that it doesn't compare."

"So that's good," I said.

"As far as it goes. There's a lot of debate about the accuracy of the science, always has been, but right now I think we can get the images displaying the bite mark thrown out. If you're really lucky it will call the remaining photos into question. Okay, thanks, sorry to interrupt your evening," she said, then gathered up her satchel and walked toward the front door.

"What, no sucker?" I said, following.

"Sorry, fresh out. Guess you'll have to take a rain check."

"I'll do that."

"I'll hold you to it." She smiled, brushed past me and out the door.

I tried to read, tried to watch TV, tried to read again. Since I was tired after last night and this afternoon's grope and grab with Heidi, I went to bed early.

Chapter Thirty-Three

At six-thirty the following morning I'd already made coffee and was sitting out on my front porch finishing my first cup as traffic slowly began to build. Even at this hour it was warm to the point of suggesting beastly for later in the day. I had a nine o'clock appointment at the office of my home arrest officer, a Miss Muriel Puehl of Sentinel Monitoring. Meanwhile, Heidi's question continued to nag away, why me?

The offices of Sentinel Monitoring were located about three miles up 35W, off Larpenteur Avenue and just inside the St. Paul city limits. One of those nondescript, one-story brick strip buildings, housing a dozen different offices where you could park right in front were it not for all the reserved parking signs. I thought I should be on my best behavior so I pulled the DeVille into the far side of the lot, then entered the office. I arrived ten minutes early for my appointment, and sure I was making a good first impression.

The receptionist was named Marcie, if her plastic nametag could be trusted. She was rather large, and unfortunately rather unattractive.

"Hey, good morning, how are you?" I said.

Marcie replied with a slight nod and cold, close set eyes. They sized me up over her hooked nose. I tried not to focus on the erupted mole growing alongside her left nostril.

"I have a nine o'clock appointment with Muriel Puehl." I pronounced it 'Pew-L'

"Pull," Marcie said.

"What?"

"Pull, Muriel's name is pronounced 'pull'."

I read each letter out loud from my appointment card. "And that's pronounced 'pull'?"

Marcie gave another slight nod. Not only unattractive, she was humorless as well.

"I have an appointment in about ten minutes. Devlin Haskell," I said.

"Have a seat."

I did and then sat for the next twenty-five minutes. Eventually an attractive woman with eyes that looked puffy from crying exited from an office behind the receptionist desk.

"Asshole," she hissed under her breath as she walked out of the office. I couldn't figure out if she meant me or Muriel Puehl.

A few minutes later Marcie called, "Mr. Haskell," as if she was searching the office for me. I was sitting six feet away from her, the only person in the tiny waiting area.

"Here."

"You may see Miss Puehl." She inclined her head toward the door.

If Marcie was rather large, Muriel Puehl was massive. A neckless blonde with a number of chins hunched over a desk. Fleshy arms easily the size of my thighs jiggled when she moved. She never looked up

149

from the file she was reading. She just pointed with a pen and grunted, "Sit."

I did, then listened to her labored breathing. The plastic chair I was in seemed uncomfortably warm. No doubt due to the sobbing woman who'd exited the office minutes earlier.

Muriel's perfume was almost eye watering and reminded me of the air freshener in the bathroom of my grandmother's home when I was a kid. I tried to breathe through my mouth as she silently read on and on.

Eventually she raised her head to the point where her chins formed one large chin which sort of forked at her chest and turned into cleavage. She stared at me for an uncomfortable length of time. The dark bags under each eye looked like carry-on luggage.

"You're a private investigator."

"Yes." I nodded, hoping to look bright and somewhat agreeable.

She sucked her front teeth.

"Interesting, your kind have caused a lot of people a lot of pain."

"Not intentionally." I smiled. I couldn't tell if she was studying me or just trying to come up with the next consecutive thought.

Finally she said, "Sign these top two sheets, initial the third in the places I've highlighted. They explain the fees to you?"

"Yes, twelve dollars a day, right?"

"In advance, payable weekly or monthly, your choice. Here, initial this." She slid another form across the desk at me. "Once you decide which option to take, weekly or monthly, you can't change. Don't have the staff for the paper work. We take credit cards. If you write a check, back date it to cover yesterday."

"Yesterday?" I slid the forms back to her.

"Plus the set up and install fee, eighty-seven-fifty." She glanced down at the forms I'd just slid back across the desk to her. "So, okay, you're doing the monthly payment. I need a month in advance, three-hundred-sixty, plus the eighty-seven-fifty. I'll save you the trouble, Mr. Hastings," she said, punching keys on a calculator.

"Haskell."

"Four-hundred-forty-seven-dollars-and-fifty-cents. By the way, trust me, this is not the place to bounce a check. That check gets returned NSF and you're back in the Ramsey County Jail. Questions?"

"No, they made things pretty clear when I was released. You'll be checking me a couple times a day. No alcohol. I have…"

"Or drugs."

"Not a problem."

She stared coldly.

"I have to push the button on the phone within five rings, punch in my code. I stay in the house. I review my schedule with you a week in advance. I have to phone forty-eight hours in advance to alter the approved schedule. I can travel to and from work. I have thirty minutes to get to my office and thirty minutes to return home."

"See that you do," she said slowly, enunciating each word.

"About my weekly schedule, I'd like…"

"See Marcie out front."

"She does the schedule?"

"No, she sets up your appointment to meet with me, then I approve your schedule."

"Would it be possible to do that now? You see…"

151

Muriel held up a meaty paw and stopped me in mid sentence.

"Please, let's follow procedure. You can set up an appointment with Marcie when I've finished."

From there she droned on for another fifteen minutes. Occasionally she picked up a pen in her chubby right hand and checked off another item on a laundry list, then read the next point in an expressionless monotone. Eventually, she finished up with the loving reminder, "Failure to comply with any of the aforementioned requirements may result in your arrest and re-incarceration. Do you have any questions, Mr. Haskens?"

She may as well have asked did I want fries with that? I shook myself awake.

"Haskell. No, no questions."

"Please initial in the box provided next to each check mark, indicating you fully understand the requirements as I've explained them to you. Then sign at the bottom, indicating you agree with the initials you've placed in each box."

As she said this she slid a long narrow form toward me. There were a number of creases in her fat wrist like she had string or something tightly tied around it.

I initialed and signed.

"Very good, Mr. Hastings, please report to Marcie." Muriel didn't bother to raise her massive chins and look at me.

"Thank you," I said, and exited.

It was more of the same from the lovely Marcie out at the front desk, except she was less charming. At no surprise, neither woman wore a wedding ring. Either they didn't come in the required size or they hadn't found a guy stupid enough. Marcie set up my appointment to see Muriel tomorrow, when she would theoretically approve my schedule. Good thing I didn't have anything else to do in my life.

Chapter Thirty-Four

Back home that evening I felt like a caged animal. As I sat on my front porch sipping ice water, a crowd of five women walked past, chatting and not listening to one another on their way to the next saloon.

"Want to come in and see my ankle bracelet?" I said, a little too loudly.

That seemed to put a spring in their step and they went quickly on their way. Eventually, I got bored with watching people enjoying themselves, became frustrated with nothing on TV and I went to bed. I tossed and turned fitfully through the night and was sipping coffee out on my front porch at six the following morning.

I had a nine-thirty appointment with the charming Muriel Puehl to hopefully approve my work schedule. I arrived ten minutes early, again.

"Yes," Marcie said at the receptionist desk. I recognized her blank look. She was oblivious to the fact I'd been in twenty-four hours earlier and had scheduled today's appointment on the way out the door.

"Devlin Haskell. I have a nine-thirty appointment with Muriel."

"I'll see if Ms Puehl can see you."

I noticed the crossword puzzle in front of her. I was going to say something smart, thought better of it, took my choice of uncomfortable seats and waited.

"Mr. Haskell?" Marcie called out twenty minutes later searching for me in the small reception area. Once again I was the only other person there.

"Yes."

"Ms Puehl will see you now," Marcie said. The same blank look on her face and a quick glance suggested she'd gotten no further on the crossword puzzle.

Muriel was reading some papers at her desk when I entered. Pink chins rolled down her chest. The air was almost syrupy with perfume. She didn't look up, simply pointed a sausage-like finger at the uncomfortable chair in front of her desk and kept reading.

I sat, watched her, counted four separate and distinct chins and waited.

"You've brought this week's schedule?" she said eventually looking up.

"Yeah. Actually, I brought two weeks I figured we might as well…"

"We approve one week at a time. I've neither the patience nor inclination for changes."

"Okay." I swallowed down the wise guy comment about her living with five cats, eating cake frosting out of the can every night, and placed my schedule on her desk.

"I see," she said, then took a few minutes to read the single page schedule a dozen times.

"You'll be allowed thirty minutes to commute to and from your office. Other than that you will be in your office or your place of residence. Correct?"

"Yes."

"Very well, you can see Marcie about your next appointment."

"Would it be possible to email my schedules to you? Might save us both some…"

"No. Please make your appointment with Marcie on your way out. Good day."

There were a number of things I wanted to ask, Why couldn't I email a schedule? Why was she so fat? Had she ever been laid? If so did the poor guy survive? Instead I settled for, "Thank you."

I made my appointment with Marcie. It dawned on me they were probably scamming the county, paid a specified amount for every client appointment. Therefore, everything required an appointment. I decided to shut up and just get out of there as fast as possible. Marcie was only too happy to oblige so she could return to staring blankly at her crossword puzzle.

I fled Sentinel Monitoring and drove to my office. I looked longingly across the street at The Spot bar for a moment and then climbed the stairs. There was over a week's worth of mail shoved under the door. A dozen circulars from grocery stores, two past due notices and a post card from Las Vegas written so illegibly I couldn't determine who had sent it. I dumped most of the pile into the waste basket, taped the post card to the wall, then went to make coffee and discovered I was out.

I hit speed dial on my cell and walked out the door.

"The Spot."

"Jimmy, Dev, can you get me two coffees, to go?"

"To go? And where you been the last few days? Christ, we're down about fifteen percent."

"Long story. Can I come over and get the coffee?"

"Yeah, how long you gonna be?"

"I'm crossing the street now," I said, hung up and pushed open the front door. Jimmy still had the phone in his hand.

"You weren't kidding."

"I'm a busy guy. You got something I can carry those in, besides the dirty coffee mug you usually serve me?"

"I've never served you a coffee in here in your life."

"You got a point."

"Here, take this," he said, sliding the pot across the bar. "It's way past time to make a fresh pot anyway."

"Gee, thanks."

"On your tab, I'm guessing."

"Is there another way?"

"Amazingly some of our customers pay cash."

"On the tab."

"Everything going okay?"

"I'm about to start on that now."

"And you think that coffee is gonna help?"

Fifteen minutes later I was thinking Jimmy had a point. I grimaced as I felt the acid burn a hole in my stomach. I swirled the coffee a little to see if there was any glaze left on the inside of the ceramic mug, then pushed the thing aside. The coffee had to have been from yesterday, early in the day.

I drummed my finger on the desk and thought about that lunatic Kiki, Mrs. Thompson Barkwell and her idiot brother Farrell Early. I wrote their names on a sheet of paper. Then wrote KRAZ off to the side. I wrote Thompson Barkwell below that, then drew a question mark in the middle. A half hour later all I'd done was retrace the question mark a few thousand times.

Had I been set up or was I once again just in the wrong place at the wrong time?

Chapter Thirty-Five

I didn't accomplish much more than that for the rest of the day. Occasionally, I looked longingly out the window at The Spot as another miscreant walked in or stumbled out. The sun shimmered off the asphalt street and the sidewalk looked hot enough to fry an egg on. A little after four, I hit on an idea and called Sunnie Einer, my resource for all things computer.

"Hello," she answered on the second ring.

"Hi, Sunnie, it's Dev. Long time no talk."

There was a long pause, too long.

"Hello, Sunnie?"

"Yes, Dev."

"How are things?"

Another too long pause.

"Sunnie?"

"Look, Dev, you know and I know you couldn't care less how things are. So get to the point."

"You okay?"

"Yes, I'm fine. I'm also busy. What do you need?"

"Well, I was wondering if you wouldn't mind looking something up for me, on the computer? It's the…"

"Do you still have that laptop you borrowed from me for the weekend? I believe it was about six months ago?"

I did as a matter of fact. It was on top of my file cabinet. I'd set the coffee pot on top of the thing earlier.

"Yes, I've got it right here, meant to bring it back. I guess I've been working overtime and it sort of got away from…"

"Is it on?"

"Well actually, not exactly. See it…"

"Not exactly? Is it on or not?"

"It's not. I think it might be broken."

"Broken? Did you drop it?"

"No it just stopped working all of a sudden. Honest. I was typing away on the thing and out of the blue it shut down."

"Did you have it plugged in?"

"Plugged in?"

"Oh God. So you never recharged the battery?"

"How do you do that?"

"You can't be this… Oh God, look, bring it over here. I'll give you a basic tutorial. The same one I give to eight year olds, although that might be a little too advanced. You can pick up dinner by the way, and some wine, I'm in the mood for Italian, and make it a nice wine."

I had trouble just turning on a computer. I hated the things. The last thing I wanted was a tutorial. Then there was the small matter regarding the condition of my release and my schedule allowing just a half hour commute to and from the office.

"How about this?" I said. "You come to my place and I'll have dinner and the computer all ready for you. That way you won't have to do any dishes or clean up or anything."

"You think my home is dirty, is that it? I teach full time, I have my son, Josh, my consulting business. I barely have time to think let alone…"

"Hey, Sunnie, I've got a problem I'm trying to deal with. No, your house isn't dirty, it's always spotless. I never said anything about your place. I'll have dinner for you, Italian as requested, with wine, a good wine. But, I need some help. I can't come to your place, I'll explain over dinner, if you can make it. If you can't, no problem, I'll catch you some other time. Then you can tell me what's bothering you. You okay?"

Another long pause.

"What time?"

"It's a little after four now. How's six-thirty sound?"

"Fine," she said and hung up.

Gee, a computer lesson from a woman pissed off at me. I could hardly wait. I wondered if Muriel Puehl had anything going on. I could invite her and make the night a complete disaster. I racked my brain to remember what I'd done to get Sunnie so mad.

Chapter Thirty-Six

It was about eight-thirty. We were sitting in front of the infamous laptop at the end of my dining room table. Remnants of our twelve-minute, conversation-less, eggplant lasagna and garlic bread dinner were scattered at the opposite end of the table. I was drinking decaf, my second, and Sunnie was on her third glass of wine. The first two had done nothing to improve her attitude. I was manning the controls on the laptop, getting the intro tutorial to her computer 101 class.

"You're kidding me. All I had to do was plug the thing in?"

Sunnie twitched a smile for half a nanosecond, suggesting anything but pleasure.

"Okay, so I want to look up marriage records. Actually a marriage, as in one," I said.

"Where?"

"Minnesota, I think."

She sighed.

"Probably Minnesota, yeah. Pretty sure, Minnesota."

"County?"

"I'm guessing Ramsey."

She stared at me a moment.

"Okay, do a search, type in…"

"Search?"

"Move your cursor up to here." She pointed with a pen to a box on the screen. "Okay, now type in Minnesota, then Ramsey County, marriage license. Do you have a date?"

"No, that's actually what I'm looking for."

"Do you happen to have the names of the individuals?" She said this in a tone that suggested she was using quite a bit of her self control.

"Click on this box. Right, now type the names in there."

I entered Thompson Barkwell.

"Okay, now click here on search, again. Okay."

I looked over at her. She continued to stare at the screen, stone faced.

"Sunnie, something's bothering you. Even I'm picking up on it and I'm really bad at picking up on signals from women."

She ignored me and tapped the screen with her pen. "Pay attention. See here. Thompson Barkwell married to a Katherine Early. That who you're looking for?"

I nodded, reading the screen.

"There's your date, looks like a little over a year ago. That all you needed?"

"Yeah, now you want to tell me what's bugging you?"

"No."

"No?"

"Thanks for dinner, I've got work to do. I'll expect the laptop back in the near future," she said, grabbing her purse off the couch and heading for the door.

"Thanks for your help, Sunnie," I called. "Nice chatting," I added after she slammed the door behind her.

Kiki and Thompson were married thirteen months and eleven days ago. It was a toss up who fled the scene first. My money was on Kiki. Only because Thompson Barkwell struck me as the type of guy who would have put up with a lot, anything as a matter of fact, once he found a woman crazy enough to go out with him twice let alone marry him. 'Crazy enough' seemed the perfect description for Kiki.

I stared at the search window on the laptop screen. I was home for the night with a table full of dirty dishes, waiting for a computerized phone call from the monitoring service. What to do, what to do? I typed in XXX and clicked search.

The call from the monitoring service came through about two and a half hours later. Time flies when you're having fun. A computerized female voice instructed me to; "Please input my personal code, then press pound." When I did that the voice replied, "Thank you. Goodbye," and hung up. A second call came through an hour and thirty minutes later and had me do the same thing. It was a good thing I hadn't gone out. Thank God for Internet porn.

Chapter Thirty-Seven

The following morning I picked up a can of coffee on the way to the office, half decaf. On the way I drove past the offices of KRAZ, just because. If there was anything to see, I missed it. I drove around the block, pulled into the parking lot and parked at the rear of the lot. A couple of beer cans crackled when I flattened them backing into the parking spot. After about twenty minutes of not seeing anything and getting nervous about the GPS capabilities in my ankle bracelet I drove to my office.

I was on my third cup of half decaf coffee and not the least bit smarter. Granted, Kiki was a lunatic, but what was she thinking marrying Thompson Barkwell? Did I really hit her, tie her up? My toxicology report suggested I was drugged. But why? Was I being set up, royally framed? Again, why?

I plugged in the trusty laptop, turned the thing on and began searching. I was reasonably adept now. Seven hours of intense practice going through porn sites, barely scratching the surface, will do that. I began searching Kiki, then Farrell and Thompson and finally KRAZ. I learned a couple of things, the most immediate of which was I was out of aspirin and had a pounding headache.

In a nutshell, the three were bit players with spotty histories of scams stretching back eight to ten years... the usual real estate and finance deals, a couple of bankruptcies. Farrell had a bar go belly up out in Las Vegas in 2006, the 'Early Bird Saloon'. In today's world a business failing was nothing at all out of the ordinary. Well, except maybe for Farrell's Vegas bar, the Early Bird Saloon, not exactly an original name, but 2006 was still a boom year, before everyone got yanked back to financial reality. How could a bar fail in Vegas?

I went to the Las Vegas Sun website, searched Farrell J. Early and read a handful of articles that suggested maybe more than food and liquor were being dealt at the Early Bird Saloon. To be specific, Ecstasy and Roofies, ironically the same menu as my toxicology report. Things apparently got to the point where even the Vegas authorities were fed up. In the final article, sort of a post mortem round up of the bar's twenty-two month history, it mentioned that Farrell, along with wife, Katherine 'Kiki' Early worked out an agreement where they would not be charged, closed the bar and filed for bankruptcy.

Farrell had a wife with the same nickname as his sister? Kiki? What were the odds? It seemed the odds were more likely Kiki would have married her brother than there were two women with the same nickname, although it all sounded extreme, even for Vegas and even for Kiki. I searched my second set of marriage records in less than twenty-four hours, both relating to Kiki.

Back in 2005 Farrell J Early married one Katherine 'Kiki' Hinz. Katherine was the only daughter of Ottmar "Loopy" Hinz, former president of the Food and

Beverage Workers union of Las Vegas. Ottmar Hinz had been unable to attend his daughter's gala wedding. Unfortunately he had just begun serving an eighteen year sentence at Nevada's High Desert State Prison. Seemed old "Loopy" had been convicted of racketeering.

One could only guess why Ottmar was called "Loopy". Apples didn't fall far from the tree, like father like daughter and all that. None of which got me any closer to being exonerated, or did it? A further search found nothing of interest. At five I tucked the laptop under my arm and headed home to practice my searching skills. On the way I called my attorney, Louie.

"Lo." Louie sort of groaned into the phone.

"Hi Louie, Dev Haskell. Got a moment to talk?"

"Lo."

"Hello, Louie, can you hear me."

"No one there, man." I heard Louie say. His voice faded as he pulled the phone away from his ear. I could hear him mumbling, the background noise of glasses clinking, music, laughter, it all suggested he wasn't at a church service. Then we were disconnected, meaning Louie hung up. I called back three more times. Louie never answered and his mail box was full so I couldn't leave a message.

The monitor call came through at about eight-forty-five, interrupting my internet viewing of 'Double D and Disorderly'.

Chapter Thirty-Eight

I'd been sitting in the KRAZ parking lot for twelve minutes, eating a couple of blueberry muffins and sipping half decaf coffee from my travel mug. I couldn't taste the difference in the coffee. I was bored. You'd think at a few minutes before nine in the morning someone, somewhere, would pull into the parking lot for work. As far as I could tell, I was the lone source of activity.

My cell phone rang. As usual I glanced at the numbers, but couldn't read them.

"Haskell Investigations." I prayed it wasn't the monitoring folks picking up on the fact I was outside KRAZ.

"Dev?" a groggy voice rasped, then cleared the throat a couple of times.

"Yeah."

"Dev?"

"Yeah. Louie, that you?"

"I was working and missed a call from you late last night."

"You weren't working, Louie, and it wasn't late. It was a little after five. You were…"

"That's late."

168

"You were in some bar somewhere. It sounded like you'd been there for quite a while."

"I was doing some research."

"Yeah, sure you were."

"Anyway," he said, again with the clearing of the throat. I had to admit it actually did make his voice sound better. "I missed your call."

No point in arguing.

"Yeah, thanks for calling back. Look, I've been doing some research myself and investigating on my own and I've come up with some things."

"Please don't tell me you're stupid enough to go anywhere near that Kiki Barkwell chick or her brother. I really don't need to hear that."

"Give me a break. How stupid do you think I am? Relax."

"Thank God. Okay, investigating what?"

"I was online…" I went on to tell Louie what I'd learned, especially the Vegas stuff, Kiki married to Farrell. The Early Bird Saloon closing then finishing up with the drug sales, the same concoction my toxicology report indicated had been fed to me. As I spoke I watched a sleek, dark blue BMW pull into the lot and glide into a parking place close to the front door.

"Look, I'm driving right now man, can you …"

Farrell climbed out of the driver's side of the BMW. He had a white gauze bandage around his index finger and right hand. I could only hope he'd slammed the thing in his fancy car door. A half second later Kiki climbed out the passenger side, looking fabulous and taking a bite out of an apple. He waited for her, then gave her an extremely unbrotherly massage across her rear. She smiled, tossed her shiny brunette hair, then glanced over in my direction. I couldn't tell if she recognized the DeVille or noticed me. If she did, she didn't seem to react or say anything to Farrell. Twenty seconds later they'd disappeared inside the building.

"Dev, you there?"

"Sorry about that. Must have hit a dead spot, you know, no phone service."

"Okay, look, I'm driving too, can you call me in about fifteen minutes? Let's go over this shit when I can pay attention, take some notes. Jesus, lady, signal or get off the God damn road. Oh, sorry 'bout that. Give me a call in fifteen, okay?"

"Yeah, I'll call you."

I waited until we disconnected before I started the car, sat for a minute, took down the license number on Farrell's BMW, then drove to my office. I phoned Louie's cell, phoned again after twenty and then twenty-five minutes. I phoned his office number at the half hour mark and left a message. Louie returned my call about an hour later.

"Yeah, Dev, man it's crazy here, took forever just to find some aspirin. Got a pounding headache. God, I hope I'm not coming down with the flu or something," he said, slurping what I hoped was coffee.

At the moment I was gazing out the window at what I guessed were three co-eds waiting for a bus across the street. One of them wore tight shorts and a grey T-shirt with purple letters, UST, University of St. Thomas, stretched across the front. She had on purple flip-flops to complete her ensemble. They all looked like they'd be a lot of work.

"Tell me again what you've got. I'm probably gonna interrupt, I'm taking notes." Louie cleared his throat.

"Okay, I started doing a search, online," I bragged. "Starting with Thompson Barkwell's marriage." I went on from there, told him about the Vegas information,

170

the Early Bird Saloon, Loopy Hinz, Kiki's marriage to Farrell. We went back over things every time Louie asked a question, and he asked quite a few. It brought up new questions. After a good half hour we were more or less finished.

"I'm thinking I should get in touch with Detective Manning, let him know this stuff," I said.

"You didn't contact him, did you?"

"Not yet. That was gonna be my next call."

"Bad idea, Dev, very bad idea."

"You kidding, this stuff puts a whole new spin on things."

"If Manning had his way you'd be in the electric chair by now."

"But this stuff could really..."

"You get where I'm coming from? The guy is not your biggest fan. Past history I'm guessing."

"Maybe a little." I saw no point in going into any detail.

"Look, let me get this to Manning. I want to have someone from our office verify this information and..."

"How long will that take?"

"It shouldn't be that long. I know you're hot to get this over with, Dev, but let's do this properly. Then we can walk away, free and clear of all charges. Someone has a burr up their ass to get you, so let's just get everything nailed down, okay?"

"Yeah, okay, it's just that..."

"Just that nothing. This is why you pay me, so listen up. Continue investigating, online. Stay away from Farrell Early and his sister, or wife or ex-wife, Kiki, whatever in the hell she is. Just stay away from her. Your job, and I know it's tough, but your job is to look like a model citizen right now. Try and fool everyone into thinking you're a decent guy. Got it?"

171

"I'm not sure I can pull that off."

"Humor me."

Chapter Thirty-Nine

As much as I hated to admit it, I couldn't argue with Louie. It made sense that his office, rather than me, should turn over verifiable information to the police as part of the on-going investigation. My particular problem was I wanted everything cleared up yesterday. I didn't want to wait another minute.

I phoned Louie's cell toward the end of the day just to check on his progress. I was staring absently out the window as a bus pulled up and a stream of tired looking women poured out after another work day. I got disconnected while listening to the recording that said his mailbox was full. I phoned his office. He was out so I left a message. The receptionist assured me "Mr. Laufen will return your call just as soon as he's able."

'As soon as he's able' seemed to cover a multitude of sins where Louie was concerned.

Later that night, I was at my dining room table, finishing up the last microwaved burrito. I'd been deeply involved in more online investigation, reviewing twenty years of "Girls Gone Wild at Mardi Gras". I still had twelve years to cover when my cell phone rang.

"Haskell Investigations," I said, turning down the computer volume.

"Dev, have I caught you at a bad time?" It was Sunnie.

"No, just watching a news report on the retail market." The Girls Gone Wild at Mardi Gras were way past being content with just a cheap beaded necklace.

"Do you want to give me a call when it's over?"

That would be about ten hours from now, if I wasn't interrupted.

"No, nothing I haven't seen before. How you doing? And by the way, thanks for the tutoring session it…"

"That's why I'm calling, actually." She sounded tentative.

"It really helped me out. I'm getting pretty good at this Internet researching."

I remained focused on the sexy figures gyrating across the laptop screen.

"Well, look, I may have come off the wrong way the other night. Lately, I've just been… I don't know, I feel I've just been pulled so many different ways…"

That's exactly what was happening to the two girls currently going wild at Mardi Gras. I hit pause.

"…take it all out on you. Not that you don't deserve it. But, I'm sorry if I might have come across as oh, I don't know, maybe a little touchy or something."

This was the place where I was supposed to say, 'You weren't touchy. I admit I held onto your laptop six months longer than I promised. I know you're busy. I know you're a single parent. I'm aware I usually call you when I need something and I expect you to drop everything and solve my problems.' But, then again, there was a limit to what anyone, especially me, should have to take.

"Look, first of all, you weren't bitchy, I mean touchy. Second, if it's okay, I'm still doing some research using your laptop, but if nothing else I'm convinced I should get one of these things. Soon as I do, I promise I'll return yours. I'm just in the middle of a case right now, and…"

"Don't worry about getting it back, I just wanted…"

Studying the paused screen I became convinced the Mardi Gras girls had implants, not that I was bothered.

"Dev, you there?"

"Oh yeah, sure. Let me ask again, are you okay? Is there something bothering you?"

"It's nothing. In fact it's silly, forget it."

Sometimes it's like pulling teeth.

"You sure? You seemed upset and you're never like that."

"No really."

"Is there something I can help with? God knows I owe you, Sunnie, you've always been there for me."

"Oh, you're sweet… sometimes. But no, it's nothing."

"Well, something's clearly bothering you. You want to just talk? I could tell you how screwed up my life is and then you can think, gee, thank God I'm not Dev. Your life will start to look about a thousand percent better."

"No, I need to work through this."

"You're sure? This isn't like you, Sunnie." Liar, liar, liar. "What is it?"

"It's nothing, really."

"Good, then you can tell me and we can move on."

"It's just that it's so silly, so stupid."

175

"Doesn't sound like it's silly to me. Whatever it is, it's upsetting you. Maybe I can help."

"Oh, I don't know."

"Try me." Jesus, I wanted to get back to the Mardi Gras. I'd asked a half dozen times, a dozen different ways. "Come on, what's the matter?"

"Well, it's Josh."

"Josh? Is he okay?" Sunnie's son, I liked the kid. We'd developed a sort of wink and a nod relationship over the years. His straight shooting, successful, educated, hard working mom dispensed common sense advice which I tempered with my street-smart, loser input. He was a good kid, just doing normal idiot guy stuff.

"He's okay at the moment, but he's hanging around with a bad crowd."

"Bad crowd?"

"Well, one person in particular."

"Some guy into drugs or something?"

"No, worse, a girl." She sneered.

"What's she been doing?"

"Well, they're always together. Her hair is ridiculous. Her language is about as colorful as yours. She's simply falling out of the few, inappropriate clothes she wears. She's tattooed and for the past month and a half seems to be physically attached to my son. He'd rather spend time with her than study or be with me."

That's my boy.

"Is her hair one of those colors not found in nature? You know, pink or blue?"

"Worse, it's this hideous curly, blonde mop."

"She wearing old hippy clothes, flannel shirts, bib overalls, work boots, that sort of stuff?" I'd just described Sunnie at a young age, except I'd left out braless.

"Worse, nothing's left to the imagination. Not that you'd need any imagination. She's falling out everywhere. She wears a thong the size of a postage stamp. How can that possibly be comfortable?"

"You saw her in her underwear?"

"You can't help but see. When she's sitting at the kitchen counter wearing those low cut jeans, her bright colored, silky thong what there is of it rides right up her rear end. Her jeans are too tight to even be remotely comfortable. God if she was my daughter..."

"You said she was tattooed?"

"Yes, some dreadful lacy thing across the small of her back. Imagine how that'll look when she's thirty-five?"

I was trying to. It sounded pretty good. So far I was on Josh's side.

"What's her name?"

"Amanda, but she insists on being called Mandy," she groaned.

This from a woman christened Bernice who insisted on being called Sunnie since she was in Kindergarten.

"How'd he meet her?"

"He met her at school. They're in the same classes."

"The U, doesn't he take advanced classes?"

"Look, I know where you're going. Yes he does, and yes she does. I'm just saying she seems more than a little too advanced for Josh, right now, that's all. And, Jesus Christ, do they have to be together twenty-four-seven. I mean give it a rest."

"You want me to talk to him?"

"Oh, sure, that would smooth things over. Mommy's bum friend can tell him what not to do…I'm sorry, I didn't mean it like that, Dev. You know how I get once in a while."

I was now solidly on Josh's side.

Chapter Forty

I was wasting my time hanging around at the University of Minnesota, waiting for a Chemistry lab to finish. I was on the third floor of Smith Hall, leaning against a beige wall just around the corner from some sort of laboratory room. I was probably the dumbest person for two-hundred yards in any direction and the only one without a backpack.

There were more than a few things wrong with the situation I found myself in. I could start with my offer to speak with Josh. Go from there, to me pretending to innocently run into him in the third floor hallway of the Chemistry building. I'd had to pay fifteen dollars or whatever the consult fee was to amend my schedule with fat old Muriel at Sentinel Monitoring. The whole thing was another one of those examples of someone like Sunnie, who didn't do what I did, knowing exactly how I should conduct myself. The only thing dumber was me agreeing to everything in the first place.

After about ten minutes a pair of heavy double doors flew open and three guys strolled out of the lab. Each weighed about a hundred and thirty pounds dripping wet, stood about six-one and had Adams apples the size of golf balls. They wore matching Star

Wars T-shirts. A moment behind them came a pack of kids, more than a few attractive co-eds and toward the end of the pack there was Josh. I presumed the infamous Mandy was the gorgeous young blonde woman walking next to him, holding his hand.

She was just as Sunnie had described, curly blonde hair, fantastic figure, an outfit leaving nothing to the imagination and surgically attached to Josh. Who could blame the boy?

I pushed off the wall before they rounded the corner in an effort to make my appearance look unintended.

"Hey, Josh, how's it going?"

"Oh, God, my Mom sent you, didn't she?" He half chuckled. Mandy seemed to somehow get even closer to him and climb inside his pocket.

God, why do I get involved? So much for the casual run-in.

"Yeah, look. I owe her. Can we talk so at least I'm covered? And you must be Mandy. I'm Dev Haskell, a friend of Josh's mom and this idiot." I nodded at Josh.

"He's okay." Josh laughed.

Mandy held out her hand, tentatively. The rest of her seemed to remain surgically attached to Mr. Lucky.

"Nice to meet you, Mandy. We need to talk, you hanging around with bums like Josh. You seem like such a nice girl, I should probably set you straight. You guys got time for coffee, an early lunch, late breakfast?"

"Mom must have really got to you, man."

"Let's just say I find myself in the doghouse, once again," I said.

"We know how that goes," Josh scoffed.

"You lead the way. I barely got out of high school so I'm lost here," I said.

We were having an intimate conversation in the midst of about a thousand other people in a giant cafeteria. Everyone had been over charged for bad coffee and some sort of lousy pastry with a name I couldn't pronounce and had already forgotten. We'd been chatting and laughing for the better part of an hour. I swore Mandy to secrecy, then told her some Sunnie tales.

"So there you have it. She was understandably pissed off because I still had her laptop and, well you know how she can get." I finished with a last swallow of coffee. It hadn't improved with age.

"You get the one word treatment?" Josh asked.

"One word?"

"Yeah, you know, how you doing? Fine. Anything wrong? No. Want something to eat? No. Did you read about the tsunami? Yes. Who needs it? After a while you get the message. She's pissed off, but isn't going to tell you why."

"Well, look, she's a mom and she's worried about you, both of you." I tried to sound understanding, it was a reach.

"What does she think we're gonna do?"

I looked at him for a long moment. Instead of saying the obvious with Mandy there, I countered.

"Aren't you the guy that smashed up her Prius? Didn't you spray paint something on the wall of your high school locker room? Remember the little rusty Volvo station wagon you totaled about a week before high school graduation? Weren't you the one who got caught mooning on the team bus junior year? Didn't…"

"What?" Mandy shrieked and started laughing.

"Okay, you can spare us all the details, Dev."

"Look, take some advice from someone who's been kicked around the block a few times. Sit down and talk to your mom. It'll make life easier for everyone. Oh, and just in case she didn't mention it, keep the grades up. Both of you." I shot a look at Mandy.

I felt the vibration on my ankle and in my pocket simultaneously.

"Pardon me for a moment, I better check in." I listened to the message, entered my code number, followed by the pound sign, just like I was instructed. Then looked at Josh and Mandy.

"That a case you're working on?" Josh asked.

"Yeah, I've got to check in periodically."

"Almost sounds like you're released and being monitored." Mandy chuckled.

I looked at her a moment.

"Oh, sorry, my Dad's in the County Attorney's office up in St. Louis County. He tells us about the low-life types with ankle bracelets having to do that stuff all the time. Most of them never seem to be able to get their act together."

"Oh, I don't know…"

"You're wearing an ankle bracelet? Cool. God, what'd you do, Dev?" Josh asked, suddenly thrilled with my unfortunate spell of bad luck.

"What makes you think I'm wearing an ankle bracelet?"

"Let me see it, man." Josh's eyes were wide. He grinned from ear to ear. Mandy's eyes were wider.

"You won't tell your mom, will you? I'm not kidding."

"God, you really are," he said, shooting a glance at Mandy. "Let me see it." Then he slid his chair back to get a better look.

I glanced around, then hiked the leg of my jeans up enough to expose the monitoring device.

Both kids bent over for a closer examination under the table. A number of heads glanced over in our direction. I didn't know if they were looking at me or Mandy's silky thong.

"What'd you do? What'd they nail you for? DUI I bet, right?" Josh said from under the table.

"Will you two get up here and stop making a scene? Everyone's looking." I was trying my best not to, but my eyes caught just the bottom of the lacy tattoo across Mandy's lower back then followed a bright green thong back down into her low cut jeans.

She sat up and smiled at me.

"So what'd you do?" Josh asked. sitting up.

"More of a little misunderstanding, then anything else. I'm just in the process of tying up some loose ends in the investigation, then I'll get this thing off."

"It was a DUI, right?"

"I don't think they bother with that just for a DUI. Well unless you were a habitual offender or something," Mandy said.

"So I was right, DUI?"

"No, look, just forget it, and whatever you do, please don't mention it to your mom."

"Oh, this is so great. She sends you to talk to us and you're out on release, fantastic!" They both started laughing.

"Look, can we just keep this between ourselves, please?" I pleaded.

"Fucking fantastic." Josh was still laughing.

"Look guys, promise me."

"We promise, Mr. Haskell," Mandy said. She was still chuckling.

"Thanks, Mandy, call me Dev. I'm becoming your second biggest fan."

"Okay, okay, we won't bring it up. Make sure to give us a good report, will you?" Josh said.

"I'll do that. Look you want to win her over? Just make sure those grades are up. You know she'll back off once she sees that."

They both nodded.

I glanced across the room, scanning the crowd. I was about to wrap things up when I went back to a woman carrying a tray to a table. My look must have given away more than I intended. First Mandy, then Josh followed my gaze.

"Forget it, Dev, she's taken," Josh said.

"What?"

"You're looking at the hot woman in that sort of rust colored sweater, right? The one over by the door sipping her coffee?"

"Josh, God," Mandy said and punched his arm.

"Her? No, I was looking at someone else. Why? Who is she?"

"I don't know her name. She's the wife or girlfriend of one of our professors," Josh said.

"Doctor Death," Mandy said.

"They're both nuts," Josh added.

"The guy's name is Doctor Death?"

"Actually it's Kevork. You know, like Jack Kevorkian, that assisted suicide guy. She's crazier than he is."

"Why do you say that?"

"We heard them going at it in his office after hours one night. We were up there using the department printer for a bunch of handouts for a class. She was screaming at him, calling him names, swearing, threatening him. She was absolutely over the edge, a nut case," Josh said.

"It was really scary. We just left and went back to my place," Mandy added.

"Yeah, she's a nut job," Josh said, glancing back at the woman for a brief moment.

"Certifiable, you can't possibly imagine," Mandy added.

Actually, I could imagine. I watched Kiki calmly sip her coffee. She took the smallest nibble from some nondescript pastry, then made a face and pushed the pastry plate aside.

"What's the guy's name, again?" I said.

"Doctor Carroll Kevork, he's in the chemistry department," Mandy said.

Chapter Forty-One

Tempted as I was to follow her, the last thing I needed was to have Kiki turn around and see me in a hallway at the University of Minnesota. That would do nothing for my attempt to look like a model citizen. I left the kids to grab and grope one another while I went back to my office and did an online search of Doctor Kevork. Most of what I found was unintelligible university-speak. Did these people ever sit down over a beer and casually chat? Probably not.

More to the point, next to a photo of Doctor Carroll Kevork was a brief bio. He was originally from the town of Dale, Indiana. He did his undergraduate work at Purdue University, and then went on to get a doctorate from Berkeley in 1999. He did post-doctorate work at MIT from 1999 until 2002. Rummaging around online some more, I learned that interestingly, in 2003 he washed up on shore as an associate professor at the University of Nevada, Las Vegas. From there he drifted to the University of Minnesota in 2008. Nothing of a criminal nature that I could find, nor any marriage records. He was the owner of a home somewhere in Minnetonka, not exactly slumming it.

Kevork's University Nevada Las Vegas and U of M gigs seemed to dovetail with Kiki and Farrell's wanderings. Was his chemistry background tied into their drug distribution? But then what about KRAZ and Thompson Barkwell? Distributing illegal drugs via radio to the conservative, evangelical far right seemed to be a bad business plan right from the get-go.

There was only one thing to do. I returned to my intensive research of Girls Gone Wild at Mardi Gras. I was still diligently researching two hours later when the phone rang.

"How did it go?" Sunnie asked not wasting time with 'hello'.

"The food was lousy, the coffee wasn't the best."

"I don't care about that, and what's that moaning in the background? Are you alone?"

"Oh, some commercial on the radio…medical stuff or something." I hit pause on the laptop screen.

"So?" Sunnie asked.

"It went very well. Josh is fine. Mandy seems like a very nice girl. She…"

"I knew you'd say that."

"Maybe because it's true. It's not like they're smoking dope and drinking all day. They cut short my clever conversation to get prepared for a class. Did you know her father happens to be a County Attorney up north? Doesn't sound like the type who'd put up with a lot of nonsense."

"Those are exactly the kids you have to watch. As soon as they get out of the house it's party time."

"You could be describing your own son, there."

Long pause.

"Sunnie, I think they're fine. I know it's hard to let go, but maybe you could, just a little. I did tell them the way to win you over was to keep the grades up."

187

"You said that?"

"Yeah, of course, if the grades are there…"

"Not that, you idiot. You said *the way to win me over*? Like I'm some pain in the ass, single mother, who's not letting go of her little boy? Not turning him over to some blonde bimbo with big boobs and loose morals?"

"Don't forget the thong."

"You saw it, didn't you? I don't believe it."

"Sunnie, I like the girl. She's pretty, she's nice and I think she's good for Josh, and by the way, Josh is good for her. See how the grades come in and…"

"I should never have trusted you."

"Okay, now you're sounding like the idiot. Stop, cut the kids some slack. I'll tell you this, the more you resist the more attractive she'll seem. You've raised him well. He has a good head on his shoulders. He can think."

"That's exactly what I'm worrying about. Now what's he going to be thinking about, after your comment?"

"Can I make a suggestion?"

"Maybe."

"How about dinner? My treat. I'll pick you up at six-thirty tomorrow night, deal?"

I thought I'd better phone Louie before I returned to my Mardi Gras research. I wanted to give him the Doctor Death connection, slim as it was. I also wanted to see about getting a little breathing room on my travels. I was going to get nicked for another fifteen bucks for my schedule change to take Sunnie out for dinner.

I drummed my fingers, listening as his cell rang. I was developing a pattern. Get the message on his cell telling me his message box was full, then phone his office where "Mr. Laufen will return my call just as soon as he's able."

Chapter Forty-Two

Dinner was everything I expected or maybe feared. After filleting me for the first fifteen minutes because I hadn't made a citizen's arrest on Mandy, Sunnie calmed down and became more of her old self. On the way home she asked, "So what's up with the no drinking? You finally in a twelve step program or something?"

"No." I half laughed. "Just decided to give it a rest for a bit. You know, drop a few pounds…the good health thing, that's all."

"Good health? You? You're kidding?"

"No." I thought I sounded defensive.

"Because I could see you look longingly at those beers over at the next table when your cheeseburger, fries and side order of onion rings arrived."

"Is this a slam because we didn't dine at some fancy joint that features grilled buzzard breast stuffed with duck shit as the chefs special?"

"No, that might have been nice, but really, I don't mind having my hair done, getting all dressed up and then eating a cheeseburger and fries. The two kids crying in the booth next to us was a nice touch. I was the only one in there not wearing jeans, and it's always tricky wading through peanut shells in five inch heels, but I managed."

"You saying I still owe you dinner?"

"Yeah, and I'll choose where."

"Well, look at it from my angle. I was with the best looking woman in there."

"Thanks."

I walked her to the door and exchanged pecks on the cheek. We'd never had a sexual relationship and neither of us wanted one. We were good friends. A moment of passion, enjoyable as it might be, would ruin the long friendship.

I drove home and waited for my monitor call. Once it came through I planned to drive by Doctor Death's place out in Minnetonka. I told myself I was just going to take a casual pass and I wouldn't get out of the car. I also knew I was lying.

The call never came through and I woke up about three in the morning on the couch, the laptop still prowling through sex starved girls misbehaving during Mardi Gras. I turned it off. Even for me after eight or nine hours it all sort of ran together. I stumbled off to bed, planning to sleep in so I didn't set my alarm.

The monitor call came through just after seven in the morning. I wasn't the happiest camper as I punched in my code and the pound sign. But, I was awake, wide awake. I decided to head west, into the wilds of Minnetonka, one of the more posh areas of the Twin Cities. I followed the MapQuest driving directions to Doctor Death's house. It turned out not to be the most direct route, but eventually I got there.

The place was a pretty substantial, two story brick home, actually situated right on Lake Minnetonka, more of a mansion than just a home. It had two wings, an attached three car garage, circular brick drive, manicured lawn, and potted red geraniums on either side of a double front door. A couple of newspapers lay next to one of the flower pots. I guessed they were most likely something highbrow like the Wall Street Journal or the New York Times. The shades were drawn on all the second floor windows. There was a little metal sign planted in the garden next to the front door, advertising the alarm service. It looked to be a pretty pricey piece of property for a college professor.

There was a lawn service truck parked in front with four guys hustling around cutting the grass and blowing clippings off the circular drive. I drove past four times, but decided against getting out and poking around. The last two times I drove by, one of the lawn crew guys starred at my DeVille. He seemed to be making a mental note. I certainly didn't need anyone taking notice of me hanging around and thought my time might be better spent finding out more about Doctor Death, Carroll Kevork, online.

Three hours latter I didn't know much more about Doctor Death than when I had started. I could make a couple of assumptions. It didn't seem to make a lot of sense that someone with a Doctorate in Chemistry from Berkeley, who had done post graduate work at MIT would settle for an associate professorship at UNLV, a school that, at least from my online research, seemed not to have much in the line of a chemistry department.

The jump from an associate professorship at UNLV to owning a two-million-plus home on Lake Minnetonka seemed to require an extraordinary leap of faith on my part. Tie in his association with Kiki and Farrell and I concluded something wasn't right.

Just for the fun of being disappointed I decided to phone Louie. I was listening to the third ring. It was almost time for the full mail box recording to begin when a groggy voice came on the line.

"Lo." Cough, grunt, cough some more. "Hell, hello?"

"Louie, I don't believe it. You're alive, more or less. I wake you up?"

There was a loud exhale, some more coughing.

"This has to be Dev, that you?"

"Yeah, it's me."

"Hey, man. Christ, what time is it?"

"Five to eleven. Listen, Louie I wanted…"

"Are you fucking kidding me?" he screamed.

I had a vision, not very pretty, of a fat, naked Louie bolting upright in bed.

"Actually, now it's four minutes before eleven. I…"

"Gotta run, bye," he said and hung up.

My next two calls went unanswered. He was either in the shower or already racing to work. I phoned his office. Left a message to call me, that I had important information. The receptionist assured me that "as soon as he was able…" I got that sinking feeling, again.

On my way home that evening I lingered for a half hour in the KRAZ parking lot. I didn't see Farrell, Farrell's BMW or Kiki. My monitor call came through about nine-thirty that night. I was out the door and driving to Lake Minnetonka two minutes later.

Doctor Death's house looked the same, except the lawn service guys were gone. The second floor shades were still drawn and there appeared to be a light on in the upper right corner of the house. Most likely a bedroom, nothing unusual about that. The newspapers were still next to the flower pot. I drove back home and walked to a bar about a block away.

"Dev, the usual?" The bartender looked underage, with a neatly trimmed, three-day beard.

"Actually, nothing to drink, Tommy. Can I just get a couple rolls of quarters from you?" I slid a twenty and a five dollar tip across the bar.

He looked left and right, took the cash as he did so, walked about three feet to a computer screen, hit the thing four times at lightning speed and came back with two rolls of quarters.

"Thanks, laundry," I said.

"When you're finished you can start on mine." He laughed.

I walked about two blocks in the opposite direction to one of the few pay phones left in the city. I inserted fifty cents and called Doctor Death's office number at the U. After four rings there were a couple of clicks and then his voice.

"Thank you for calling. This is Associate Professor Doctor Carroll Kevork. I'm unable to take your call at this time. My office hours are Tuesdays and Thursdays between one-forty-five and three o'clock. If you wish to make an appointment outside those hours please press zero at this time. Leave a detailed message after the tone and I shall return your call at the earliest convenience."

In case he didn't seem like a pain in the ass with just two-and-a-half office hours per week, the affected posh accent did the trick. He was from southern Indiana if I recalled. I didn't like the guy and I hadn't even met him, yet.

"Wrong number," I said once the recording began, then waited until a tone signaled the end of the recording time, hung up and redialed. I was almost through the second roll of quarters before I got the recording that said his voice mail was full. Thank God, listening to pompous Doctor Death's message some thirty-plus times did nothing to endear him to me. I walked back home, took a couple of aspirin and went to bed.

Chapter Forty-Three

I was slurping breakfast coffee from my travel mug, parked in the far corner of the KRAZ parking lot. I had crumbs from a couple of blueberry muffins scattered across my chest. The crumbs were about the only thing I'd seen moving in the past half hour, not counting the trash blowing across the parking lot. Surprise, surprise, Louie actually called me back.

"Yeah, Dev, returning your call." Louie sounded all business.

"Louie, thanks. To tell you the truth it's been so long I've forgotten why I phoned you."

"Real funny."

"Hey, were you able to verify that information and get it over to Detective Manning?"

I thought I suddenly heard files being rummaged through and Louie sounded a little flustered.

"Well, we're on that, working the thing. It shouldn't be too long, now."

He was breathing heavily and I had the sinking feeling he was pawing through his very messy desk looking for his notes.

"You lost the notes, Louie, right?"

"I'd say it's more like I just momentarily misplaced them. They're here, somewhere. I'm almost sure of it."

"Hey, Louie, does it resonate with you that I'm the guy charged with kidnapping and rape? Not to mention the fact that I'm the key suspect no, make that I'm the guy charged with Thompson Barkwell's murder. I've had to hit up a good friend to pop for bail money and I've got a cop investigating this who already has me tried and convicted in his mind. And you can't find your notes? You're supposed to…"

"Here they are, told you."

"Read 'em back to me."

"What?"

"Read 'em back so I know you're not bullshitting me."

"You're kidding?"

"No, I'm not. Come on, Louie. You haven't even passed this stuff on to be verified by anyone, have you?"

No answer.

"Well?"

"No, I, I haven't Dev. I was just about…."

"God damn it, read it back to me."

"You dug up the 2005 marriage records in Las Vegas, Nevada, of Farrell J Early and one Katherine "Kiki" Hinz, daughter of Ottmar "Loopy" Hinz. Ottmar was unable to attend…"

"Okay, stop. Louie, I want to add a few more things to your notes." I went on to tell him about Carroll Kevork, his stint at UNLV, then his move over to the U of M about the same time Farrell and Kiki appear on the scene. I wondered out loud about them dealing Ecstasy and Roofies since Doctor Death was a chemistry nerd and there were rumors of Kiki and

197

Doctor Death in a relationship. Then I ended up with, "Louie, I want you to get someone in the office to verify that stuff. Today. I want you to call me, and tell me who will be doing it, and I want their phone number. Got it?"

"Yeah, not a problem, Dev."

"I'm counting on you Louie. All my hopes are pinned on you."

"I understand. Look, could we maybe keep this between the two of us? I'm sort of not the most popular guy around here at the moment." He was whispering.

"My lips are sealed, Louie. Unless you screw this up, then I'm coming down on you like a ton of bricks."

"Thanks, Dev, I won't let you down."

I wasn't so sure.

"I'll expect your call with the guy's name and number, sooner rather than later."

I was in my office, looking out the window at absolutely nothing when Louie called me back forty-five minutes later. He gave me the guy's direct dial number along with his name, Nelson.

I asked, "What's his first name?"

"That is his first name. Last name's Tornvold."

"He Irish?"

"No, I think…"

"I was kidding, Louie. Hey, were you able to get me some breathing room with those Sentinel Monitoring folks? Every time I walk down the hallway to use the can I have to call in and pay them fifteen bucks cause it's not on my approved schedule."

"I'm working it. I really am, Dev, but I'm dealing with some thick headed witch over there…"

"Muriel?"

"Oh, you've met her."

"All four hundred pounds covered with cat hair."

198

"There's a surprise. So you know what we're dealing with. I've explained your business, such as it is, more than once to her. We're in the process of going through their appeal review. It's gonna take a few more days. Just continue to keep that low profile, upstanding citizen thing going." He slurped something.

"I'll do my best. Tell your pal Nelson I'm calling him later today. I expect that shit to be verified and on its way to our friend, Detective Manning."

"That's gonna take some time, he…"

"Then you shouldn't have lost those notes on your desk, Louie. I'm going nuts here, so tell him to get moving or maybe I should just mention the fact that you sat on this for…"

"Okay, okay, let's stay positive here."

"Then get it verified and over to Manning."

Chapter Forty-Four

I didn't feel that much better after talking to Louie. In fact, I didn't feel very good at all. I decided to screw Muriel at Sentinel Monitoring, figuratively, and drive out to Doctor Death's mansion.

On the way there I picked up a pay-as-you-go phone. It was navy blue with shiny chrome-like trim. You had to fold it open to talk on it. Folded up, the thing was about the size of a pack of matches. I told the kid at the counter I'd left my identification at home, slipped him a five, then paid ten bucks in advance for twenty cents a minute calls. The kid, all of sixteen, didn't blink. I'd the feeling it was probably a pretty standard transaction.

It was a good forty-minute drive, mostly on a four lane freeway after the morning rush hour, before I got to Minnetonka where all the 'swells' lived. The shades were still drawn on Doctor Death's second floor and I pulled in and parked in the circular drive. It looked like the light might still be on in the corner room, but I couldn't really be sure in the mid-day sun. Now there were three newspapers at the front door, the past three days of the Minneapolis Star. There was a sticker on what looked like one of the living room widows. The sticker matched the little alarm system sign in the front garden. Through the window I could see a fireplace with two nice off-white couches positioned on either side, a large oriental rug, a couple of end tables with lamps, some sort of large flat screen above the fireplace mantel. It looked like pretty nice digs

I pushed open the mail slot next to the front door. It was crammed with circulars and a few envelopes. I grabbed the envelopes, then walked calmly to my car and drove off as if I rifled people's mailboxes everyday. I pulled into a grocery store parking lot and fanned through the envelopes. One was addressed to resident, one was a credit card offer from Citibank addressed to Carroll Kevork. The third envelope held a form letter from Wells Fargo Bank explaining new policies and charges for direct debit cards. Basically worthless except it suggested Dr. Death had at least one account at Wells Fargo.

There was a pay phone alongside the grocery store. I phoned Doctor Death's office at the U, listened to his pain in the ass recording, then got the message that told me his mail box was full. I pressed zero to schedule an appointment. A nice lady came on after two rings.

"Department center, how may I direct your call?"

"I'd like to make an appointment with Doctor Carroll Kevork."

"One moment please, I'll transfer your call."

She dumped me back into Doctor Death's message. So much for higher education. I punched zero again.

"Department center, how may I direct your call?"

"I would like to make an appointment with Doctor Carroll Kevork, his voice mail is full. It seems I can't leave a message."

If the nice lady remembered who I was from twenty seconds earlier she gave no indication.

"One moment please, I'll transfer your call."

I was dumped into some recorded message that asked me to input the first three letters of the last name of the individual I was trying to reach. I did that. The next recording instructed me to press one upon hearing the name of the person I was trying to reach. Doctor Death was the fifth or sixth name I listened to. I was becoming numb. I pressed one. The recording instructed me to press one to leave a call back number, two to leave a message or zero to return to the switch board. I pressed two. The recording instructed me to wait for the tone before leaving a message. I waited for what seemed an interminably long time. Finally I heard the tone.

"Doctor Kevork, this is Mr. Myles Wesley at Wells Fargo Bank," I said in a rich guy accent. "I'm calling today to alert you to an accounting error, in your favor for the amount of one-hundred-and-forty-nine dollars. Would you please call me and let me know where you would like these funds deposited? Or should you prefer, we can issue a check made out to you. My direct dial number is…" and I left the pay-as-you-go cell number.

The three newspapers and the full mail box had me wondering if Doctor Death had fled the scene once Kiki visited him the other day. Or, he was just lazy, never checked his mail and had just stopped reading all the bad news in the newspaper.

I drove to my office and called my new best friend, Nelson Tornvold, and left a message. I took it as remotely positive that his mail box wasn't full. I phoned Louie's office number, "Mr. Laufen will return your call just as soon as he's able." Some things never changed.

Nelson phoned me toward the end of the day. He sounded about twelve years old, but a diligent twelve.

"Yeah, Mr. Haskell. This is Nelson Tornvold, I'm returning your call."

"Nelson, thanks for calling back. I was checking to see if you received anything from Louie Laufen. He had some files…"

"Yes, sir…um, Mr. Laufen gave me these notes, a couple of pages, told me to verify names and dates. I think they're from his interrogation with you. Then I'm to formalize them, write a cover letter for him. The information I have is that this is all going in a packet directed to a Detective Manning, at Saint Paul, homicide. I've got a case file number to reference, B-A-R seven-four-seven-seven?" He waited for an answer.

"I have to take your word on the file number. Can you repeat that to me?"

He did and I wrote it down.

"So, that will be going over to Manning, at homicide, yet today?"

"It should, I'll have it ready for Mr. Laufen's signature shortly. Then as soon as he signs it we'll messenger it over."

"You can't just send an email?"

"No, sir, paper trail and all that sort of thing," he said earnestly.

I was guessing 'all that sort of thing' covered a multitude of sins, but I didn't want to go there.

"Has everything checked out?"

"Yes sir. I mean the records and dates were all verifiable. I'm sure someone on the other end will be doing the same thing I did, verifying. But it all checks out."

"Nelson, thanks, don't let me hold you up from getting Louie Laufen's signature and sending that stuff over to Manning."

"Yes, sir."

I felt like recommending young Nelson for Louie's job.

Chapter Forty-Five

My monitor call came through at 9:50 that evening. It had been dark for almost forty minutes and mercifully there was a slight breeze, surprisingly pleasant weather. As soon as I hung up I got in the car and drove out to Doctor Death's house. I cruised past twice, then headed for home. I could see the newspapers were still piled at the front door and the same second floor bedroom light was on. I was pretty sure the good Doctor wasn't home.

Another monitor call came in at 6:20 the following morning. I was convinced it was that witch Muriel, getting back at me because I had the temerity to request a review of my schedule arrangement. I couldn't get back to sleep, so I lay in bed for forty minutes before I finally got up.

I was parked in my usual space in the far corner of the KRAZ parking lot. By this point I was able to recognize some of the litter that had been there for a while. I tuned to seven-forty on the radio dial, the Blast of Freedom as they referred to themselves, listening as Farrell ponderously read from a script that made no sense to me at all. He lost me somewhere between Pilgrim's Rights and the Sword of Damocles, then the plea to make a stand for as little as a twenty dollar cash donation, followed by the cautionary reminder not to send checks lest the Communists and Anarchists in Washington monitor your active financial support of freedom. Farrell actually stammered over the word anarchists. Who could be stupid enough to listen to this drivel day in and day out? Present company excepted.

I was clearly in the world's dullest parking lot, not a thing happening. I drove back out to Doctor Death's house, just to see if he'd picked up his newspapers yet. There were four of them at the front door, newspapers. I pulled into the circular drive, got out and rang the doorbell. I didn't expect anyone to answer and I wasn't disappointed.

I forced my way through some trimmed hedge affair at the side of the house and clomped through a garden around to the back. I walked down a set of terraced stone steps that led to a broad back lawn running a good hundred feet out to the shore of Lake Minnetonka. There were colored flowers, impatiens, on either side of the shady steps. Along the lake the back lot had close to seventy-five feet of shore line. Two large oaks, close to where I guessed the property lines ran shaded a good portion of the back. One of the oaks had a heavy limb running out toward the water. A rope and tire swing hung from the limb, both looking relatively new.

There was a second story cedar deck across the entire rear of the house. A broad staircase with a ninety degree turn half way up led to the deck. As I climbed the steps I could smell the cedar.

I pulled on a pair of surgical gloves as I surveyed the upper deck. On the railing side sat a large gas grill, with a grey plastic cover pulled over it. A large black metal table with an umbrella raised in the middle was just beyond the grill, and seven matching metal chairs were arranged around the table. A crystal tumbler with maybe two inches of brownish liquid, a leaf and a dozen bugs floating on top sat on the far end of the table. I sniffed the glass, Bourbon…lucky bugs.

The house looked dark. I could see through the windows inside to a kitchen, but other than a digital clock on the ovens it didn't look like anything was on. The lights were off. Even though it was late morning the rooms still seemed dark enough to warrant an overhead light. I walked the length of the deck. All the windows were locked, and nothing seemed to be happening inside. There were two sets of sliding glass doors. The living room set was locked. I could look in through the living room and see my car parked in the circular drive out the front window. I walked back along the deck to the sliding kitchen door. The door was open about an inch. I listened carefully for a few more minutes, then slowly slid the door, half expecting an alarm. The only sound was my heart pounding like some base drum.

Once I stepped inside I quickly walked in the direction of the attached garage. In a hallway just off the kitchen was a solid metal door. I guessed it led to the garage. Next to the door was the control panel for the alarm system. It gave a digital read out of the date and time, and next to that was a green light. The alarm was off. Attached to the wall below the control panel was a wooden cut out in the shape of a house with four brass hooks. A set of car keys hung from one of the hooks. There was something else, a smell. I was pretty sure I knew what it was.

As I walked through the house, I could feel the central air. The kitchen was clean. Other than the crystal tumbler with some bourbon outside on the deck there was nothing to indicate human activity, nothing in the sink. Black granite counter tops reflected cherry wood cabinets and ceiling fixtures. I opened one of the cabinets. It was empty, so was the next one and the one after that, they were all empty. I opened the large brushed chrome refrigerator. It was turned off, spotless and empty as was the freezer.

The living and dining rooms held elegant, matching furnishings with nothing out of place. In the dining room there were three crystal glasses sitting on a long walnut cabinet. The glasses matched the one out on the deck. The cabinet held nothing but a half-pint of Jack Daniels, maybe just a third full.

The front hallway felt larger than my entire first floor. At the far end a white carpeted staircase led upstairs. The smell was a bit stronger. As I climbed the stairs the carpeting felt thick, plush and ended about three feet beyond the top step. From there the floor was just dusty chipboard subflooring.

The smell on the second floor was approaching the gag point. There were six bedrooms on the second floor, five of which were empty, not so much as an IKEA chest of drawers, anywhere. The walls were sheet rocked, plastered, but not primed or painted. Capped electrical wires extended out from holes where outlets or ceiling fixtures should have been. All the shades were drawn. Although the door frames were installed and the bedroom doors were hung, none of the rooms, doorframes or the upper hallway for that matter had any trim attached.

The sixth bedroom, the one in the upper corner, held more than I bargained for. There was a thin mattress on the floor and a rumpled sleeping bag. A jumble of socks, T-shirts and boxers were piled against the wall. A table lamp with no shade sat on the floor.

The light was on, plugged into an orange extension cord that came up through a hole in the floor. I covered my nose and mouth with my hand and ventured in.

A black metal chair, an exact match to the seven out on the deck sat in the far corner of the room. What was left of Carroll Kevork, Doctor Death, sat with his ankles and wrists taped to the chair and a six-inch strip of duct tape over his mouth. I recognized him, or what was left of him, from the website photo. It looked like some nutcase had played tic-tac-toe on his body. Both ears, his nose, arms, chest, well, you get the picture, were carved and sliced. Blood was splattered across the walls. On the floor, small foot prints outlined in dried blood wandered around the chair then faded as they tracked out toward the door. Congealed blood was crustily pooled beneath the chair.

A familiar looking knife had been tossed into the corner. I'd seen it once before. It was bigger than a steak knife, not quite a carving blade, but still capable of doing some very serious damage. The knife came with a bright red handle, the kind sculpted to fit your fingers and hold a blade that gleamed viciously. The blade was crusted with blood. Kiki.

I became aware of a noise. At first I thought it was radio static, then realized it was flies buzzing around. Lots of them all of a sudden. I backed out of the room, down the staircase, through the dining room and out the sliding kitchen door. I somehow had the foresight to slide the door almost closed behind me. Out on the deck I sucked in huge gulps of fresh air, and then made my way to the car as fast as I could, hoping I didn't attract any attention.

I looked in the rear view mirror as I pulled away and saw the puddle of oil that had dripped from my engine onto the circular brick drive. The oil left a large

stain the size of a dinner plate. I was pretty sure Doctor
Death wouldn't care.

Chapter Forty-Six

    Driving back home on I-94, I could not seem to get the smell out of my nose. For the umpteenth time I ran through a check list in my mind. Had I closed the door? Left anything behind? Worn the gloves at all times? Fortunately, I'd called from the untraceable pay-as-you-go cell and disguised my voice when I left phone messages on Doctor Death's office number. Still, I thought I should call the police, although try as I may, I couldn't come up with how that would help me in any way.

    I got home, pushed a chair up against the front door, then wedged another chair under the back kitchen door knob. Then sat and thought, Kiki, Kiki, Kiki while I ate butter-brickle ice cream directly out of the carton with a spoon. My monitor call came through about nine-thirty that night and sort of snapped me back to reality. Other than the ice cream carton I must have been staring at nothing for the better part of the evening. I punched in my code, hit the pound sign and went to bed, not that I could get to sleep.

    I must have drifted off because the ringing woke me. It was a phone, a phone close by, but I didn't recognize the ring tone. It took a few moments to track down, coming from my dresser, the pay-as-you-go phone. I let it ring. It stopped on the fifth ring. I hadn't set up any voice mail on the thing so it must have disconnected. I checked after a couple of minutes, no message, caller unknown. It was three-forty in the morning. There was only one place I'd left that number, on Doctor Death's recording to schedule an appointment. I had said I was from Wells Fargo, attempted to disguise my voice, sounding like some banking jerk. I spent the rest of the night awake, wondering how effective my attempt had been.

I woke to the sound of my cell-phone ringing, Sentinel Monitoring. I punched in the numbers, then pound, the thing was ringing again when I came out of the bathroom.

"Haskell Investigations."

"Yeah, Dev, Louie Laufen. I just signed off on everything and your packet is waiting to be messengered over to Manning in Homicide this morning."

"Would it help if I ran it over there?" I glanced at my watch, nine-forty-five.

"Really bad idea. No, in fact that could only make things worse. It'll be over there in the next hour or so. Everything checked out, so this is great news for us, but expect something, maybe all of it to be questioned initially. Once they comb through it, they'll see how solid we are."

"Hey, pass on my thanks to your boy Nelson. He did a hell of a job."

"He's a good kid. You learn anything else that might help? I'd be more than happy to pile it on."

"No, nothing. I'll keep looking into things, but I haven't come up with anything, yet. What do you think about the guy at the U?" I immediately wished I'd never asked the question about Doctor Death.

"Kevork? What do I think? I think it's interesting, but at this stage just hearsay. I'm not saying there isn't something there, but Manning's going to put it to the side until he can tie it in, solidly. By the way, that's not necessarily a bad trait."

"Guy's a prick."

"Probably, but he's a straight shooting one. I know you two rub each other the wrong way, but he's not gonna railroad you, Dev."

"We'll see."

I listened to three of the KRAZ broadcasts from the safety of my office. One was worse than the next. I got home a little before six that evening. There was a note on the door from Heidi, asking me to give her a call.

"Hello." She sounded way too cheery to have this go my way.

"Hi, Heidi, Dev…got your note on my door."

"Oh yeah, thanks for calling."

"Course. What's up? Why didn't you just call me?"

"Didn't want to bother you. Besides, I wanted to pick out the color and get it."

"Color?"

"Yeah, paint for my bedroom. I need it painted, tomorrow. That is if you've got the time."

She said the last part like she knew I didn't have much else going on.

"Time, well, yeah, I guess. I mean, you want to think about it, do you want me to pick up paint or anything?"

"I already told you, I picked up the paint."

"Okay."

"Waterbury Cream."

"Okay."

"It's sitting right here in the front entry. Can you be here tomorrow morning?"

"I could be over there tonight if you want." I was thinking positive, maybe painting with benefits.

"No." She sounded awfully definite.

"Tomorrow morning?"

"Yeah. Look, I got a ten o'clock appointment so be here around nine-fifteen, okay?" It wasn't really a question.

"Yeah, nine-fifteen." What the hell, I had a lot to think about and could do it while I painted.

Chapter Forty-Seven

I supposed there was something to be said for
attacking a simple task, uninterrupted, work away, just
letting one's mind percolate. I was of the impression I
could have achieved the same result staring out my
office window or maybe sipping a beer. Nonetheless, I
reported to Heidi's. Her Mercedes was parked out on
the street. I parked behind it and rang the doorbell
promptly at 9:30.

"Where the hell have you been? I told you I had an
appointment this morning."

She was dressed in a matching pink T-shirt and
tight, pink shorts with a white belt. She wore white
sandals with little jewel things on them. She carried a
straw purse large enough to hide a small child inside.

"Since when do you go to client meetings dressed
like that? You going to the beach or something?"

"I didn't say it was a client meeting."

"Oh, what are we up to?"

"None of your business. The paint's in my
bedroom. I'll expect it finished and cleaned up by the
end of the day. I'm entertaining tonight, so I'll need
you out of here by six."

Heidi ripped through male partners like a chainsaw. I was her long standing fall-back position and sometime counselor when it came to the finer points of relationships, which was a frightening thought in itself.

"Anyone I know?"

"No."

"Who is he?"

"I told you, none of your business," she said, strutting down her front walk and climbing into her car.

I stood at the door watching. She climbed back out of the car and yelled at me over the rooftop. "I'm not kidding, Dev, I need you out of here by six, no later." She jumped in her car and raced off before I could give any sort of a wise guy answer.

The place was gleaming it was so clean. I checked her refrigerator, usually empty, but today it held a number of white carry-out food containers. The largest container held a heat and serve meal, some kind of chicken thing with sauce and peppers, while another box was crammed with salad greens. There was a bake and serve loaf of French bread and some kind of fruit and chocolate dessert deal. Four bottles of white wine were chilling on the bottom shelf. The dining room table was set for two. Silver candle holders with red candles were placed on the table, fresh cut flowers on the cabinet. Whoever the lucky guy was, I hoped he had rested up.

Later in the afternoon I was actually ahead of schedule and about halfway through the second coat. I had the window open, airing out what little fumes there were. The phone rang, not my cell but the pay-as-you-go. I let it ring three times, then hit the accept key. I didn't say anything, just listened. It was quiet on the other end, except for some faint breathing. It sounded feminine, which sounded kind of crazy and that made me think, Kiki.

I remained quiet for the better part of two minutes, straining my ears. All I heard was the breathing. I didn't think it was intentional, not heavy or rasping, not trying to intimidate me or anything, just breathing. Then from somewhere in the distant background, I heard a car honk, just a couple of beeps. Whoever it was hung up. I put the phone down and thought for a few minutes.

It could have been the U of M. Or the police, if they'd found Doctor Death. Either one might be calling in response to the bogus Wells Fargo message I'd left on his line. It could have been Farrell, I doubted it. My money was on Kiki. Whoever it was. I did know one thing, I'd been stupid to hang onto the pay-as-you-go phone and I was going to get rid of it on my way home, tonight. I got back to the business at hand, hustled and finished painting in forty-five minutes. I was just wrestling Heidi's gigantic antique wardrobe back against the wall when I heard the kitchen door open.

"Dev, you still here?" she called. I heard the rustle of shopping bags coming from the kitchen.

"In here, just putting things back together."

She appeared at the doorway and I took it all in. Her hair looked gorgeous, her nails were done, she had a new pedicure and she was nicely tanned.

"You look great. Were you out in the sun?"

"No dopey, spray on. You don't have tan lines this way."

"You get that done before or after your wax?"

"Be... shut up, you pervert."

"Just checking. Who's the victim?"

"The room looks great," she said, ignoring my question. "How soon can you be out of here?" She stepped into the room, took off her earrings, placed them on her dresser, then kicked off her sandals. She unbuckled the white belt on her shorts and started to walk out of the room.

"Don't mind me. I'd be happy to check out that all-over tan for you?"

"Interesting offer, but umm, no thanks I want you out of here so I can get ready," she called from the kitchen.

I checked my watch it was twenty minutes before five. I was almost an hour and a half ahead of schedule.

"I've got a little time. I could wash your back in the shower for you, if you like?"

"No, I don't like," she said, coming back into the room. She carried three or four shopping bags. One I recognized, bright pink, Victoria's Secret. "How soon before you leave?" she asked.

"Hey, I can be lots of fun. Date underwear?" I nodded at the Victoria Secret's bag.

"You are still on double secret probation with me, so please get out. Come on, Dev, get going, please. I've got a really big night planned."

"Okay, okay, just let me carry this stuff to the basement…"

"Just leave it, I'll take care of it and straighten up. Thanks, the room looks great," she said, moving her arms as if to shoo me out the bedroom door.

"My loss," I said, then gave her a peck on the check. I looked wistfully at the Victoria's Secret bag then headed toward the front door.

She followed me, like she was herding sheep, just to make sure I left. "Thanks," she said as she closed the front door behind me, then snapped the lock while I was still standing on the front porch.

My monitor call came through about eight-forty that evening. I spent the rest of the night running through the cable channels, over a hundred options and not a damn thing that interested me.

Chapter Forty-Eight

I was still wrapped in bed sheets when my phone woke me a little before six-thirty the following morning. This was getting ridiculous. I listened for the monitor message.

"You asshole!" That didn't really narrow things down much, except it was a woman screaming.

"Huh?"

"Oh, shut up, you knew what would happen."

"Mom?"

"Shut up. You figured out a way to ruin my night, didn't you?"

"Heidi, Jesus, calm down. What the hell time is it?"

"A lot later than when you're stupid call came through, fuckwit."

"What are you screaming about? God, can you just tone it down for a minute and tell me what happened?" I was still half asleep.

"What happened? You hid that stupid little phone under my bed, then had one of your fake boob, slutty, stripper girlfriends call, didn't you?"

"I honestly don't know what in the hell you're talking about."

"Oh, really? This isn't yours? A navy blue and shinny…"

Shit, my pay-as-you-go phone.

"…some drunk slut called and then just sat there breathing not saying a fucking thing."

"That's my phone, but I didn't leave it there on purpose, honest. In fact I'd planned to get rid of the thing."

"Well, not to worry, I'm gonna smash it. Course it serves you right, by the third time she called I let her have it."

My mind was spinning so fast with questions I didn't know which one to ask first.

"She got the message," Heidi snarled.

I had no doubt.

"What did you, no, wait, Heidi, back up and tell me from the start what happened."

"What do you think happened? The first call came through a little after one, right in the middle. It interrupted us, totally ruined the moment."

"Sorry."

"I got things back on track after about twenty minutes then the second call came in. I…"

"Did you say anything?"

"You mean like hello? Like a normal person would? Yes," she said. She seemed to be calming a little, maybe.

"Then what?"

"Whoever she was on the other end, the stupid cow still didn't say a fucking thing, but I could hear her breathing. So I just hung up."

"How do you know it was a her?"

"What, you going both ways all of a sudden, having guys call you in the middle of the night?"

"No, of course not, but why do you think it was a woman?"

"I just know, Dev, okay? Anyway, now I've got to do some heavy duty explaining. Idiot Robbie thinks it might be a boyfriend or something and…"

"Robbie?"

"That's who I was with."

"Was he over eighteen?"

"Not funny, and stop interrupting. It's none of your damn business, anyway. So I'm trying to get him calmed down, explain the phone belonged to you, that you'd been working here during the day, and the God damn thing rings again and I go ballistic."

I've been on the receiving end of Heidi going ballistic. It was not a fun place to be.

"I pick up the phone and just let the bitch have it. I screamed, he's not here bitch, Dev Haskell isn't here, but before he left I fucked out what little brains he had. Then she hangs up, so there you go, you'll probably have a lot of explaining to do. I can only hope."

So much for subtle.

"You okay?" I asked. It was more rhetorical than anything else. If it was Kiki, she'd gotten whatever confirmation she may have wanted. If it was the cops, they probably had my house surrounded.

"Yeah, I guess, sort of."

"I'm sorry, Heidi, I didn't do it on purpose. You know I hadn't finished cleaning up, and you whisked me out of there so damn fast. I guess I just left the thing lying around. I didn't mean to, honest."

"So who is she?"

I ignored her question, playing for time.

"How did Robbie take it, did he get back in the saddle?"

"Very funny, not. No, as a matter of fact he got dressed and got back in his car."

Probably had an eight o'clock class wherever he went to high school, but I kept that thought to myself.

"Oh, I'm really sorry, Heidi, really I am." Served her right I thought, what a bitchy thing to do, still...

"Ahhh, he wasn't that great."

"Make it up to you?" I asked.

"Not today, I'm still really pissed off at you. You mean it though? You really didn't leave it under my bed on purpose?"

"No, believe me, it's a long story. I was planning to get rid of the thing, and just completely forgot about it when you shoved me out the door."

"Well, there you go, that leaves two of us unsatisfied. Hey, I gotta run, client meeting later this morning."

"Wait, can I get that phone back from you?"

"I'll leave the damn thing inside my back door. But I'm warning you, if it's there by the time I get back home, I'm trashing it. Got it?"

"Yeah, got it."

Chapter Forty-Nine

I picked up the phone at Heidi's back door a little after nine. I'd just gotten back into my car when the monitor call came through. I responded, then drove to the office. The same three coeds were waiting for the bus. They looked half asleep and no more fun than the last time I saw them. It was too late in the morning to leer at the girls going to work.

I scrolled through the incoming calls on the pay-as-you-go phone. All four were identified as caller unknown. I had to get rid of this thing, permanently. It took me about five minutes before I figured out how to open the damn thing up. I took out the battery, then removed the SIM card and cut it in half with a pair of pliers. I kept the two sections of the phone separate.

I drove across the High Bridge, tossed half the phone into the Mississippi river from the city side of the bridge, tossed the other half into the water on the far side. I dropped the battery into a trash can up by the St. Paul Cathedral. Then tossed half the SIM card down a sewer on Selby Avenue, the other half I flushed down the men's room toilet in Milton Mall. Then I drove back to my office and stared out the window for the rest of the day.

On the way home I drove past KRAZ. Farrell's
BMW was parked close to the front door. I pulled into
the parking lot and tuned my radio to seven-forty and
waited a couple of minutes until 5:30 when Farrell's
'Voice of Freedom' or 'Pilgrims Rights' or whatever
they called their broadcast polluted the air waves.

It was just as bad as I remembered. Part way
through his rant Farrell got caught up in a coughing jag
that burned up a good half minute. It was the highlight
of the broadcast. He continued on, unfazed, droning
along in close to a monotone. Not that it mattered, who
could stand to listen?

I twiddled my thumbs for another twenty minutes
after the broadcast. Finally, afraid I was really pushing
my luck if I remained, I left. I grabbed a couple of
necessities at the grocery store on the way home, frozen
pizzas, lime Dorito chips and a box of Snickers ice
cream bars. I came in the front door and when I went to
close it behind me I noticed something silky hanging
from the inside door knob, in the pattern of an
American flag, a thong. I didn't put it there. A list of
names ran through my mind, a short list. Very short.

I phoned Heidi from my front entry.

"Hello."

"Pretty funny, look, I said I was sorry."

"Not sorry enough, and I still fail to see the
humor." She still sounded pissed. "You didn't just ruin
the moment, you ruined the night. By the way, you
missed a spot in my bedroom, by one of the outlets."

"I'll take care of it. No, I'm calling because of
what you left for me, at my place "

"Left for you?"

"Very funny. Yeah, today, when I came home, I
just got it."

"You're sounding more obtuse than usual. What in the hell are you babbling about?"

"Please tell me you were inside my place today."

"No can do, Dev. Your place? You kidding? I'm just coming out of an all-day meeting, on the way to my car. Your place? I don't have time to screw around like that. What are you talking about?"

"Look, Heidi, I'll paint your entire house, don't play games with me. This is really serious, so give me a straight answer. Did you leave something inside my front door today?"

"No, I didn't, I already told you. I've been in a client meeting the whole damned day. Honest to God, my head's killing me, if I have to smile and nod at another stupid suggestion one more time I'm going to explode."

"You didn't leave a thong on my door knob? Looks like an American flag."

"A thong? Like a flag? Not really my style. You're not dating that Marine Corp chick again are you? Wasn't she the one who threatened to shoot you if you ever tried to contact her again?"

"That's beside the point and anyway, I'm not seeing her. In fact, I haven't seen her in at least a year."

"Look, no offense, but you're sounding kind of crazy. For what it's worth, I wasn't slumming in your neighborhood today, okay? And you are still on my shit list, bye." Click.

I could think of three other women who had keys to my place. The first two hung up on me when I called. The third one explained, in rational tones, that the only thing she would think of bringing over was her boyfriend to beat me up. I put them all in the 'unlikely' column. Heidi was still my best bet, and I believed her when she told me she'd been in meetings all day. That left a frightening thought.

I decided to call an old friend named Felix Alkers. He was a locksmith and owned a little one-man-shop called Prevention Installations. I'd met him a few years back while we were both waiting to testify in a case that ended up settling at the last minute. We'd sent one another the odd bit of business since then. I left a message on his phone. Everyone who called had to do that. Felix never answered. He phoned me back about ten minutes later. I was in the process of walking around the first floor, making sure all the windows were locked.

"Haskell Investigations."

"Prevention Installations returning your call, is this Dev?"

"It is, Felix. Good to hear your voice."

"Likewise. What can I do for you?"

"The usual, need a new set of locks for a front and back door. Nothing too special, Schlage will work. That's what's in there now."

"Okay, when do you want this done? I could maybe get to it in the next forty-eight hours. That work for you?" he asked.

"Actually Felix, I was hoping you might be able to do it tonight."

"Tonight? This your place?"

"Yeah, I…"

"You're not having trouble with some woman again, are you?"

"Well, let's just say…"

"Save it. I'll have to charge you time and half, Dev. Plus cost of the hardware. I'll give you a discount, won't put a mark up on materials. I'm looking up your account as we speak. Yeah here it is, did 'em both about two years ago for you. Well…" He chuckled. "At least, you seem to be moving up the food chain. Time before that I think it had only been about ten months and you had to have 'em changed."

"You can make it over here tonight?"

"Yeah, let me check at the shop. I think I got replacement sets on hand. I should be there in an hour, hour-and-a-half tops."

Felix was knocking at my front door in forty minutes. He was a solid, square built guy, though you'd never think of him as fat. He sported a crew-cut. If I had to guess, I'd put Felix just north of sixty years old. I figured in his younger days he may have played some hockey. The nose had been broken once or twice, and some pucker scars ran across his chin suggesting two to three stitches apiece. He had both sets of locks, front and back, replaced within thirty minutes.

"Just toss the check in the mail, Dev," he said. Then tore off the original copy of the invoice he'd just written up while sitting at my kitchen counter. Sixty bucks a pop for the locks, ninety bucks for the labor. Two-hundred-and-ten-dollars for thirty minutes work and I was thanking him.

"Don't mention it, Dev. Good to see you again."

"Now the old keys won't work in these, right?"

Felix looked at me like I was nuts.

"No, it's the same make as you had in there before. You can insert the old key, but it's not gonna unlock your door. Now, here's your new keys, four of them. Why don't you give me your old ones now, so you don't mix them up? They all look the same."

That sounded like a pretty good idea. Obviously Felix had seen me in action. I took the old house key off my key ring, took a second one off a hook by the kitchen sink and handed them over.

He chatted for a minute or two about the work he planned to do on his rose bushes when he got home tonight. I had tossed the flag thong on the table in the dining room where it still sat as we passed to the front door. It was sort of crumpled up, but there was no mistaking what it was. Felix glanced at it, but didn't comment. He shook my hand at the door and thanked me again.

"Maybe be a bit more on the cautious side when handing the keys out to your lady friends." He followed that advice up with a wink, and then waved over his shoulder as he walked to his van.

I watched him drive off, closed the door and snapped the dead bolt into place on my new lock. I pulled at the door slightly, just to make sure it was secure. My monitor call came through a little after ten. I went to bed and was asleep before eleven.

Chapter Fifty

It was dark in the bedroom and my eyes snapped open the instant I heard the rattling. It was subtle. I wondered for half a moment, thinking it might be the wind, then I heard it again. I slid out of bed and grabbed a snub .38 in a web holster I kept in my top dresser drawer. I tiptoed toward the stairs, hearing the sound again as I moved down the hallway. There was someone at my front door, trying the lock.

I peeked around the corner and looked down the staircase. I didn't see anyone. I waited for three or four minutes, started to convince myself it really must of have been the wind on this still night when I heard the noise again. This time more distant, but definitely there. I stood in the dark looking down through the large, beveled glass window of my front door. No one was out there, then I heard the rattle again. This time the back door.

I flew down the staircase and quietly moved toward the rear of the house. The noise was definitely coming from the back door, this time a little more forcefully. I stepped into the kitchen, but couldn't see anyone on the back porch. Over the course of the next hour I moved back to the front, then returned to the kitchen, checked the front again. Whoever it was seemed to have left.

My monitor call came through at seven-ten in the morning. Not a problem. I was already up and on my third cup of coffee. I'd never gone back to sleep. It had started to rain around five and the grey morning felt even worse with the steady drizzle coming down. I punched in my code, hopped in the shower and then drove to the office.

I watched the office girls going to work. There were some nice looking women huddled under umbrellas waiting at the bus stop. It was still about forty-five minutes too early for crabby coeds. Occasionally someone drifted into The Spot for a liquid breakfast. No one had left the place, yet. At five-past-nine I phoned Louie's office.

"Louie Laufen, please." I was prepared for the 'he'll call when able message.' But to my surprise she said, "One moment please, I'll connect you with Mr. Laufen."

The phone rang twice, followed by a nasty spat of coughing before I heard,

"Yeah. Hello."

"Louie?"

"Dev?"

"Louie, you just on your way home from last night?"

"I wish, I'm in trial today. Thought it might be nice to prepare. What do you need?"

"Any word from Manning on that stuff you sent over?"

"You mean that stuff where your pal Farrell married his sister in Vegas?"

"Yeah, although she's not actually his sister. That's just how they presented her to me." I couldn't believe I was explaining Farrell and Kiki's actions.

"Well to answer your question, no." Louie cleared his throat into the phone.

I desperately wanted to ask about Doctor Death.

"Not unusual," Louie continued, "I'd give them a week to check things out. They'll take their sweet time, but eventually they'll realize you're the wrong guy."

"You sound a hell of a lot more optimistic than I feel."

"I may have an inside track, nothing concrete, but I'm picking up some rumblings."

"Like what?"

"Nothing solid, yet. Let's just say rumors are your buddies at K-R-A-Z maybe aren't all they're cracked up to be. Things seem to be going in a couple different directions right now. Listen, Dev, your job is still the same, pretend to be an upstanding citizen, okay?"

"Can you tell me anything besides you heard a rumor there might be rumors?"

"No, that's about as good as it gets, for now. Listen, I gotta run, anything else that can't wait?"

"You can't tell me anything? Maybe just give me a…"

"No, like I said nothing to tell. Peace, love, dove, brother," he said and hung up.

Chapter Fifty-One

I'd like to say I spent the night scrolling through boring cable channels, but in actuality I slipped onto an Internet porn site around eight-thirty, promising myself it would be no more than fifteen minutes. Sunnie's laptop seemed to be working a little slower tonight so I didn't get to bed until a little after one. I woke at about two-forty-five. I thought I'd heard a car in my driveway, but then drifted back to a fitful sleep. I was finishing my coffee at the kitchen counter the following morning when the monitor call came through. I punched in the code, then drove to KRAZ and nibbled blueberry muffins sitting behind the steering wheel in the far corner of the lot. It was a gorgeous morning, sunny but not beastly hot, very pleasant. Despite the trash around the place I almost thought I could pick up the scent of flowers or perfume. Farrell's BMW was already parked in its usual spot when I arrived, pretty early in the morning for old Farrell.

A sleek silver Audi pulled in next to Farrell's car a little before ten and a gorgeous brunette climbed out, Kiki. She nibbled an apple, and was dressed in tight fitting jeans, heels and a sort of slinky top with spaghetti straps. Even from this distance she looked delicious as she made her way to the front door. Her entire appearance lasted less than thirty seconds. She never glanced in my direction. That was a good thing since just my watching from this distance violated her bogus restraining order.

Another car pulled in, some nondescript SUV, nothing too fancy. The guy got out, stood for a moment and gave my car a long glance before he walked toward the building. That was enough attention for me and as soon as he stepped inside I left.

As I drove to the office Farrell's voice droned on the radio. I had learned absolutely nothing, other than Kiki, crazy as she was, still looked great.

I was at my desk a little before noon, reading through my mail, which consisted of a grocery store circular featuring a special on Brussels sprouts, chick peas and beets. I wondered what sort of clientele they were attempting to reach.

There was some high pitched, feminine screeching coming from in front of my building, nothing desperate, just loud and obnoxious. I looked out the window and saw the three coeds lumbering across Randolph toward a waiting bus, giggling, screaming and in general disturbing everyone's peace. Once the bus pulled away I continued to watch as it disappeared up the street.

My car was parked at the curb, just a few spaces from my office door. I looked at it out the window. Something wasn't right. The headlight seemed to be broken on the passenger side. The bumper looked dented and was hanging at an odd angle.

I was swearing and grumbling as I raced down the stairs and outside to inspect the damage. Some idiot must have backed into me the other night at the grocery store and took off. I'd never even noticed.

It got worse as I walked closer. The head light was broken. The front of the car dented, the grill damaged. Down along the edge of the bumper there looked to be rust. I scraped at it with my thumb nail, hoping. Unfortunately, it wasn't rust, it was dried blood, I knew as soon as it flaked off. I could only hope a dog had been hit. Closer examination suggested that wasn't the case. There was a bit of hair around the outside edge of the headlight, threads snagged on the underside of the dented bumper. Someone had really been nailed. I hadn't had a drop to drink for so long I'd lost an inch around the waist. It hadn't been me behind the wheel, but that didn't change the facts.

I decided I'd better get the car washed, so I hopped in. There was that smell again, subtle, but none the less there. Flowers? Perfume? I had a pair of shoes on the back floor I used for softball. That wasn't it. On the way to the car wash I thought it might be a better idea to see Louie first.

Chapter Fifty-Two

I'd never been to Louie's office, but I knew where it was located. The building was just across Fourth Street from the Ramsey County Courthouse, in the City Hall Annex. Another former commercial building the city took over as business receded and the downtown area went on life support. The Annex sat next door to the former Lowry Hotel, another Real Estate scam some developer had been milking for the past fifteen years and the city would ultimately pay a high price for their naïveté.

Whoever did the layout for the Annex didn't have romance as a strong suit. The walls were painted a sort of puke green. It might have been government olive drab at one time, now thinned out to stretch coverage and look even more unattractive. Louie's office was up on the sixth floor, behind an eighties-style glass door labeled 613. The numbers were rectangles, black with a silver background. The kind of peel and stick address numbers that used to be popular in hardware stores until the buying public judged them as too ugly. At which point the city apparently loaded up.

There was a small lobby just inside the office door and mismatched plastic chairs against two bare walls.

Two black women sat on one side, while a fat white girl with a swollen eye madly texting on her cell sat across from them.

A heavy set woman with dyed black hair, a bouffant hairdo and bad skin sat hidden behind a computer screen at the receptionist counter. I approached the counter and waited politely until she had finished typing. Only she never finished, she just kept typing.

Eventually I said, "I'd like to see Mr. Laufen, please." I had aged just standing there.

She typed just long enough to where I thought she might be deaf, then glanced up at me.

"And you are?"

She turned away, answered the phone, then forwarded a call to some place, probably the wrong place. As she spoke on the phone I recognized her voice. I'd left probably a half dozen messages with her over the past two weeks. She hung up the phone, glanced at me again and looked surprised I was standing in front of the receptionist counter.

"Yes?"

"I'd like to see Mr. Laufen. I'm a client of his, Devlin Haskell."

If she picked up on my name she was doing a good job of hiding the fact. She returned to the phone, punched in four numbers, waited, presumably listening to it ring for a good long while, then hung up.

"Do you have an appointment?" She seemed to be staring about a foot to my right at the wall behind me.

"No, I don't, but he's representing me on a matter and I…"

"He's not here."

My tax dollars at work. If this is what they offered as a first impression of the place, rumpled, bourbon-soaked Louie was beginning to look stellar.

"Do you know when he might be back?"

She shook her head, still seeming to stare just to my right. I moved a half step in that direction.

"Could I leave a message for him? Have him call me when he returns?"

She suddenly shrugged, not in an 'I don't care' sort of way, more like a nervous twitch. She returned to her computer, clicked through a half dozen screens, then waited, hands poised for the attack just above the keyboard.

"Could I leave a message?" I spoke slowly, deliberately.

"Yes."

I guessed that was my cue. "Please have Mr. Laufen call me."

"Name?"

"Devlin, D-E-V-L-I-N. Haskell, H-A-S-K-E-L-L." I spelled it out carefully, slowly.

"Message."

"Please. Have. Mr. Laufen. Call. Me. It. Is. Important." I paused between each word.

Her fingers raced across the keys. She paused a second, then hit the enter key, then returned to her typing. Apparently I was finished.

The girl with the black eye was still texting, frantically. I smiled at the two black women. "Good luck," I said and left.

Outside on the street I phoned Louie. His message center was full. I was positive I'd have a coronary if I phoned his office. Instead, I drove to a self-car-wash down on West Seventh Street that featured high pressure hoses. I washed my car three times over the

238

course of forty-five minutes. I crammed the nozzle behind the dented bumper, shoved it inside the broken headlight, ran it along the grill and spent a lot of time washing under the wheel wells. I knocked a good deal of rust off the frame and hopefully any traces of whoever had been hit.

I remembered waking up last night, thinking I'd heard a car in my driveway. Had it been mine? The night before, someone trying to get in, the thong on my front doorknob. I was thinking Kiki. If she had drugged me, tied me to the bed, it seemed reasonable she could have made a copy of my keys. I just couldn't figure out why.

I drove back to my office, but kept going when I saw two squad cars from a couple of blocks away. They were parked at an angle, almost in front of the door, one facing against traffic. As I passed the building there was another squad down a ways on Victoria Street, a cop standing near the fire escape at the end of my building. It looked like they had me surrounded, except I wasn't there. I kept going, no point in heading home.

I swung by an Ace hardware store, the one down on lower Grand Avenue.

"Can I help you?" a guy asked. He wore a red polo shirt, Ace Hardware monogrammed on the left breast. I was maybe four feet inside the door.

"No, I know what I need, thanks."

He nodded and directed his attention to the woman behind me who said she was looking for bird seed for songbirds.

I walked down the aisle, taking a left just before the last nail and screw section. Tools hung on racks, pliers, wrenches, screwdrivers. At the far end of the aisle were three different sized bolt cutters. I chose the medium size, raised the leg of my jeans and snapped off my monitor bracelet. I returned the bolt cutter to its hook and left.

I took Kellogg Boulevard through downtown, then turned to cross the river on the Wabasha bridge. About halfway across I tossed the monitor bracelet out the window and over the railing into the Mississippi river. I briefly wondered how much stuff was down there on the bottom of the river, guns, knives, a car or two and now my monitor.

Chapter Fifty-Three

"What the hell are you doing here?" Heidi asked. She was halfway up her front walk before she saw me.

It was about seven-thirty and the bottles of chilled wine I'd picked up a couple of hours ago were now lukewarm, at best. The condensation from the bottles had made the paper bag useless. I had lined the wine bottles up against her front door, hoping the evening shade might slow down the warming process.

"Nice way to talk to someone who shows up with a peace offering."

"Yeah, why are you suddenly acting so nice?"

"I can't do something nice without being hassled? How's that work?"

"It's just that it's so unlike you, you caught me a little off guard."

"Look, I thought you might like a glass of wine, maybe some laughs. I wanted to get that spot you mentioned in your bedroom taken care of. You know, by the outlet cover."

"Really?"

"Hey, I can take off if you got something going. I didn't mean to barge in on your night." I stood to leave.

"No, no, that's okay, yeah come on in. I can use the company. It's been a brutal couple of days."

We were in her kitchen, sitting at the counter. It had taken me longer to wash the paint brush than it did to touch up around the outlet cover. She seemed to be relaxing after the second glass. She'd kicked her shoes off, dialed in some nice music, laughed a couple of times.

"So, ever find out who left their underwear on your door?"

"I got a couple of ideas," I said.

"I can't believe you blamed me."

"I didn't blame you, I was just hoping, that's all."

"You're so full of it."

"Not kidding."

"Really?"

She got up and went to the refrigerator for another wine bottle. It was sometime after midnight when we staggered into bed.

"Gotta run, meeting," Heidi whispered in my ear the following morning. "Help yourself to breakfast and lock the door on your way out."

She was dressed, just putting on earrings and then she was gone. I drifted back to sleep for a few more hours.

When I woke I lounged in bed for a long moment smacking my teeth and assessing the extent of my hangover. I got dressed and wandered into the kitchen. I should have known better than to look for food. There was a half package of cream cheese in the back corner of the refrigerator. On the bottom shelf something housed in a white Styrofoam container was growing a fuzzy science experiment. I wasn't hungry enough to risk it. I took four aspirin from the bottle she'd left on the counter, then locked up on my way out.

I phoned Louie's cell and amazingly he answered. Actually he coughed a number of times.

"Louie?"

"Hello."

"Louie?"

"Dev?"

"Yeah, listen can we meet?"

"I think we better. I got a call from your close personal friend Detective Manning. He's looking for you, along with the rest of the department."

"What'd he say?"

"Oh, you know, the usual first thing in the morning sort of phone call. You're missing and in violation of your release agreement."

"Anything else?"

"He casually mentioned since you've disappeared and aren't wearing the ankle bracelet anymore so there's a warrant issued for your arrest. They've posted a BOLO, Be On The Lookout for you. He sort of wondered if maybe I knew anything. Since apparently as your attorney, I'm the last guy to know anything, I really couldn't help him out. Care to enlighten me?"

"I'm not sure, but I've got some suspicions..." I went on to tell Louie about my damaged car, the cops at the office.

"So let me get this straight. You wake up and discover your car has been in an accident. And you have no recollection?"

"I know it doesn't sound too good."

"Possibly the understatement of the year. Does the term absolutely horseshit have any connotation?" Louie said.

"That a legal term?"

"I think we better meet, but probably not at my office and definitely not at yours."

"You name the place, I'll be there," I said.

"There's a bar, the Coal Bin, over on…'

"I know the place."

"I got a motion in court late this morning that I gotta deal with. Can you be at the Coal Bin about one-thirty?"

"I'll be there."

"And Dev, keep that car out of sight. They'll be looking for it."

Chapter Fifty-Four

I knew one of the dumbest things I could do right now would be to go to the KRAZ parking lot. At least that's what I told myself as I sat parked in the far corner. Farrell's BMW was in its usual place. Kiki's Audi was parked two spaces away.

I climbed out of my car and walked over to Farrell's BMW. I didn't touch the thing, but I did notice sand collected beneath the wheels. I was guessing it was washed up there after the rain the other morning. Lodged on the grill was a round plastic lid, a small hole in the middle like it might have been from a soft drink cup. The BMW hadn't been moved in a couple of days.

I left the parking lot, tuning in seven-forty on the dial to listen to the KRAZ broadcast. Farrell, sounding as dull as ever, appealed for cash donations, followed by the cautionary reminder not to send checks lest the Communists and Anarchists in Washington monitor your active support of freedom. He stammered over the word anarchists. He seemed to do that a lot, the stammering.

The Coal Bin was a dismal little neighborhood joint that sat on a bleak corner of a back street, in sight of the old Northern States Power plant and the river. It had been pouring drinks since at least the end of prohibition. The sign above the corner door, illuminated in the middle of this muggy summer day, proclaimed Rusty and Marge as the proprietors. Rusty's name had been spray painted over so long ago that you could read it again.

I pulled into the small rear parking lot a half hour early and parked on the far side of a large green dumpster. In order to see my car, you'd have to drive in the lot and somehow hit it.

Inside, the Coal Bin was what you'd expect, four guys sitting down the length of the bar on red vinyl and chrome stools, three stools apart, all staring at their beers. There wasn't a hint of conversation. I felt like asking if the glass was half-empty or half-full?

A large woman, north of sixty, nodded, then wiped the bar, sort of directing me where to stand when I ordered. She had glow-in-the-dark red hair and didn't smile. I guessed she probably doubled as the bouncer.

"A Summit," I said.

She grabbed a mug, pulled the tap, then set the beer in front of me. Not a wasted motion.

I retreated to a dark booth in back and sat facing the door. I was on my third mug when Louie finally arrived.

"Louie," the red headed bartender/bouncer squealed as he walked in.

"Marge, my beauty, how's it going?"

They exchanged insults, and then she pushed a mug and a shot he'd never ordered in front of him.

"Gotta meet with this guy," he said, and waddled over in my direction, sloshing beer.

"Been here long?" he asked, then drained a third of his beer before he sat down. It was close to two-thirty.

"Not to worry. She seems a fan." I glanced toward the bar.

"I'm in here once in a while, kind of off the beaten path. Allows me to sit in here and sort of think uninterrupted and shit, you know?"

"I do."

"Okay, Dev, tell me what's going on." He took another healthy sip, dropping the level of beer to about the halfway mark.

"Well, I came home the other night, found a thong on my doorknob…"

Louie listened as if he heard this sort of thing everyday, nodded occasionally, sipped the bottom half of his beer. I told him everything, seeing Kiki at the U. The newspapers stacked up at Doctor Deaths house. I described Doctor Death dead and taped to the chair. Told him how I spotted the dents in my car, my suspicions about Kiki. I finished up with, "So, once I saw the cops at my office, I figured my chances were slim to none and kept on going. I cut the monitor bracelet off, dumped it and called you."

Louie nodded for a moment before he tossed his shot back. He didn't so much as blink when it went down.

"Well, let me tell you, you're Mr. Popular. Seems everyone wants to talk with you. I already told you about the BOLO. Manning issued an arrest warrant for you, although that seems kind of fast if you just dumped the bracelet late yesterday. I'll check it out. I've got to pick up the autopsy report on Barkwell later this afternoon, anyway. They'll do an autopsy on that guy from the U. What'd you say his name was, Kevork?"

I nodded.

"They'll do an autopsy on Kevork, when they find him. To my knowledge they haven't, yet." He looked at Marge, signaling another round with just a slight nod. "Gotta tell you, Dev. You could use some help in the girlfriend department. Man, I thought I was screwed up."

I couldn't disagree.

"Talk to me about the car. You washed the thing, found hair and threads, you said?"

"And blood." I nodded.

"Not good, man, not good. Probably a smart guy would disassociate himself from that vehicle. I'm not suggesting get rid of it or hide it. That would be illegal, but you catch my drift. With the sort of testing they can do today, you could wash that thing a thousand times, then burn it and they'd still be able to find something."

I nodded, message delivered.

Marge arrived with a tray, two beers, and another shot. Louie handed her a ten.

"What is that shit?" I nodded at the shot glass.

"Sambuca, calms the tummy," he said, then drained close to half his mug.

"The key is Kiki," I said.

"Well, yeah, and the husband. Her first one, that Farrell guy. It's just not adding up, why go through all this bullshit? And then of course, if we ever figure out why, the question is how to get them? They seem to have been way ahead of everyone thus far."

"Life insurance?"

"You mean on Barkwell? Nelson checked, the guy didn't have any. Probably thought insurance was some sort of pinko plot." Louie shook his head, suddenly snatched his beer and drained it, then eyed the shot of Sambuca.

Chapter Fifty-Five

I'd bought a couple of ice cream trucks a while back, a no questions asked, cash transaction, which was how Walter handled all his transactions. I walked into his office, actually The Trend bar late that afternoon. A nicely dressed gentleman was seated on a stool at the far end of the bar, sipping coffee and reading the paper. As I entered the conversation level dropped, but as I began to move toward the back of the bar things really got quiet.

"Hey, Walter," I called and waved from between the shoulders of two very large, very solid black guys who had just stepped in front of me to block my progress. Both of them were looking down at me from a distance of about six and a half feet.

"Who's there?"

"Me, Dev Haskell, friend of Dog's," I said, then half waved my hand.

"Fool with them ice cream trucks?"

"That'd be me." I waved again.

"Come on back here. Shit, you waving like that, thought it was Casper the Friendly Ghost."

People started talking again, and the two stone pillars who'd blocked my way moved just enough so I could squeeze between them. "Excuse me," I said, feeling like an idiot as I spoke.

"What can I do for you?" Walter said as he looked me up and down.

He was dressed in an off white suit, a beige sort of tie with a matching silk stuffed into the front coat pocket, matching beige shoes. Understated.

"I need some wheels, Walter. Mine's, well, sort of high profile right now."

He looked at me for a long moment, then shook his head, "So I heard. It would appear you've got just about everyone after your ass right now."

"What'd you hear?"

"Nothing you don't already know. Out on bail for murder, rape…was there a kidnapping in there, and a sexual assault? You were black, they'd have already locked your ass up for life. Sounds like you're having a hell of a fun time. Guessing you violated your release stipulations, most likely a restraining order on top of that. That about sum it up."

It did.

"I need a vehicle, something understated. You know, something that blends."

"Not the usual market I'm in. S'pose you'd be needing this pretty damn soon?"

"Like yesterday," I said.

"I got something that might do the trick, I think."

"Terrific."

"Not so fast, man. You know the gig, cash. Be six large."

"Walter, you know where I'm at. I can't get that to you right now. They'll have everything frozen. I can do half, maybe."

"Problem is, you went and did the respectable thing and trusted a bank, now look what it got you."

"Yeah, I know. Look, can you help me?"

"I'm not in the help business."

"I know that, but I could sure use your help right now, Walter. You can have my vehicle, the one I'm driving now."

"Your vehicle? A DeVille, right? Red, with a blue door on the passenger side?"

I nodded.

"Hell, that damn thing wouldn't be able to go a city block before it was pulled over. You think you're doing some sort of favor dumping that thing on me?"

"I don't really want it to fall into the wrong hands."

"Tell you what, you get me four, large, you owe me another six. Which I'll need to see in a week."

"Six? In a week?"

"Take it or leave it," Walter said and then returned to his newspaper.

I was out of options and running out of time.

"I'll take it."

"Be back here nine tonight, I'll have something," he said, never looking up from the paper.

I kept a 'Go to Hell' fund in an empty gallon paint can out in my garage. I wasn't sure if my place was being watched, so I parked over on Dayton Avenue, cut through the backyard and in through the side garage door. If they came for me now I was cornered. I waited for a couple of minutes, but the only thing I heard was traffic out on the street. I let my eyes adjust, went to the shelf of paint cans, pried open the one labeled ceiling paint and counted out four large for Walter. I shoved the lid back on, walked quickly back to my car and left.

I parked in the lot at University and Snelling. There was strip mall there, Rainbow Foods, the Dollar Store, Office Max. It was almost six, and plenty of cars were in the lot. I had three hours to kill before I went across the street to The Trend and paid Walter.

I did a quick check of the trunk, made sure there was nothing in there that could be linked to me. I opened the blue passenger door, checked the glove compartment. There was a wallet in there, not mine. I opened it and Farrell's driver's license stared back at me. Another set up, probably Kiki and Farrell adding burglary or armed robbery to my growing list of offenses. I transferred twelve bucks cash to my wallet, then stuffed Farrell's wallet in my back pocket.

A '95, red, Cadillac DeVille with a blue door on the passenger side isn't exactly subtle. Even in the crowded parking lot it looked like an aircraft carrier docked there. I debated removing the license plates, but thought that might attract even more attention, so I just left the thing there with the keys under the floor mat.

I entered The Trend at nine on the dot. No one tried to stop me as I walked to the far end of the bar. Walter looked to be in some semblance of discussion with two twenty-something's, both attractive white girls. He held his hand out to halt me maybe ten feet away, and continued to talk to the girls. Then, just like in the movies he dispatched them with a nod of his chin, signaled me forward by wiggling a couple of fingers.

"How's it going, Mr. Dev?"

"Guess I'm about to find out. I'm still here."

"Fortunately, I was able to find something understated that I think will fit your needs," he said.

"Understated is good."

"Terrance will show you to the sales room," Walter said, then flashed a mouth full of white teeth when he grinned.

I was aware of a massive presence suddenly looming alongside me. Terrance, I presumed. I looked over and then up into a large, unsmiling face, plastered onto a gigantic head all of it supported by a muscular neck about the size of my waist. Terrance had been one of the pillars that blocked my way earlier in the afternoon. He indicated with a nod of his shaved head that I follow.

We walked across the street to the parking lot and then over a couple of rows. We weren't twenty yards from where I'd left my car. The DeVille stuck out like a sore thumb. Terrance stopped next to a tiny, faded blue, Ford Fiesta.

"This is it? A…a Ford Fiesta? You gotta be kidding me, right?" I said.

Terrance didn't seem like the kidding type. In fact he didn't seem to have much of a sense of humor at all.

"Four large," he said.

"Look, Terrance, I don't know…"

"Four large, asshole."

Who was I kidding, I handed him the cash. He stuffed the wad in his pocket, pulled out a set of keys attached to a ring that said "Jesus Saves" and placed the keys in my hand.

"Walter said you guys would take my old car."

Terrance nodded.

"That's it over there, that red DeVille. Keys are under the floor mat."

"A DeVille? Shit." He looked down at me and shook his head, then turned and walked back to The Trend.

I walked around the little Fiesta. It had Tennessee plates. Across the bottom they read 'State of American Music'. On the rear bumper, next to the license plate was a sticker, black letters on a white background. The bumper sticker almost looked homemade, except it was spelled correctly. "What Would Jesus Do?" followed by a big cross with lines suggesting sunlight coming from behind. I figured a smart guy like Jesus probably wouldn't be caught dead in this thing.

I attempted to climb into the Fiesta, but the seat was set so close to the steering wheel I had to pull myself out and push the seat back. It did start, eventually, which was about the only positive thing you could say. The odometer read a-hundred-and-forty-three-thousand. I reminded myself I still owed another six-grand on this dog, payable in a week. I immediately became depressed.

Chapter Fifty-Six

Just for the fun of it I drove past the KRAZ building. The parking lot was empty, with the exception of Farrell's car which apparently hadn't moved since I checked it out earlier in the morning.

I drove past Kiki's house. All the lights were off. She was probably out looking for some innocent guy to slice up. If she was home, her car was in the garage and she was wandering around the house in the dark. I saw absolutely no benefit in hanging around.

I drove out to a highway rest area just south of Saint Paul and pulled into the parking lot. I settled down to make myself comfortable, if that was even possible in the Fiesta. I figured the Tennessee plates would make sense to any State Trooper who saw me sleeping in the car. I dozed fitfully for the next few hours. Finally, stiff and cramped, I drove to a Denny's just as the sun came up. I was in search of a greasy fried breakfast and a reasonably clean restroom. I was sitting in a booth reading the menu with maybe a half dozen customers scattered around the place.

One couple looked to be pretty drunk. The woman suddenly sat up straight, raised her voice and slurred, "Don't you tell me what to do."

The guy she was with ran a hand through his hair and looked like he was incapable of telling anyone anything.

"Coffee, sir," a waitress said. She was in her mid-fifties with a voice that had a two-pack-a-day-rasp. She sort of wrinkled her nose as she stood over me, then took a slight step back. She poured my coffee and I heard her exhale after she turned to walk away.

At nine I called Louie on his cell phone. It sounded like I woke him up. I hung on for about an hour while he coughed and cleared his throat.

"Lo," he finally said.

"Louie, Dev."

"Oh, yeah, Dev. What the hell time is it?"

"A little after nine, I…"

"Shit, gotta boogie man…"

"Louie, wait, wait, don't hang up. You get that autopsy report?"

"You mean from Manning?"

"I don't know who you were getting it from. I thought the Medical Examiner would send it to you."

"Hmmm, yeah probably," he said, like he hadn't thought of that.

"So, did you get it?"

"No, I called Manning, left a message, he was going to get back to me, but I never heard anything. Ended up closing the Coal Bin last…"

"Closing the Coal Bin? I left you there before three in the afternoon. You telling me you stayed there drinking for the next eleven hours?"

"I had some dinner."

"They don't do food there."

"Had a bag of pork rinds. Look, I…"

"Louie, get that autopsy report will you? If Manning doesn't have it or you can't reach him, the

Medical Examiner will have it. In fact maybe try there first. They should have sent the thing to your office automatically."

"Yeah, I'm on it. Look I gotta fly, man."

I hung up not really flushed with confidence.

I parked the Fiesta out on the street, just for a change of pace, then sat back and watched absolutely nothing happen in the KRAZ parking lot. Farrell's car was still sitting there. I guessed that it had never left. I dozed off a couple of times for no more than a few minutes, then turned the radio to seven-forty to catch Farrell's droning rant over the noon hour.

I was trying to remain focused, but it was becoming increasingly difficult. Farrell was describing the international banking conspiracy KRAZ had uncovered and was about to bring public if only you could send in a cash donation, no checks. Send the donation to their Post Office Box. He had just finished giving the mailing address a second time, when he suddenly launched into a coughing jag in mid sentence. The on air hacking went on for at least a half minute, then simply picked where he'd left off. I'd heard it all before, the coughing. A few days back, the same thing, the exact same thing.

Whatever I was listening to, I'd heard it before. It was being replayed, so where was Farrell?

I remained parked on the street until late in the afternoon. The only thing I learned was the front seat of a Ford Fiesta can become damn uncomfortable. I phoned Louie, but his mail box was full, again. I phoned his office and left a message. My phone rang about an hour-and-a-half later.

"Mr. Haskell." The voice was icy coming over the air waves, and I cringed when I heard the Ivy League accent.

257

"Yes."

"Mr. Haskell, this is Daphne Cochrane, Ramsey County Public Defenders office." I pictured her wearing a sneer and sitting up ramrod straight at her clean desk, a sharpened pencil and a blank legal pad in front of her. She probably shuddered when she heard my voice.

"Yeah."

She cleared her throat, then said, "Mr. Haskell, your case has been reassigned to me."

"Where's Louie?"

"Mr. Laufen is no longer with the Public Defender's Office. I've been…"

"What happened?"

"That is a private matter between Mr. Laufen and Ramsey County."

"Sounds real private. Look, no offense, but I don't want you to represent…"

"I can assure you, Mr. Haskell, whatever protestations you may elicit, they could not possibly be greater than mine in this whole, sordid situation."

"I want to talk to Louie, Mr. Laufen."

"It's really not a matter of what you want, Mr. Haskell. Rather it has become a matter of what you must do. As your court appointed attorney, I'm advising you to admit your crime and surrender yourself to the proper authorities, immediately. This office…"

"Would you please have Louie call me?"

"I have absolutely no way of contacting Mr. Laufen, and I certainly have no…"

"I haven't done anything wrong, Daft."

"Please, don't use that tone with me, Mr. Haskell. You are in serious violation of a number of…"

258

I had a feeling where the rest of the conversation was going so I hung up. I wondered about Louie, but didn't have to wonder long.

Chapter Fifty-Seven

He was in the back booth, just behind the one I'd sat in yesterday. I wasn't sure, but I thought he was wearing the same clothes, only they looked a lot worse. He needed a shave and a very long, very hot shower. Close to a dozen empty beer mugs and a half dozen shot glasses littered the table in front of him. There were maybe eight customers in the Coal Bin, every one of them staying clear of Louie. Marge, with the nuclear red hair, was pouring a shot of Sambuca as I walked in. She brought the shot, along with another mug of beer over to Louie.

"I'll have a Summit and better get a black coffee for Louie," I said to her once she headed back behind the bar.

"He ain't gonna like that."

"Humor me."

I walked to the back booth and slid in across from Louie. He looked at me with glazed, bloodshot eyes, but I wasn't sure he could see me. He gulped down a fair portion of beer and then slammed the mug down. Beer dribbled down the corner of his chin. It wasn't like him to waste alcohol.

"So, counselor, seems you've had a busy day."

He attempted to focus for a brief moment then his head rolled from side to side and he belched.

"Just doing the public's biding," he said and grinned idiotically. He lurched a hand toward his mug, missed the handle and pushed the mug across the table in my direction it clanged off the empties scattered around but he seemed not to notice.

"Here, Louie, compliments of your friend," Marge said, then sneered at me.

"Love me?" Louie asked her.

At this point I had real concern for him.

"Louie, drink this," I said, placing the coffee mug in front of him.

He took a sip, and another, after the third sip he said, "Jesus, that's coffee. I need a beer."

"I know the feeling, but I think we should probably just go home, drink some there…what do you think?"

We sat for another year or two. I got two more cups of coffee into him.

"Louie, what do you say we head back to your place, crash for the night?"

"Sounds like a plan," he said, then attempted to get to his feet and immediately fell back into the booth.

"Here, let me give you a hand," I said. I almost threw my back out wrestling him into the Fiesta.

"What the hell's your address?" I was attempting to buckle him into the seat. The car was leaning toward the passenger side at close to a forty-five degree angle and I wasn't sure the seat belt was long enough to reach around him.

"Damned if I can remember."

I'd been here before with people, usually dates I'd deliberately over served, which was something that never seemed to work in my favor.

"Louie, Marge sent over a gallon of Sambuca to your place. She wants us to go get it. What's the address."

He rolled his head in my direction, attempted to focus, then mumbled what I could only hope was his address and we were off.

I parked in front, and then led him up the front walk using his tie as a leash. It worked, more or less. He attempted to pull his keys out of his pocket and dropped them on the front steps where I scooped them up. I opened the door, entered his living room and led him to a dilapidated couch. He wobbled for a brief moment, then collapsed face first onto the thing and was snoring in fifteen seconds.

I examined his bed, decided not to chance it, showered quickly and settled into a tattered recliner in the opposite corner of the living room.

It was bright and sunny out when Louie's coughing woke me. He was sitting on the edge of the couch, in a T-shirt, red boxers and black socks. Not the vision you'd want on any given day and certainly not the first thing in the morning.

"Oh, fuck me," he groaned.

I thought that pretty much summed things up. He sat there for a few minutes, coughing, clearing his throat, in general trying to focus before he rose to his feet. I thought it was pretty awful when he was seated on the edge of the couch, but the view once he stood was even worse.

"Tuck yourself in, man, Jesus."

"Screw it, you want a beer?" he asked, lumbering into a small kitchen. I heard the refrigerator door open. It grew quiet for a long moment. Then he groaned, "God damn it." The refrigerator door slammed shut. He reappeared a minute or two later empty handed.

"Guessing you heard what happened?" he said, scratching himself as he stood in the kitchen doorway.

"Depends. I heard you were taken off my case."

"Pricks fired my ass."

"Oh, that. How come?"

"Various infractions. I'm not sure really which one set them off. I mean there could be tons of reasons, but that heartless bitch…"

"Daphne Cochrane?"

"…was involved."

"She's the one who called me. Told me to plead guilty and turn myself into Manning because…"

"Actually, that's still pretty good legal advice."

"But, I didn't do anything. Between him and that weasel cop Heller, those two would lock me up and just throw away the key."

"Yeah, not your biggest fans. I meant the turn yourself in was good advice. You got your pal in there, LaZelle. He wouldn't let anything happen to you. Daft has a tendency to forget the innocent until guilty part when dealing with the lower strata of society."

I let his lower strata comment pass.

"I'm not turning myself in until I figure out what happened. It still isn't making any sense to me."

"It's about to get worse," he said.

"What do you mean?"

"I'm guessing Daft didn't tell you."

"She didn't say shit, except that I should plead guilty and turn myself in, immediately. Told her I didn't do anything and all she said was 'don't use that tone with me'. Like she's some damn school teacher."

"Yeah, that sounds like her," Louie said, then gave a tremendous belch. "Oh, man, much better, much better."

"So, you said it's going to get worse?"

263

"They found your pal, Farrell," Louie said, lumbering back to the couch.

"Found him?"

"Hit and run. Someone phoned in an anonymous tip, gave the description, a red, '95, Cadillac DeVille, a blue door on the passenger side. Sound familiar?"

"That's my car."

"You think?" Louie said.

"That's probably the damage to my front end, right?"

"Pretty fair guess."

"Someone phoned it in. Let me guess…a female voice."

"You got it. Amazingly similar to the report of shots fired at that bullshit press conference those clowns had. I'm guessing voice comparison would match this to the press conference call and the report of your vehicle driving over by Thompson Barkwell's place. Amazingly, all the calls were made from some untraceable, bogus phone. Seems like someone is really pissed off at you."

"I seem to have that effect on people. Did you ever get Barkwell's autopsy report?"

"No, I was busy getting fired."

"Think the Medical Examiner knows you've been fired?"

Louie shook his head, rubbed his eyes.

"Doubt it. They'll know soon enough, though. Daft will probably have it up on Face Bag and Tawter, and the bastards will probably have me disbarred by the end of the day."

"Louie, let's get cleaned up and go get that autopsy report, while we still have time."

"What? Do you think you're going to actually accomplish something? I think I'd rather go back to the Coal Bin," he said, then yawned and scratched himself.

"Even if it's nothing, that would accomplish more than sitting on my ass and feeling sorry for myself."

"As your former legal council I advise you to flee the country," he said, groaning to his feet.

"You serious?"

"No, they'd probably nab you at the border anyway. Come on, you can drive me back to the Coal Bin."

I stared at him with my mouth hanging open.

"Oh. Jesus, will you relax, I just gotta pick up my car," he said.

Chapter Fifty-Eight

Louie saw me and waved as he stepped in the door, then marched directly over to the booth I was sitting in.

"Been waiting long?" he asked.

"'Bout three hours." I finished the last of my drink.

"Here, you can read through this while I grab something. You want anything?" he said, then dropped a file on the table in front of me.

"Maybe another coffee." I opened the file and started to slog through the technicalities of Thompson Barkwell's autopsy report while Louie ordered.

He returned, carrying two Big Mac's and my coffee. He also had French fries, some onion rings, a giant pink shake and some sort of dessert thing. He spread it out across the table and started cramming food in his mouth.

"Skip that technical bullshit," he said, spitting a mouthful of French fries in my direction before slurping some of the pink shake. "Get over to page four. That's the part that's interesting. Tells you the contents of the guy's stomach."

"Barkwell's?"

"Who else?"

"Just wondered. I can hardly wait." I turned to page four, about halfway down Louie or someone had highlighted a paragraph.

'...partially digested rice and what appears to be the severed tip of an index finger. The finger tip appears to have come from the right hand of an adult Caucasian, aged between twenty-five and fifty. Separation occurred at the first joint. Examination suggests that severing possibly occurred from the deceased biting the finger tip and swallowing. Inner cheek, gum and tracheal bruising are consistent with the insertion of, and possible probing with, a foreign object. Possible effort to retrieve?'

"Someone cut a finger off and stuck it in some rice dish that Barkwell ate?" I said.

"Not exactly. He had a meal, part or all of which was rice. At some point, someone stuck their hand in his mouth. Your invoice was crammed in the guy's mouth, when they found him, right?'

"Yeah?" I wasn't getting up to speed with this.

"Somebody crams your invoice into his mouth. He reacts, maybe it's a reflex, maybe he's pissed off, maybe he's just hungry, but he chomps the guy's finger and then swallows the damn thing. Whoever it is tries to get it back."

"Tries to get it back? What the hell for?"

"Fingerprints for a starter? Maybe they're just pissed off, I don't know. We do know he swallowed the damn thing so they weren't able to retrieve it."

I was suddenly thinking of Farrell getting out of his BMW the other day, rubbing Kiki across her ass, all that gauze wrapped around his right hand and the index finger.

"It was Farrell."

"Or the broad," Louie said, then crammed the final half of a Big Mac into his mouth.

"No, it was Farrell." I went on to explain while he chewed.

"Well, then they should be able to put this together when they do the autopsy on Farrell," Louie said. He was licking his finger tips, getting the last bit of whipped cream with chocolate sprinkles. His appetite seemed to be unfazed by our topic.

"Maybe a phone call to the police would be helpful. You know, like in the movies…you've been kicked off the case, but you want to see the pursuit of justice all the same," I said.

"That's the movies," Louie said.

"I need your help here, Louie. These people are trying to railroad me."

"Don't feel like the Lone Ranger. I'd say so far, they've been pretty damn successful in screwing up both our lives."

Chapter Fifty-Nine

"Kiki, Kiki, Kiki, Kiki, Kiki."

"God, would you knock it off, you're weirding me out, here," Louie said.

We were sitting in Louie's car, amongst all the food wrappers, files, gas receipts and random debris, parked in the KRAZ lot, waiting for something, anything to happen.

Farrell's car hadn't moved and sat aging in place. Ideally Kiki would show up, spot us, realize the error of her ways and immediately confess, but so far that hadn't happened. Right now, I was ready to settle for someone making a wrong turn and driving into the parking lot.

"So, is this what you guys do all day?" Louie asked. He followed a Styrofoam cup dancing across the parking lot.

"Pretty much. It's not all gorgeous women and wild exciting…"

"I could get used to this gig, man. Just sit around, do nothing."

"Yeah, sort of like being a high buck lawyer."

"I wouldn't know anything about that," he said.

We had the radio on, some feminist talk show dealing with what was wrong with men. All the phone lines were jammed and they were going to extend the discussion into the next hour.

A minute or two before 5:30 I tuned the radio to KRAZ. On cue the patriotic music started and then we heard Farrell's voice, giving their post office box address, before slipping into a rant on banker controlled communist Washington.

"This the same shit you heard before?" Louie asked.

"Hard to say. It all sounds the same to tell you the truth. It's so damn dull I usually nod off before he's even finished. I didn't catch on until he made a mistake, flubbed a word, coughed, something like that."

"Absolute crazies is what they are," Louie said. He was shaking his head as he listened to Farrell's monotone rant.

"So, if Kiki isn't here, how are they doing this?" I asked.

"I'm guessing it would be pretty simple to access their computer from somewhere off site, especially if she was involved to begin with. She could be replaying this shit and sunning herself on a beach right now."

"In other words, multitasking," I said.

"They've been known to do that."

"You think she's gone?"

"I'd say there's a reasonable chance she may have fled the state. I would if it was me," he said.

"I'm thinking about how she got my car," I said, drumming my fingers on the glove compartment. I had it open as a tray for my empty coffee cup.

"And?"

"Like I said, I'm thinking."

"Hotwire it, I guess," Louie said.

270

"Except, I'd notice someone had been screwing with the ignition, wouldn't I?"

"Yeah, probably."

On the radio Farrell suddenly stumbled over the word 'anarchists' then kept on reading.

"There, I heard that shit before," I said.

"What?"

"Him screwing up 'anarchist', and then he just keeps right on going. Come on," I said, and stepped out of the car.

"Where're you going?"

"Up to their office. I'll lay you odds no one is even in there."

"You sure?" Louie was still seated behind the wheel, calling to me out the driver's window.

"Come on, man."

By the time we'd climbed the stairs to the sixth floor, Louie was scarlet faced and looked like he was going to have a coronary right there in the hallway.

"Jesus, my heart's beating like a rabbit," he said, gasping for breath.

"Must be the altitude. Come on, it's just down here." I led the way.

The wooden door to the office was locked. The handwritten sign 'KRAZ National Headquarters' was still crookedly taped above the mail slot. Looking through the slot I could see a pile of envelopes and circulars on the floor. The lights seemed to be off.

"Damn it, I don't have my tool kit," I said.

"Tool kit?" Louie said as he was slowly waddling down the hall behind me.

"Yeah, to get inside."

He gave me a long look, and then knocked on the door. No answer.

"I knew it," I said.

"Here." He pushed me aside, glanced back down the hall, then gave the door a solid hip check, then another and it suddenly flew open, bouncing off the front of the desk just a foot and a half inside.

"Problem solved," Louie said and smiled.

I stepped inside, listened for an alarm, but didn't hear anything. Louie made his way to the chair behind the desk and sat down.

"God, those steps damn almost killed me. How high up are we?" He was still breathing heavily.

"Six floors."

"Six, that all?"

"Six."

"Gotta be more like ten. I'd get up and check, but I'm too exhausted."

The pile of mail hadn't been touched in four days. Beyond that I couldn't tell that anything had changed. The place looked as messy and disorganized as ever.

"This has all the earmarks of people slipping under the radar," Louie said, looking around.

"Well, yeah, except two of them are dead."

"Plus your pal over at the U."

"Doctor Death."

"Yeah, that makes three," Louie said, looking sideways at the desk like he was going to go through the drawers.

"Can't be long before Manning washes up on shore, here. Don't touch anything in this place."

"Oops, okay, just my fat ass on this chair."

I did a very quick walk through the place and came up with nothing.

"Might as well go. We're not gonna learn anything else here," I said. Louie was still huffing and puffing in the desk chair.

Chapter Sixty

"You know we've gone back and forth, over and over this shit. Maybe we're making it too hard," Louie said.

"Meaning what, exactly?"

It was after ten that night. We were back at Louie's, working our way through the better part of a case of Summit Extra Pale. Louie was flaked out on the couch. Empty beer bottles lined up on the floor in front of him. I was running a couple of beers behind and straining my ears. I thought I heard some sort of rodent scurrying around inside the ratty recliner where I sat and I was listening for the thing.

"I'm not sure," Louie said, then tilted the bottle up and drained a good third. "The radio deal is a hoax. At least with Kiki...probably was with Farrell, too. I'm guessing Thompson Barkwell believed it, but they just used him. Sweetened the pot with Kiki, told him she was Farrell's sister. He probably couldn't believe his good luck, dumb bastard. But why? Sell drugs to Evangelical Christians and the Tea Party? That just doesn't seem to work," Louie said, burped and then drained the rest of his beer.

"It's something. That's not it, but it's something."

273

"The other thing I don't get…" He'd grabbed another beer and opened it using his key ring. "Why continue running the radio spots?"

"Make it seem like Farrell was still alive," I said.

"Okay, so then why would you call the cops and tell them he was run over by a car? Your car as a matter of fact, and then have the radio spots still playing? It just doesn't add up."

"That's the only thing you've said that makes any sense. None of this adds up."

"Do the broadcasts say anything? Is there information imparted? Are they…"

"No, you heard the damn thing today. Just a monotone rant. Hell, if the guy didn't make a mistake or cough his chain smoking lungs out, we never would have picked up on it. Fifteen minutes of him just droning on and on and on. Then all that bullshit a half dozen times about sending cash donations to…"

"That's it," Louie said, suddenly sitting upright, kicking an empty bottle over on the floor and spilling beer down the front of his shirt in the process.

"What do you mean, that's it?"

"Cash donations, the post office box. That rant. If it's picked up and beamed across North America, how many crazies you think send them cash?"

"I don't know maybe one or two. Who in their right mind would?"

"What if it's more than that?"

"More?" I said, sitting up.

"What if it's one or two percent?"

"Percent?"

"People send them cash, it's untraceable. That's what they used to fund your drug guy…"

"Doctor Death?"

274

"Yeah, and that's another cash business," Louie said.

"But Thompson Barkwell? The guy was a flake, but I don't think he was into drugs. Well, unless they were suppositories."

Louie groaned, then said, "Maybe Barkwell found out they were skimming funds. It's all cash coming in. I'll lay you odds they didn't put it in a bank. Maybe Doctor Death wigs out when Barkwell's killed. Maybe that was why they tried to pin it on you and…"

"Jesus, Louie, maybe the guys in black helicopters did it. You know, the *real* government just like Farrell rants about, international bankers or whatever it…"

"The post office box," Louie said.

"What?"

"Where the money goes…their post office box. She's still collecting cash donations, Dev. That's why those rants are still running on the radio. Cash is still coming in and your girlfriend Kiki is collecting it."

All of a sudden Louie didn't sound so far fetched.

Chapter Sixty-One

We took Louie's car to the KRAZ parking lot the following morning. We didn't expect to see Kiki, but on the off chance she showed up, we'd be there waiting for her. There was no sign of her. The broadcast came on in Farrell's usual monotone drone. As soon as he mentioned the address to mail cash donations Louie turned off the radio.

"Let's go, man."

"Go where?"

"Five-five-one-oh-seven, the zip code."

"You're going to drive around a zip code area?" I asked.

Louie gave me a long dead-pan-look.

"No, I thought we'd maybe go to the post office there. Check their box, you know? Maybe grab her when she picks up the mail."

"Yeah, that's what I thought," I said, not sounding too sure.

"And you're the private investigator?" he said.

The post office KRAZ used was on Eva Street. The building looked fairly small from the front and if I had to guess I'd say it was built in the late seventies. It sat just off of Plato Boulevard, across the river from downtown in a light industrial area. As you walked in the front door there was a sort of lobby with a couple hundred post office boxes set into the wall, each one numbered. Beyond that a door that led to a counter where you could buy stamps and conduct business.

From what we could tell there were three sizes of postal boxes. The one for KRAZ, number fourteen-seventeen, was the largest size.

"That can't be because they're getting so much mail coming in, can it?" I said.

"Maybe they're subscribing to Penthouse or the New Yorker," Louie said.

There was a small glass window in the box and we could see envelopes when we peeked in. Lots of envelopes.

"Jesus, frightening," I said.

"Let's wait in the car. She sees us in here, she'll run."

"I got an even better idea," I said. "We park in the lot across the street."

We did that, parked in the lot across the street, then sat there for the rest of the morning. Then we waited all afternoon. A guy locked the inside door to the postal counter promptly at five, then turned out the lights. At seven, another guy locked the door to the outer lobby where the Post Office boxes were and turned out that light.

"Any other bright ideas?" I asked.

"I thought that was your department. Yeah, actually I got one. Let's find a bathroom, with a bar attached."

"Not the Coal Bin," I said.

Chapter Sixty-Two

Early the following morning we were parked across the street from the post office, hiding behind a five-inch wide tree trunk. Around 8:15 we watched a half dozen people arrive for work at the building behind us. Then we watched the 9:00 rush at the post office. Forty-five minutes later things had settled down and customers were barely dribbling in.

At my prompting Louie called Detective Manning a little after 10:00 and left a brief message, mentioning the finger tip and Farrell Early.

About 10:45 a guy came out of the office behind us and walked up to Louie's window. He was dressed in nice khaki slacks and a starched, open-collar blue shirt. Shined shoes. He wore a gold wedding band, had closed cropped hair and looked to be in his late thirties. He also carried a cell phone in his right hand and I guessed he was ready to call 911 at the least provocation.

"May I ask what you two gentlemen are doing here?"

The words were polite, but the way he said gentlemen suggested anything but.

I pulled out my wallet, reached past Louie, flashed a badge, then counted to four and snapped my wallet shut.

"Sorry, we're working surveillance. We'd appreciate it if you kept this under your hat."

"Someone's gonna rob the post office?" he said, and then gazed across the street as a woman wrestled a baby stroller out the door.

"No, just looking for an individual. I think we're drawing a blank, but you can never be too careful. Appreciate your help all the same."

"Let me know if you guys need anything. Name's Bob Ross," he said, nodding and backing up.

"Where'd you get that bullshit badge?" Louie asked once Bob went back into his office.

"Toy store, six of 'em in a bag for barely two bucks."

Louie shook his head.

Bob came back out about fifteen minutes later with two steaming mugs of coffee.

"Listen, you guys need anything, feel free to come on in…bathrooms, coffee…hope you take it black. I didn't think to ask cream or sugar."

"Thanks, Mr. Ross," Louie said.

"Appreciate you looking after us," I said.

Bob ducked back inside.

"Nice enough guy," Louie said, and sipped his coffee.

His phone rang sometime after three that afternoon and jerked both of us awake. He glanced at the number.

"Christ, my former office, probably calling to give me the date on my disbarment hearing. Hello," he said, after letting it ring two more times.

I was about six inches from Louie so it was impossible not to listen. Not that I learned anything.

"Yes. No. I have no idea. I see. I understand. Did they? Oh, really? No. Yes. What time? Thank you."

"Everything okay?" I asked.

"Yeah, as a matter of fact better than okay. They want to meet with me tomorrow. Seems some things have been brought to their attention."

"Such as?"

"I'm guessing the autopsy report for starters and that finger, just a guess. Mentioned they got a call from Manning. He wanted to know how to reach you?"

"Did you tell them?"

"You're sitting right next to me. Did you hear me tell them?"

"Guess not."

"If they want to know how to get a hold of you they can talk to your attorney. If they can stand her attitude."

"Was it Daft who called?"

"No, Jerry Hamel…he's the big cheese. He didn't mention Daft, but I'm guessing she's going to be getting a lot of personal attention in the near future. Her advice that you plead guilty, which by the way would give you life with no chance of parole, is against all rational thought. If Hamel hasn't heard about it I'll lay it on him tomorrow. Anyway, the meeting is at eleven."

"Now, if we could just deliver Kiki," I said.

"Yeah, that would help."

I dashed across the street and looked in the KRAZ box, then quickly returned to Louie's car.

"There's a lot more mail crammed in there than yesterday. That thing looks to be just about over flowing," I said.

"Well, there you go…figure each envelope holds a cash donation, even if it's just ten bucks…"

280

"There's gotta be a couple cf grand sitting in there right now just waiting for Kiki to pick it up."

The interior doors were locked promptly at 5:00, and the lights turned off. At 7:0C the same guy as last night locked the lobby door and then hit the lights.

"Any dinner plans?" Louie said.

An hour later I had the recliner fully extended eating sausage pizza with extra cheese. Louie had just started working on a new case of Summit.

"You're not having a beer?" he asked from the couch.

"No, I'm going back out in a bit."

"Not back to that post office?"

"No, I'm gonna swing past Kiki's place and…"

"Thought you said she wasn't there?"

"I'm pretty sure she isn't. But, I just want to make sure."

"Suit yourself," Louie said, then shrugged and drained his beer.

Chapter Sixty-Three

Later that night I parked around the corner, about four doors from Kiki's. I sat in the Fiesta for a long time. It was just as boring as the day I'd wasted watching the post office, only darker.

I walked past the front of her house and then down the alley, nothing. After I lost count of how many times I'd made that pass I walked up onto the front porch and rang her doorbell. I could hear the thing go off inside the house, a Big Ben chime. No one came to the door. I tried the knob and it was locked. I walked through her back gate across the yard and up the steps onto her back porch. Her back door was locked, and so was the garage door. I peered inside her garage with the help of an alley light. No car, the place was empty.

She could have gone to a late movie, just been out on a date or she could be shacked up somewhere with a pair of twin brothers, but she was probably already out of the state.

I went back to Louie's and slept fitfully in the recliner. The following morning I found myself seated behind the wheel of the Fiesta in Bob Ross's parking lot as people arrived for work.

Bob brought me coffee a few minutes after he arrived.

"See you switched vehicles," he said, indicating the Fiesta.

"Trying to keep a low profile."

"Well, this thing certainly does that." He laughed. "Offer still stands. Feel free to use the bathroom or anything else you need."

"Thanks, Mr. Ross."

I dialed in KRAZ a little before the mid-morning broadcast. It was twenty minutes later when I realized I hadn't heard Farrell's voice. I crossed the street to check the KRAZ box. It was still stuffed with envelopes. As the day slowly passed the clock seemed to come to a complete stop. After sitting there for what felt like a month, a guy drifted out and locked the inner lobby door, then turned out the lights. Another month later, at 7:00, he returned and locked the front door and turned off those lights.

Apparently Kiki wasn't in desperate need of the funds in the post office box. I drove past her house on the way back to Louie's. The lights were off and the place looked dark and quiet. Louie's house was dark, too. Fortunately it never dawned on him to lock a door, so I let myself in.

I fell asleep a-half-dozen beers later. I'd been watching a baseball game, theoretically, when I nodded off. There was an exercise show on the television when Louie shook me awake.

"You want a beer?" He held two open bottles. I took one, stretched and yawned.

"What time is it?"

"Little after one. Here's to you, man," he said, raising his bottle.

I nodded then sipped.

283

"You want the good news or the not so good news?" he said.

"Give me the not so good news first."

"They can't find your girlfriend."

"Kiki?"

"Yeah." He chugged down a good portion of his Summit.

"What happened?" I asked, watching him almost empty the bottle.

"That autopsy on Thompson Barkwell, the finger tip checks out as your buddy Farrell's. Manning's guessing Farrell was drugged when he was run over, but we won't have confirmation from the Medical Examiner for a couple more days."

"No kidding?"

"Yeah. You were right about the bandage. It's his, the tip of his right index finger."

"He told you this, Manning?"

"No, I was down at the morgue, looked at the guy on a slab, saw it for myself. They took a print of the tip. It's a match, man."

"How'd he look?"

"Farrell?"

"No, the medical examiner…yeah, Farrell."

"Dead." He drained his beer. "Need another?"

I'd barely taken a sip and shook my head no.

"He was pretty banged up. The car either nailed him doing about sixty or ran over him a half-dozen times. They'll figure it out. They're pretty good at that shit," he said, then walked into the kitchen. I heard him open the refrigerator door and heard the bottle clink as he pulled it out and closed the door.

"Anyway," he said, strolling back into the living room and dropping onto the couch. "Manning's waiting on an autopsy report from Hennipen County, your Doctor Death guy."

"Carroll Kevork, from the U."

"Yeah, that's him. Autopsy should be coming across in the next couple of days."

"How'd they find him?"

"Outstanding warrant, possession with intent…Sherriff was out there to serve the warrant and picked up the scent, literally, if that translates."

"No, I'm not…"

"The sheriff could smell the body. They got a search warrant, found him inside, just like you described it. Guessing he'd been there about a week, not pretty."

"They think I…"

"I didn't say anything, just acted surprised. Far as I know they got no idea you were ever there. I sure as hell didn't offer to tell 'em."

"Where's all this leave me?" I asked.

"Probably in that recliner tonight, the good news is, I'm kicking you out tomorrow."

"What about the charges against me?"

"Dropped, or will be. They're hot to trot on your girlfriend. Manning calls her the Black Widow. Get it? Two of her husbands and a lover are…"

"I get it, Louie."

Chapter Sixty-Four

I slept in and left Louie's before noon. I didn't want to go home until I heard for certain everything was okay. He finally returned my calls late in the afternoon.

"Yeah, Dev, what can I do for you?"

"Louie, I'm ready to blow what's left of my brains out, here. I've been wandering aimlessly around the damn Mall of America for hours waiting for you to call."

"Then you should feel exactly like every other idiot out there. Are you in one of those bars?"

I was sitting on a wooden bench in some brick sort of courtyard area next to a bunch of potted ferns. A player piano was automatically playing a version of 'Stardust', again, the keys moving up and down, the piano sound bouncing and echoing off three stories worth of shops and fast food joints I had no interest in. It was giving me a hell of a headache.

"Did they drop the charges? Can I go home?"

"Pretty much."

"Pretty much? What does that mean?"

"You're free and clear on the hit and run with Farrell J Early. You're free and clear on the murder of

Thompson Barkwell. On the kidnapping, sexual assault and rape charges they're still out there, but only because they can't locate the always charming Kiki. Give those another forty-eight hours and they'll disappear."

"Even with those photos?"

"They're viewing them as a creative effort. Apparently they found about a hundred similar shots of her when they went through Farrell's place. He and your gal had some sort of ongoing kink thing happening. If you put him at the scene the night you were drugged, it all makes sense."

"The black eye and the bite mark?"

"They're guessing Farrell tied her up and did that shit, probably consensual, trying to frame you. They did the bite impression thing on him. It most likely will be inconclusive, but it creates enough doubt with the photos they found. It'll be pretty much a dead issue, pardon the pun."

"No problem." I could feel myself relaxing.

"That just leaves one charge pending…"

"What's that?"

An older woman sat down on the opposite end of the bench. She was dressed in a pink velour sweat suit with one of those fanny pack things around her waist and a red, white and blue visor that read '*John 3:16!*'

"The monitor bracelet you cut off. It's actually a misdemeanor to remove the thing."

"A misdemeanor?"

"I can get it taken care of, I think."

"You think? Come on, I was facing two murder counts, a kidnapping and a rape. They tried to throw in the sexual assault…"

The woman at the end of the bench quickly got up and left.

287

"Dev, I told you all of that is going away. We just got this one little thing to take care of."

"So can I go home?"

"Yes, Manning made a point of assuring me it was okay."

Chapter Sixty-Five

I had been cleaning since I got back home hours ago. It wasn't the first time the police had searched my house, but it was the first time they'd ransacked and trashed the place. Furniture was turned over, books tossed off shelves. The contents of my file cabinet were heaped in a large mound in the middle of the floor. Some jackass had left the refrigerator door open. That wasn't good. Fortunately they missed the freezer.

I wondered who I could call and thought of a clean-freak friend, Kathy. It had been a few months since I'd seen her, but this was an emergency. I phoned, but she had apparently blocked my number.

I called Sunnie, thinking I might be able to entice her with the promise of returning her laptop. She didn't answer so I left a message.

I phoned Heidi, almost as worthless as I was when it came to cleaning.

"Dev?"

"Heidi, how's it going?"

"What do you want? And where the hell have you been?"

"Actually, kind of a long story. I wondered if you wanted to come over? I…"

"It's pretty late."

"It is? I had no idea. I was doing some cleaning and …"

"Call me tomorrow, bye."

I went back to repositioning furniture and getting my files back in a semblance of order. I had the living room pretty much put together, the refrigerator emptied and everything out in the trash when I heard a knock at my back door.

Maybe Sunnie heard my message and was coming to the rescue.

I opened the back door. A woman was there. I couldn't tell who, because she had her top pulled up in front of her face, exposing herself. I caught the top of her bleach blonde head before I focused on her flat tummy and the rather formidable pair of breasts she swayed from left to right.

"Well, hello there," I said and continued to stare.

"God, you are so incredibly stupid," Kiki replied as she dropped her top, shoved a pistol in my face and pushed me into the house. She backed me up against the kitchen counter. I kept my hands raised over my head. The pistol wasn't just big, it was huge, some sort of automatic and she held it with both hands.

"Great dye job, Kiki. Going for the dumb blonde look? Hey, I know you're not Farrell's sister and I…"

"Spare me."

"I know he tied you up, bit you on the ass to set me up, put the…"

"Oh gee, really? Right now that's the least of your problems, Dev."

"What do you think you're doing here?"

"Actually, since I have this gun, just about anything I want to do. Jesus, you're a pretty lousy housekeeper," she said looking around.

"I had help. You know, Kiki the cops are gonna be watching that post office box. You're never gonna get those funds, so you might as well get out of here, now."

"Let's hope they do a little better job watching that box than you and that fat guy, both of you asleep in the car yesterday."

"They will." I didn't sound very convincing, but couldn't think of anything else to say.

"Tell you what…you got any gin?"

"In the freezer," I said and then nodded toward the refrigerator.

"Sit down on the floor," she said, and motioned with the pistol.

I sat down in a corner, my back against the cabinet.

"You can put your hands down, Dev. God, you're making me nervous."

"Kiki, I honestly thought you'd be long gone by now."

"What? And miss out on saying goodbye? I've got a few loose ends to tie up, and then I'm on my way, someplace warm."

"Hell?"

"Funny, real funny. You're a funny guy, Dev."

She pulled the gin out of the freezer.

"This isn't my brand."

"Yeah, if I recall you were a Bombay Sapphire girl, right?"

"Good boy. Suppose I'll have to make do with this lower shelf crap."

"Chilled glasses on the door of the freezer," I said.

"Oh, wow, that helps." She placed two frosty stemmed glasses on the counter and filled them with gin. "I like mine dry. Something a little extra for yours," she said, then pulled out a small packet from her pocket, powder wrapped in saran. She dumped it

291

into one of the glasses, stirred the gin with her finger, then handed the glass to me.

"Sweet dreams," she smiled.

"I'm not drinking that shit."

"Okay, whatever." She pointed the barrel of the pistol just about between my eyes. The barrel looked like a subway tunnel and I was pretty sure I could see the bullet just a finger squeeze away from my forehead.

"You know, on second thought," I said and chugged the gin down, then shuddered. It burned and froze at the same time, a weird sensation. There was a heavy sludge residue from whatever the powder was along one side of the glass.

"Have some more," she said, pouring gin into my glass with her left hand, keeping the pistol on me with her right.

"I should probably be a gentleman and share," I said.

"Not to worry, I'll take care of myself. Thanks all the same. Swirl that around for a bit, yeah that's right. Good boy, now drink it down. All of it, come on, all of it. Good."

"Now what, Kiki?" I coughed and tried to catch my breath.

"Now we just wait. You are getting sleepy, very, very sleepy," she said, then laughed.

"Hate to disappoint, but I don't think it's going to work. You're not gonna pull this off. Everyone's looking for you," I said.

"Oh darn, and all this time I had my heart set on a place in the sun."

We talked about a few other things, I think. We must have, I just can't remember.

When I woke the sun was bright. I had no idea if it was morning or afternoon. All that remained of Kiki was an apple core on my kitchen counter. I was groggy and my head felt like it was ready to explode. I was still on the floor with a white plastic trash bag twisted and knotted around my ankles. It took me the better part of five minutes to get the damn thing off.

I found my cell on the dining room table, phoned Louie and left a message. I phoned Manning and left another message. Louie phoned back about thirty minutes later. I'd moved as far as the living room couch by that time.

"You okay? You sounded like shit on the message, couldn't understand a damn thing you said."

"Shit, Kiki," I said.

"What are you worried about her for? If she hasn't already blown her brains out she's probably on the ledge of some skyscraper convinced she can fly. Hey, I…"

"No, she was here," I said, then coughed and hacked into the phone.

"Jesus, you gonna make it? What do you mean she was there? Where? Your place?"

"Yeah, last night."

"You serious? Did you…"

"Knocked at the back door, came in at gun point, drugged me with something, I don't know what. But she was here."

"Did you call the cops?"

"I, I left a message, I think."

"Jesus, stay put, I'm calling 911. Then I'm calling you back, okay? Dev, okay?"

My phone was ringing, annoying the hell out of me.

"Hello." More coughing and groaning.

"Dev, stay put, buddy, cops are on the way."

"Louie?

Chapter Sixty-Six

They kept me in the hospital overnight for observation. Then released me the next day and Louie gave me a lift home.

"I don't know if you're really lucky or really an idiot, Dev."

"That's always the question, isn't it?"

"Why did you let her in, in the first place?"

"Who, Kiki? She had me distracted, a sort of disguise, then before I knew what was happening she had a gun in my face. Things sort of went downhill from there."

"Jesus, I suppose she could have just shot you."

"We discussed that option."

Louie looked over at me, shook his head and then said, "Manning thought it was pretty funny."

"Yeah, nice sense of humor."

"Well, at least they found her car," Louie said.

"Where?"

"The airport."

"The airport? God, she could be anywhere."

"Or even still here in town."

"Don't even think like that," I said and shuddered.

"Manning said they got her key ring. He thinks your house and car keys are on it. That's good for you."

"I don't know. What a nut case." I said.

"Well, if she had your car keys, access to your car, your house, it sort of ties everything together."

"I suppose, in some bizarre way," I said.

He dropped me off in front of my place. I was ready for some aspirin and a nap. My house was still a mess, but I could live with that for a few days. I clicked the remote on, stretched out on the couch in front of the television and promptly fell asleep.

Sunnie's phone call woke me late in the afternoon.

"Dev, sorry I missed your call last night, I was out to dinner with the kids."

"The kids?"

"Josh and Mandy...we were celebrating. They both made the dean's list. I'm so proud. All their hard work is paying off."

"So you're changing your tune?"

"You mentioned the laptop," she said, changing the subject.

"Huh? Oh, yeah, I wanted to get that back to you and wondered if you could help me with a computer thing."

"Probably. Do you have dinner plans? All I've got is leftovers, but there's plenty."

I was at Sunnie's door with a bottle of wine and her laptop later that evening.

"Don't take it personal," she said after dinner. "But let me make sure this laptop is still working. What did you do, spill coffee or something on top of this?" she said, wiping her hand across the top of the laptop.

"It was working okay, but it seemed to be getting slower and slower as I was doing my research. Maybe you need a new set of batteries."

She gave me a look of disbelief as she turned the thing on.

"Oh, my," she said after clicking a couple of different places. "What were you doing? This thing is loaded with viruses. I'm not sure I even want it in the house."

"Just doing some research."

"Research? Where? I'd better wipe this whole thing. Oh my God, what is Girls Gone Wild? Double D and Disorderly? That was your research?"

"It's sort of a complex issue that…"

"Complex, you were watching porn. Oh icky."

"I may have glanced at something. You know, by mistake."

"I'll bet. God, Sex Craved…"

"They all just sort of popped up."

She sprayed a cloth with some sort of disinfectant, then wiped the laptop down.

"This is going to take a while to cleanup. How could you do this on my laptop?"

"It's not like you have to watch…

"Don't even answer, creepy, you're just perverted."

"Your point?"

"You mentioned something else you need, perv!"

"Yeah, can you do a color scan on my drivers license?"

"Yes, but why?"

"Case I'm working on…I want to see if the holograms pick up."

"They won't"

"Yeah, but I need a sample."

"And it's your license?"

"Yeah. What? You don't trust me?"

She didn't say anything, but glanced at the laptop. A growing list of things in red letters were displayed on the screen, the porn sites I'd visited over the past month. It didn't look good.

When I got home I cut out my image from the driver's license Sunnie had scanned. I taped it in place over the image on Farrell's license, trimmed the excess and slipped it into my wallet next to the fake police badge.

Chapter Sixty-Seven

The following afternoon I went to the KRAZ post office box about two minutes before the post office closed. I checked the box through the little window. It was empty, except for a single sheet of folded paper.

"What can I do for you?" the guy behind the counter asked. I was pretty sure he was the same guy who locked the door and hit the lights at the end of the day.

"Box fourteen-seventeen…I got all the way down here and forgot my keys. Can you help me?"

"Are you authorized?"

"Yeah, K-R-A-Z, Thomson Barkwell and me, Farrell Early."

"Do you have some I.D.?"

I flipped open my wallet, my scanned photo taped on Farrell's license, hiding behind a grimy little plastic window. The badge sat next to it. I counted to myself, at three he looked up at me, down again at the badge, then back up. "Not a problem. Fourteen?"

"Fourteen-seventeen, K-R-A-Z."

"Let me get it for you."

It felt like an hour while I waited but it was more like three or four minutes. He was whistling the tune

'Crazy' when he returned with a large, white plastic box with metal handles. The thing was about the size of a case of wine bottles and stuffed to overflowing with envelopes.

"Looks like it's been a while. There were so many we couldn't fit them into your box anymore," he said, hoisting the container onto the counter and pushing it across to me.

"Out of town for a bit. Thanks, appreciate your help."

"Let me lock up behind you," he said and held the door for me as I walked out.

By the time I was getting in the Fiesta he'd turned the lights off and had closed for the day.

Sitting at the kitchen counter it took me the better part of an hour to open the envelopes and remove the cash. I reminded myself more than once that every time I opened an envelope I was committing a Federal Offense. I removed a little over eight grand cash, the majority in tens and twenties, a couple of fifties. I spent the next two hours shredding envelopes and notes.

The following afternoon I went to the bank and exchanged the cash for hundreds. Then I drove two trash bags of shredded paper to the recycling center over on Pierce Butler Road. On the way back I stopped at The Trend.

Just like before I was stopped twenty feet inside the door by Terrance and some other giant.

"Terrance, I'm here to see Walter, make things right."

Terrance didn't so much as blink, then he took a step back so Walter could look at me.

Walter nodded and reached for his coffee cup.

"Another ice cream truck?" Walter asked when I stood in front of him.

"No, sir, just here to pay off my debt, is all."

"Don't," he cautioned, as I reached into my pocket. "Terrance will deal with that. Anything else?"

"Nope, nothing, other than thanks, I couldn't have done it without your help, Walter."

"So I hear. Listen, you stay in touch, Dev."

I smiled, followed Terrance outside and down the street. We'd walked the better part of a half block. We were behind a bus shelter filled with squirming kids when Terrance stopped.

"Just shake my hand," he said.

I palmed six grand, not an easy thing to do, and shook Terrance's hand. The cash seemed to disappear in his large paw. Then he turned and continued on his way. I walked back to my Fiesta, got in and drove home.

When my phone eventually woke me the sun was almost down. Scattered clouds drifted in the sky, their edges a vibrant pink in the final moments of sunset. I answered my cell, prostrate on the couch.

"Haskell Investigations."

"Hello, Dev."

"Who's this?" I asked, afraid I knew.

"I need someone to rub lotion on my back. Interested?"

"No, not really, Kiki."

"Oh, come on. You're not mad, are you?"

"No Kiki, I'm not mad."

"Hey, thanks for the drinks the other night. How's the head?" she said.

"I guess I'll live."

"Only because I let you," she said, then laughed and hung up.

I checked the front and back doors. They were locked. I pushed a chair up against them, just to be on the safe side. Then dug in my wallet, pulled out Amanda Nguyen's business card and dialed the number.

"Hello."

"Hi, Amanda, this is Dev Haskell. Please, don't hang up."

"What makes you think I'd do that?"

"Just the way things have been going lately, I…"

"From what I hear they've been pretty much going your way all of a sudden."

"Yeah, actually they have. That's kind of why I called."

"Oh really?" She laughed. "I suppose you're looking for that sucker I promised."

THE END

Thanks for taking the time to read Bite Me. If you enjoyed the read please tell 2-300 of your closest friends. Don't miss the sample of Bombshell that follows my shameless self promotion.

Help yourself to these stand alone titles.

They're all available on Amazon.

Baby Grand
Chow For Now
Slow, Slow, Quick, Quick
Merlot
Finders Keepers
End of the Line

Irish Dukes (Fight Card Series)
written under the pseudonym Jack
Tunney

The following titles comprise the Dev Haskell series;

Email: mikefaricyauthor@gmail.com
Facebook: Mike Faricy Books
Facebook: Dev Haskell
Twitter: @mikefaricybooks

Here's a taste of <u>Bombshell</u>, another Dev Haskell novel, enjoy.

Bombshell

<u>Chapter One</u>

"I'll have a pint of Summit and a Cosmopolitan," I said. With all the thumping music in the place I had to lean halfway across the bar just to give my drink order.

The bartender nodded, maybe gave a slight sigh, I wasn't sure.

"That Cosmo for you?" the woman next to me asked then she yelled across to the bartender, "Two Summits."

She stood about five three, brown hair, glasses, very nice figure. She had on really tight little shorts over black hose patterned to look like slinky nylons and a garter belt.

"Do I look like the Cosmo type?"

"Yeah, I knew it as soon as I saw you. You're probably a big 'Sex in the City' fan. I'm Justine," she said and held out her hand.

"Dev."

Her eyes bored into me as I shook her hand. The music fired up again, so loud we had to speak into each other's ear. We were in danger of getting body slammed by a half dozen twenty-something girls jumping up and down behind us. They were shaking their hair, waving their hands over their heads and screaming "woo, woo," as they twirled around.

"You come here often? You don't really look the type," she half shouted.

"Woo, woo," the girls screamed, oblivious to all but themselves.

"I've managed to avoid this place thus far. Not exactly my style. I knew I was in trouble as soon as I had to pay the cover charge at the door."

She nodded toward my beer and the Cosmopolitan landing in front of me. I handed the bartender a couple of fives.

"Twelve-fifty." He seemed to smile at the joke.

"Twelve?"

"Twelve-fifty," he smiled again.

I gave him another five and shook my head.

"Apparently she's got expensive tastes. Maybe you should think about finding a girl who likes beer."

"Fortunately she has some good points, too," I said into her ear.

"Don't we all," she said and gave me that stare again.

I raised my pint glass in a toast to Justine, knocked a couple of inches off the top and carefully picked up the Cosmopolitan.

"Be good," I said.

"I have a lot more fun when I'm bad."

"You're telling me," I said, then thought it might be a wise idea to retreat to my table.

I delivered the Cosmopolitan to my date, Carol. She was nestled into a gang of girlfriends all talking about stars whose names I didn't recognize. Each one held a different colored, overpriced drink in front of them. I reached over the shoulder of some long haired guy who had taken up residence on my stool and handed Carol her Cosmopolitan.

"Watch out, Dev you almost spilled," she snapped. She turned, shook her head and rolled her eyes at the guy on my stool. He smiled back at her, gave his head a shake to send his hair back over his shoulders, then he used a finger to push a misbehaving strands behind each ear.

"Dev, this is Nicholas, he's from France," Carol yelled over the noise.

I nodded and figured Nicholas was attracted to Carol by the same things that had attracted me.

"Dev, get Nicholas a drink, will you? What are you drinking?" Carol screamed then placed a hand on his wrist just as the music stopped.

"There is French beer, no?" Nicholas said, looking up at me hopefully.

"I don't think so," I said.

"No Caracole? No Saxo?" He sounded put out.

"No. Summit, Leinenkugel, Grain Belt and they got Guinness.

"Pity. French beer is the very best" Nicholas directed this toward Carol.

Carol smiled like she understood, like it was a fact everyone automatically knew, nodding as if she had a refrigerator full of French beer in her kitchen.

"Oh, I just love your dreamy accent. Maybe you'd like a Cosmopolitan, here try a sip of mine," she said and offered up her eight dollar drink.

"I think I may try the Martini, yes?" he said, suggesting he'd never had one before.

"That sounds so cute."

"A Martini?" I figured that would be at least six bucks.

"Yes, a vodka Martini, a double." He sounded like he may have ordered one before.

"A double?" I asked.

"Where are the olives from?"

"The olives? A jar." I was liking Nicholas less with every passing second.

"Dev, stop it. Just go and get Nicholas his Martini." Carol glared, and then graced Nicholas with her smile.

"And two olives," Nicholas reminded holding up two fingers.

Carol gave me her look that said, '*Don't even think of causing a scene*,' then turned back to focus on Nicholas.

"Double vodka Martini, your cheapest bar pour. I better have another Summit, too," I said to the bartender.

"She's onto Martini's now?"

It was Justine, again. Actually, I was glad to see her.

"No, some jackass took my stool and somehow I end up buying him a drink, a French guy."

Justine looked over my shoulder and took a long sip from her beer. As she moved to say something in my ear she brushed firmly against me.

"That guy with the long hair and the big ears?"

I hadn't noticed the ears, but now that she mentioned it "Yeah, the guy with his back to us."

"He's chatting up the girl in the red?"

"Yeah, the one with the dreamy look on her face."

"I'm guessing those aren't her God given attributes."

"You can tell that from across the room?"

"Hello, yes. God they're fakes," she said and shook her head.

"Yeah, they are, but that never really bothered me."

"Ten-fifty," the bartender said, setting Nicholas's Martini and my beer down in front of me.

I handed him a twenty. The look on my face must have given me away.

"Just isn't shaping up to be your night, is it, Cosmo?"

"Not exactly. Can you stay put for a minute while I deliver this to Pepe Le Pew over there?"

"Yeah, promise you won't be long."

"Not a problem, believe me."

"Merci," Nicholas said, quickly grabbing the drink out of my hand then returning to Carol's charm.

"Be careful, Dev. God, you'll spill again. Did he get any on you, Nicholas?" Carol said.

I could only hope, but didn't wait for an answer and wandered back to Justine at the bar.

"So how long are they here?"

"Actually, she's with me, so…"

"I got a beer says no way."

"What?" I gave a shrug, then turned to look at Carol. She was laughing, stroking Nicholas's arm. She saw me, raised her almost empty glass, signaling for another Cosmopolitan.

"Whoa, better get on that," Justine said.

"Maybe not yet. You here alone?"

"More or less. She glanced over her shoulder toward a group of women dancing. One of the women wore a white veil and a sign around her neck that read 'Child Bride'. She was twirling round and round in the center of the group. None of them seemed to be feeling any pain.

"So what do you do?"

"I'm a medical assistant by day. But at night, I'm a derby Bombshell, baby." She cocked her hip, struck a pose and fluttered her eyes at me.

"Huh?"

"Roller derby, I skate with the Bombshells."

"You're kidding."

"No, it's really fun. Don't tell me you didn't notice I was a Bombshell? What do you do?"

"You mean when I'm not getting drinks for jerks? I'm a PI."

"PI?"

"Private Investigator."

"You mean like a detective, like in the movies or CSI?"

"Yeah, exactly, only about a thousand times duller."

"Do you carry a gun?"

"Sometimes."

"Can I see it?"

"Fortunately I left it at home. Otherwise I would have blown my brains out about three minutes after coming into this place."

"You know, do you have a card? We might have a need for your services."

I dug a card out of my wallet and handed it to her.

"Devlin Haskell, Private Investigator," she read.

"That's me."

"So you find people and stuff, solve mysteries and crimes?"

"Sometimes. Like I said, it's a lot more boring than the movies."

"Think you'll be able to find your date?"

"What?" I turned to look at two empty stools where Carol and Nicholas had been sitting. I couldn't spot them out on the dance floor. I guessed they'd wandered back the crowd somewhere.

"You might be able to catch them if you hurry. I think they were headed for the back door."

"Catch them? I got a better idea. I think I owe you a beer if I recall."

"You do."

Chapter Two

I was sitting at Nina's nursing a coffee, watching the early morning crowd squirt a sugar substitute into their lattes and cappuccinos. Aaron LaZelle, lieutenant in vice with St. Paul's finest sat across from me. I decided to speak my mind.

"You know, with you making the exorbitant amount you do as a senior member of the police force, you'd think you could at least spring for coffee. I'm a taxpayer after all."

"Do we really want to get into the taxes you pay? I know a few IRS guys, this time of year they got a little time on their hands. They could check into it, do an audit or two and make sure you're not paying more than your fair share." He looked around, stared at an attractive dark haired woman in tight jeans and a T-shirt waiting in line to place an order.

"On second thought thanks, but no thanks. Like your caramel roll?"

"Always," he replied.

"You know anything about women's roller derby?"

"You mean where they skate round and round with jams and jammers? They've got those great names and look really hot."

"Clearly you know more than me."

"Actually I don't. It's been years since I was at one of those. Pretty fun if I recall. I think they actually do a lot of charity work."

"Charity work, like praying and stuff?" I said.

"Yeah, that's right, they conduct a prayer service. No they fund raise, donate a lot to food banks, maybe a kids program, the kind of stuff you'd be really involved in." He shook his head, looking back at the same dark haired woman. She'd moved forward in line a couple of spaces.

"I like kids and shit."

"Yeah, sure you do. Admit it, you like the mommies."

"Well yeah, that too."

"Are you doing something with roller derby? No offense, but couldn't most of them kick the hell out of you?"

I ignored his comment. "I met a girl last night. She does it, roller derby I mean. Seemed like a nice girl."

"Well then she won't be interested in you. If she was so nice what was she doing in one of the sleazy joints you frequent?"

"God, it was the Dew Drop. I still haven't gotten my hearing back."

"What were you doing in that place?"

"Wasting time and money. You know you have to pay a cover charge just to get into that place so you can spend more money on overpriced, bullshit drinks?"

"Yeah, I'd guess you were a little bit out of your usual demographic, but once inside you got to hang with the beautiful people."

"I think I was one of the few straight guys in there."

"Not surprising. Excuse me for a minute," he said. Then he stood up and walked over to the counter just as the dark haired woman was picking up her coffee.

"Kristi." I heard him call, but then couldn't hear anything else. The look on her face suggested Aaron might be saying something a little more official than hello. They stepped outside. I could see her through the front window standing on the sidewalk, nodding, then shaking her head and nodding again. She suddenly leaned forward and gave him a kiss on the cheek, nodded a few more times, waved and walked down the street. Aaron watched her for a long moment before he strolled back in.

"Business?" I asked.

"Manner of speaking," he said, then stuffed the last of the caramel roll into his mouth and licked the tip of his thumb and forefinger.

"She a working girl?"

"Sign of the times. Architect by training, escort by necessity. She's a nice kid, I played hockey with a couple of her brothers."

"So are you checking her pricing or what?"

He shook his head and glanced around the room.

"No, just told her we got a sting coming up, working the Internet, told her to watch out and be careful."

"When does it start?"

"It doesn't. Nothing like that in the works. The only thing we got coming up is more budget cuts."

"So why'd you tell her…"

"It's like pulling someone over for speeding. Everyone else slows down. Same deal. I'm just reminding her to be careful. You know how much architectural work is out there right now? Zero."

"So she's got an online ad?"

313

"An ad? No, a website, takes credit cards. They all do. That's the business model now. You were telling me about the Dew Drop."

"Yeah, you remember Carol?"

"Is she the Kindergarten teacher?"

"Kindergarten? No, that chick dropped me six months ago. Carol does something with the State, I forget what. I can never remember the department. Anyway, we went there to meet some of her pals." I went on to tell Aaron about the noise, the dancing, Carol leaving with the French guy, Nicholas, and me meeting Justine at the bar.

"Sounds perfect. Carol dumps you and you meet someone else before she's out the door. You are a real piece of work, buddy."

"Yeah, well anyway, I'm gonna give this Justine a call. And, I should probably play the wounded lover with Carol…try for a final sympathy roll in the sack."

"God knows that opportunity doesn't happen too often in your life."

"Actually, I think this could be a first."

I walked the half block back home from Nina's. On my way I called Carol, ready to play on her sympathies, tell her how heart broken I was.

"Bon Jour, I'm unable to take your call just now. Please leave a message, Merci."

I didn't mean to leave a sigh as my message on her cell, it just sort of came out that way. She was already learning French? I'll give you some Merci, I thought, then climbed in the car and drove to my office.

I had three days worth of verifying job references for a small company staring me in the face. Times being what they were the company was overwhelmed with applications from qualified people. My job was to check out employment histories and references. It amounted to a lot of drudgery and absolutely no romance, just like my life at the moment.

I'd been looking out the office window for maybe forty-five minutes, staring at St. Kate's coeds, waiting for the bus and watching people dash into The Spot for lunch. A liquid lunch. The Spot didn't serve food. I was telling myself I should do the same when my phone rang.

I put on my best 'feeling down' voice and answered.

"Haskell Investigations," I said. I pictured Carol pacing back and forth in the hallway of some State building, embarrassed, afraid of what I might say. She'd probably spent the better part of the morning working up the courage to call me, wondering if I'd hang up as soon as I heard her voice.

"Hi Dev, Justine. You know from last night. Are you free to talk?"

"Justine? No, I mean yes, yeah."

"You sure? I don't want to interrupt."

"Nothing that can't wait."

Outside the Randolph bus had just pulled away. It would be at least twenty-five minutes before any more women would be waiting on the corner. On my desk I had a mountain of boring applications and references to wade through. I had time, plenty of time.

"Okay, just as long as you're sure."

"Yeah, nice to hear your voice. I was going to give you a call and see if you wanted to get together."

"Well, actually that's maybe why I'm calling. I mean, I made some team calls this morning. We'd like to talk with you, see if we could hire you for a security gig. That is, if you've got the time. I'm really sorry, but it's on pretty short notice. We'd need you in two days. For maybe a day and a half, tops."

315

I looked at the pile of job applications I had yet to verify. I stared at the two darts imbedded in the wall a couple of inches to the right of my dart board. The mail man had already come and gone, leaving nothing for me except a grocery store circular and some credit card offer.

"In two days? I could probably adjust some things. I'd have to make a couple of phone calls, put a number of people off and reschedule."

"You sure? I mean we were hoping we could sit down with you tonight, go over some stuff. I'm sorry this is all coming up so fast."

"Tonight? I think that could work. I'll make it work. You tell me where and when. Let me make some calls and I'll get back to you this afternoon if there's a problem."

"You sure? I don't want to…"

"Justine, I'm moving you up to the top of the list. Can I call you back this afternoon?"

"I really appreciate it. Thanks, Dev," she said and hung up.

I wandered over to The Spot to celebrate with a liquid lunch.

Chapter Three

There were five of them sitting around the table when I arrived, teammates from the Bombshells all drinking beer. Not a Cosmopolitan in sight. Justine introduced them using their roller derby names.

"Helen Killer, Maiden Bed, Branci Manhattan and Cheatin Hart," she said.

Each woman nodded at me as Justine pointed. They were all attractive, very attractive. I had the feeling I was about to land the cakewalk job of all time.

"Nice to meet you, ladies. Justine, I don't think you ever told me your Derby name."

"Spankie," a chorus trumpeted back.

"Really? Ladies, just call me Dev. So, Justine, I mean, Spankie mentioned you had a need for my services."

"We've got the Hasting Hustlers coming in Thursday and there have been problems wherever they go."

"Hastings…you mean the town eight miles downriver from St. Paul?" I asked.

"No, not really. More like the town in England, where the Battle of Hastings took place in ten-sixty-six, Harold the Second and William of Normandy. It changed British History. Well, and the rest of Western Europe."

I think it was Maiden Bed who just gave me the school lesson, but maybe I was mixing her up with Cheatin Hart. I suddenly couldn't remember names. Well, except for Spankie.

"Define 'problems wherever they go'," I said, thinking some sexy creature with a nickname like Nasty Nicki or Lotta Luv and I was going to get paid to watch them while they showered.

"Their big name star is Harlotte Davidson," Helen Killer said. I remembered her name because she was the first girl introduced to me.

"Big draw," someone said.

"Huge," one of the other girls added.

"We're lucky to get them in here. It'll just about make our year with this one bout. Anyway, one of the things they require in the contract is security."

"Security?" I asked, thinking it might make a lot of sense to be with Harlotte in the shower room.

"She's had some sort of stalker after her for almost a year, now."

"Stalker?" I said.

Nods all around the table.

"What does he do, hang around in the hotel? Try and get into the locker room and leave her love letters or take naked photos?"

"If only," Justine said.

"Spankie?" I asked.

She shook her head then seemed to shudder almost imperceptibly.

"Well, he mailed a couple of fingers."

"Fingers?" I half shouted.

"Then, you guys remember? He slipped that one under her door?" I thought Brandi Manhattan said that.

"That was down in Chicago," Justine added.

"Has anyone contacted the police?"

"Here?"

I nodded.

"Yeah, we got the usual. We can pay one of their off duty guys to hang around outside the door, that sort of stuff. They said they'll keep an eye out, but there isn't much they can do. I mean most of it has come through the mail. Not like there was a return address you could drive over to and ask some jerk what the hell he was thinking."

"Except for Chicago, when it was slipped under the door."

"Fingers?" I asked, again.

"Yeah, and always the middle one. like he's giving her the finger or something."

"Creepy," Helen Killer chimed in.

"Does she have security? Someone with the team, that sort of deal."

"Yeah, but they want us to provide someone local. I mean I get it, it makes sense. Their guy can watch Harlotte. He'll know the practice routine, the hotel, all that sort of stuff, but he's not a local guy."

I was still stuck a few paces back thinking fingers? What the hell?

"Fingers, and always the middle one?"

Nods all around.

"This happened more than twice?"

More nods.

"I think two through the mail, then Chicago," Justine said.

"So I'd just follow her around, with the Hustlers' security, that it?"

"Maybe, you tell us, you're the Private Investigator. What would you normally do?"

"I'd just follow her around, with the Hustlers' security." I detected a slight widening of their eyes so I embellished. "Work as the local interface with the police. I know most of the players on the force. I'd want to coordinate with the Hastings Hustler's security folks about what they've been doing thus far. Find out what they're worried about, deal with any of their immediate concerns."

"Worried about? They're worried about some nut case sending human fingers through the mail and finally getting bold enough to slip one under the door. I mean, right under the damn door. That's what they're worried about."

"Yeah, I get that. But are they worried the same guy is going to take a shot at her during the bout. Where do you skate? Are there metal detectors? Is this finger deal just centered on their star attraction, Harlotte? Did she or any of her teammates receive threatening letters or phone calls? Look, we can sit here all night and go over what we might do, might not do and at the end of the night we could be completely wrong," I said.

"So now what?" Justine asked.

"I'd like to contact these people, talk to them before they arrive, maybe get some things lined up in advance. The better prepared we are the better off everyone will be. You got a phone number where I could reach them?"

"I can have that information for you tomorrow morning," Justine said.

Chapter Four

Her condo was on the fourth floor of a five story building- red brick Victorian sort of thing with gargoyles, black trim, stain glass and gables, built in eighteen-eighty. It was the perfect place for a Halloween party.

"You want a beer or something stronger?" Justine asked.

She kicked off her shoes at the door, tossed her purse on a black leather couch, one of two sitting perpendicular to a fireplace with a glass topped coffee table between them. The room was long with a three panel bay window at the far end and a stain glass window above that with some kind of flower pattern. The streets light from four stories down cast colored reflections across her living room ceiling.

"Beer's just fine for me."

A hallway ran straight ahead along the length of the condo, exposed brick on one side and doors to various rooms on the other. Track lighting along the ceiling lit the hall and highlighted three framed paintings hung on the brick wall. The paintings were roller derby scenes. Girls skating around a banked track wearing hot pants, you could feel a sense of speed and action just by looking at the things, the paintings.

"You do these?" I asked, staring briefly at the paintings before following her into the kitchen at the far end of the hall.

"No, some California guy. That's me in them, in the purple jersey. He did ten of the things if you can believe it, gave me a deal. He had a show and everything. I guess it went pretty well." Her voice was muffled as she bent over and reached into a gigantic refrigerator.

"Here's to you," she said and handed me a bottle.

A few beers later we ended up on one of the couches, legs resting across the coffee table. A couple of table lamps with stain glass dragon flies on the shades dimly lit the room. Light from the lamps reflected off the glazed fireplace tiles.

"You think there'll be any trouble?" she asked.

"You mean with Harlotte Davidson and the fingers?"

"No, I mean because I'm almost out of beer, yes with Harlotte and the fingers."

"I hope not. I don't think there will be. But, I'll give you this, it's pretty damn strange."

"Yeah and not the sort of publicity we're looking for."

"I don't know. You could probably get a sellout crowd showing up just to see if anything was going to happen. People dig this weird shit. Look at all the folks into the whole vampire thing," I said, then sipped.

"That is so not the sort of fans we're looking for. We've worked really hard to get beyond the image of strippers on roller skates and then something like this comes along."

"Maybe it's someone who gets their kicks getting headlines. You know, their fifteen minutes of fame sort of deal. If that doesn't happen, if you keep it quiet, maybe the guy will just go away."

"Or get more aggressive," she said.

"There is that."

"Who would let some guy cut off their finger?" she said, then shuddered, swallowing her beer.

"I've been thinking about that. At first I was thinking, it's him, you know some nut case doing it to himself, but there are too many middle fingers for one guy. Then, I thought maybe homeless people, druggies, but that seems sort of far fetched. I'm guessing someone with ready access."

"Ready access? To fingers? You gotta be kidding. How does that work?" She shuddered.

"Maybe it's someone who works in a hospital maybe a morgue or a funeral home, something along those lines."

"Oh, that's comforting."

"Just thinking out loud."

"You hear back from Miss Cosmopolitan?" she asked, moving quickly away from the subject of fingers.

"No, tell you the truth I'm not really interested, I guess." I saw no benefit admitting I heard Carol's stupid French phone message. I could only hope little old Nicholas was just that, little.

"Need a hug?"

"What?"

"Get over here, stupid," she said and took her glasses off.

Many thanks for sampling. Dev's about to make a series of his usual bad decisions and suddenly he'll be in over his head. You can help him out by getting a copy of <u>Bombshell</u> and finding out what happens.

Please visit me on Amazon
or
contact me directly at;
mikefaricyauthor@gmail.com

34400912R00182

Made in the USA
San Bernardino, CA
27 May 2016